MW01625485

MARYSUE
RUCCI
BOOKS

## Also by Laura Dave

*The Last Thing He Told Me*

*Hello, Sunshine*

*Eight Hundred Grapes*

*The First Husband*

*The Divorce Party*

*London Is the Best City in America*

# The Night We Lost Him

A Novel

Laura Dave

MARYSUE
RUCCI
BOOKS

NEW YORK • LONDON • TORONTO
SYDNEY • NEW DELHI

An Imprint of Simon & Schuster, LLC
1230 Avenue of the Americas
New York, NY 10020



First Marysue Rucci Books hardcover edition October 2024

MARYSUE RUCCI BOOKS and colophon are trademarks of Simon & Schuster, LLC



Simon & Schuster: Celebrating 100 Years of Publishing in 2024

For information about special discounts for bulk purchases, please contact Simon & Schuster Special Sales at 1-866-506-1949 or business@simonandschuster.com.

The Simon & Schuster Speakers Bureau can bring authors to your live event. For more information or to book an event, contact the Simon & Schuster Speakers Bureau at 1-866-248-3049 or visit our website at www.simonspeakers.com.

Manufactured in the United States of America

1 3 5 7 9 10 8 6 4 2

Library of Congress Cataloging-in-Publication Data

Names: Dave, Laura, author.
Title: The night we lost him: a novel / Laura Dave.
Description: First Marysue Rucci Books hardcover edition. | New York : MSR, Marysue Rucci Books, 2024.
Identifiers: LCCN 2024014850 | ISBN 9781668002933 (hardback) | ISBN 9781668002940 (paperback) | ISBN 9781668002957 (ebook)
Subjects: BISAC: FICTION / Thrillers / Suspense | FICTION / Women | LCGFT: Thrillers (Fiction) | Novels.
Classification: LCC PS3604.A938 N54 2024 | DDC 813/.6—dc23/eng/20240404
LC record available at https://lccn.loc.gov/2024014850

ISBN 978-1-6680-0293-3
ISBN 978-1-6680-0295-7 (ebook)

*To Josh and Jacob,*

*They're all for you*

The way the high-wire walker
must carry a pole
to make her arms longer
You carried me    I carried you
through this world

—Jane Hirshfield

# The Night We Lost Him

# Prologue

He knew any biographer would decide that the story of his life could be summarized by this: When Liam Samuel Noone began accruing his fortune, the first thing he did was buy a piece of land as far away from his hometown as he could possibly get.

Of course, there were places technically farther from Midwood, Brooklyn than the Central California Coast. But Liam felt reborn the first time he arrived in Carpinteria. His pulse quieted, his chest released—a small, yet seismic shift. He drove through the secluded beachside town in a haze—the world around him windy and soulful, cypress trees sweeping every which way, a messy canopy.

Liam was in the early days of taking over the company, and he'd flown out west to meet with a potential investor. They were in discussions to build a boutique hotel together eight miles up the road in Santa Barbara—a hillside retreat, private and luxurious, with forty-eight stand-alone cottages, winding mountain trails, outdoor fireplaces, and cobblestone walkways. A stone-wrapped restaurant.

He was meeting with the investment partner, a former classmate named Ben, at Ben's oceanfront vacation home on Padaro Lane. They sat outside on the back deck, eating poached eggs and studying blueprints, Liam's suit no match for the chill coming in off the ocean. He drank extra coffee, refusing Ben's offer to borrow a coat.

At some point, Liam looked east and spotted a cottage, perched cliffside at Loon Point. It was lit up by the rising sun—the incandescent yellow ricocheting off the bluff front, landing on its white rock and citrus grove. The rose gardens.

The property encompassed a large parcel of land, five exquisite acres, endless ocean views, the Santa Ynez foothills in the distance.

An old woman lived in the one structure on the property, a Craftsman bungalow, a white wooden sign by the front door with the bungalow's name, WINDBREAK. Liam knocked on the front door and asked her what she wanted for her home. She said she wanted to live there peacefully without people knocking on her door asking her what she wanted for her home. He smiled at her and apologized. *I can't afford it anyway,* he said.

Which was when she let him in.

Now, more than three decades later—how can that much time just *pass*?—he walks over to the northeast edge, his favorite vantage point, the ocean expansive beneath him, the ancient olive trees and the wind and the sharp breeze, wild all around him.

He takes a deep breath, swallows the tears pushing in from the back of his throat as he remembers that day.

He isn't normally so nostalgic and has never been much for fantasy. But he feels himself doing it: pretending, again, that he is still that riled-up young man, knocking on an old woman's door, wanting to start a new life. As opposed to the older man he now is, an empty house behind him, no one to answer how he'd gotten it wrong. How he'd ended up here, emotional and weary, but willing to say out loud (to finally say out loud) all the things he wished he could undo. It isn't regret, exactly. It isn't anything as clichéd or inactive as regret. No. It is penance.

That is why he keeps playing the moments back on an unforgiving loop: the moments he is trying to return to, to relive. The first moment at eighteen, then at twenty and twenty-six and thirty-seven and forty-five. Fifty-eight. Sixty-one. Sixty-eight. In the ways that matter, it is all the same moment, isn't it?

The same choice. You move toward your destiny or you move away.

He digs his feet into the white rock, a light rain starting to fall. When exactly did this place become a referendum on what he'd failed to do? It would be easy (and probably wrong) to name that shift as a recent occurrence. But however it happened, slowly and at once, Windbreak is now the place that reminds him of himself the most. The irony of that! Instead of the escape he assumed it would be, a reprieve from the childhood home that he'd run from, it has turned out to be the opposite. It is his time capsule.

He turns and looks at Windbreak, the small Craftsman, all the lights on: two bedrooms, two bathrooms, a galley kitchen. A house, a cottage, that is smaller than the guesthouses on any of the neighboring properties, let alone the eight-thousand-square-foot main houses. Everyone assumed he'd knock the small house down eventually, build anew. This bungalow, perfect and misplaced, wasn't nearly big enough to house a large family. It wasn't big enough for his families certainly.

But it wasn't as simple as building a larger home. He was always nervous to bring his daughter here when she was small, and then the boys when they were. The palisades were no security from the drastic edges. That cliffside was too precipitous, eighty feet down to the ocean and the rock and the California coast. What if they fell? What if any one of them with their small quick legs and ready elbows went over the edge before he could catch them?

That's what he told himself, at least. Is it even the truth? Or is the truth simpler? He always liked to be here alone. Alone or with her.

He peers out over the edge, the waves lapping eighty feet below, the bluffs jagged and beautiful and strong. And he knows that, no, it isn't just selfishness. He's certain of that. He's certain that he was trying, in his way, to protect his children. Even when he failed (and he doesn't kid himself, he failed far more often as a father than he succeeded), he did want to protect them.

When, mere moments later, Liam Samuel Noone is pushed over that edge, airborne and pivoting, this is in fact his last thought. For all his faults, his very last thought.

*Better me, than them.*

# – Part I –

The architect works in the territory of memory.

—Mario Botta

# Open Houses

"So what do you think? Can it even be salvaged?" she asks.

I'm standing in the doorway of a five-story brownstone in Brooklyn, perched at the edge of Cobble Hill. In my professional opinion, the brownstone is remarkable as it is: an extra-wide with steel windows, original banisters, wainscot ceilings some twelve feet above. And an eighteen-hundred-square-foot rooftop garden, which looks over a lush and lovely corner of Henry Street.

I turn to look at Morgan, my client. "What do you mean by *salvaged*, exactly?"

"Well, you're the expert, but the place obviously needs to be gutted. It's dumpy, you know?"

Morgan shakes her head, apparently waiting for me to catch up. She is beautiful and young (twenty-five, maybe twenty-six) and wearing the same blue knee-high boots that she's been clad in the few times we've met in person. Each time, she has seemed increasingly unhappy about being Brooklyn-bound. I don't know if it's this brownstone she doesn't like, or the idea of leaving Manhattan in general. But this move is clearly not one she is excited for.

She is moving to Brooklyn, she keeps telling me, because her fiancé, a business guy of some sort, is pushing for it. He has decided he wants to leave Tribeca and their North Moore Street loft and flee to the outer borough. I have yet to meet Morgan's fiancé, even though he was apparently the one who insisted that Morgan hire me. He wants to get married on the rooftop here. And, while they're at it, to completely renovate the five floors beneath it.

"When do you think it can all be done?" Morgan asks.

"Which part?"

"You know. All of it."

She motions to indicate the entire brownstone as she clips down the steps, down into the sunken living room.

"Let's start by talking about what you're imagining," I say. "Then we can get more granular and make sure we're on the same page in terms of schedule and planning. Sound good?"

"Sure . . ."

She sits down on the sofa, seemingly accepting this plan. But then she pulls her phone out of her bag—already bored with the details we haven't begun to discuss. She taps into Instagram, her five hundred thousand followers staring back at her. And she is lost to me.

I start unloading the brownstone's original blueprints anyway. The previous owner is an architect I've known since graduate school. He spent the better part of three years remodeling this space for his own family, not anticipating that his wife's job would send them to Colorado shortly after they moved in. There are, of course, many ways to design a space, but I can feel the attention he paid to every detail—the way the living room is relaxed and spacious, the rounded corners, the olive tree balancing out the fireplace, the natural light coming in from three directions.

You may think of noteworthy architecture as constructing the most novel, sculptural buildings. But I lean first and foremost into how people's environments can positively impact the quality of their lives. I am focused, most fundamentally, on building spaces that can be healing. I specialize in neuroarchitecture. Most of my clients are interested in this particular architectural approach, which is all about designing spaces to benefit overall well-being.

Whatever Morgan means by *dumpy*, I doubt that she is interested in exploring this type of calculus.

"Is your fiancé still joining or is it just going to be the two of us?" I ask.

Instead of answering, she holds her phone out, in selfie position, and puckers up. I step out of camera view as quickly as I can.

"He should be coming."

This is when her fiancé walks through the front door, the winter wind following him in. He is good-looking—tall and broad with a strong jaw, intense eyes. He is older than Morgan, nearly thirty, and wearing a sports jacket, with a hoodie peeking out beneath it, making him look younger than he is.

He is also, it turns out, my brother.

Sam nods in my direction. "What's going on, Nora?"

"You've got to be kidding me," I say.

Morgan sits up and looks back and forth between us. "Do you two know each other?" she asks.

"Nora's actually my sister," he says.

"Your *sister*?"

I smile, motion between them. "Do you two know each other?"

It's a little unfair. I can count the number of times I've been in the same room as Sam. We didn't see each other often while we were growing up. We see each other even less now that we're adults. I'm the only child from our father's first marriage. Sam is one of two kids from his second. You could argue that Sam and his twin brother, Tommy, are the reason there was a second marriage—their mother's surprise pregnancy a small tip-off to the fact that my parents' relationship wasn't exactly working.

"*Sam.* What the fuck?" Morgan says. "You didn't think this was something you should've mentioned?"

I'm not sure if the "this" she's referring to is my brother hiring me without telling her who I am—or whether she's referring to Sam even having a sister in the first place. I'm leaning toward the latter, but before Sam can answer her, Morgan's phone buzzes with an incoming call. She mumbles that it's their wedding planner. Then she disappears into the hallway to talk with her.

I turn back toward Sam, who gives me a smile. "It's good to see you," he says. "How have you been?"

"Why do you have to be so shady?" I ask.

His smile disappears.

"I've been trying to reach you for over a month. You haven't returned any of my calls. But I'm the shady one?"

He has called me—that part is true. Since our father died, I've avoided his voice messages and a couple of cryptic emails. Our father hadn't wanted a funeral, so I've avoided seeing my brother in person too.

The truth of the matter is that I don't want to get into anything with Sam. History has shown me it's best not to get into anything with him—or anyone from my father's second family. From my father's third family, for that matter.

"I need to talk to you," he says.

"You bought an eight-million-dollar brownstone to have a conversation?"

"It's a pretty important conversation."

I start reaching for the blueprints, putting them back in their tubes. "I'm late for my next client."

"Morgan actually had you block out the rest of the afternoon, so . . ."

I don't often take on residential projects like this brownstone anymore. But Morgan had paid a hefty retainer up front—the kind of retainer that gives me the latitude to do more of the work that I love the most, the kind of retainer that allows her to request extra hours of my time.

"Happy to void the check," I say.

"Can we just sit and talk for a few fucking minutes?"

"I thought I made my position clear," I say. "I don't want Dad's money. I didn't want it when he was alive. I certainly don't want it now."

"I'm not here about that," he says.

I look up, meet his eyes. A familiar hazy-green. My father's green. They have the same eyes, same light hair, same skin. It stings, but I force myself to push that down.

It's easier when I remind myself that my brother is only ever here about that. Even on the other side of our shared loss, he's certainly not suddenly interested in us having a relationship. Which, as far as I'm concerned, is fine. I have no interest in having a relationship with Sam. And I have even less interest in having anything to do with my father's company.

As I replied when I forwarded Sam's latest email (Subject line: **We need to talk**) to my father's lawyers, Sam can have anything of our father's he wants. They all can.

"Take care of yourself, Sam," I say.

I start walking toward the front door. The door that will lead me outside and down the front steps and away from here.

"Would you wait?"

I keep walking and I'm almost free. I'm free of him again and his family again and the world of them again.

And then, my hand on the doorknob, my brother says one thing. The only thing that would stop me.

"Nora. Dad's death?" Sam calls out. "His fall . . ."

I stop moving. I don't take my hand off the doorknob. But I do stop moving.

"It wasn't an accident."

# You Can't Pick Your Famil(ies)

The last time I saw my brother in person was more than five years ago.

We were at a dinner party to celebrate our uncle Joe's birthday. Joe is technically our father's cousin, but they grew up like brothers. They were raised together, went to high school together, lived together after they finished college, and spent the last several decades working together. If brothers tended to bicker, though—especially brothers who were as connected as they were—they managed to be mostly exempt from conflict. They weren't only brothers. They were best friends.

My father was hosting Joe's birthday dinner at Perry St, a restaurant just off the West Side Highway, one of his and Joe's longstanding favorites. Sam was seated next to me, at the far end of the table. He had recently started working for our father, and he was overseeing the rollout of a new property in Hawaii: a small beachside enclave on the North Shore of Kauai.

Sam flew back to New York for the dinner—which he seemed unhappy that my father had insisted he do, particularly because Tommy was spending most of the meal away from the table, pacing back and forth on the sidewalk on a work call.

Sam kept eyeing Tommy through the window. Tommy also worked for our father. He had been working for our father longer than Sam had. I couldn't tell from Sam's expression whether he was jealous that Tommy had a reason to not be at that table. Or whether Sam was feeling competitive that Tommy had a reason to be away from the table that didn't include him.

Either way, I was more interested in talking to Grace, who was seated on my other side.

"Your father tells me that you just opened your own shop?" she said. "That's really exciting."

I'd always liked Grace. She was quiet and whip-smart and had been working with my father since I was a little girl. She had been working there nearly as long as Joe—she and Joe, my father's two most trusted advisors. From the way my father described it, Joe helped him keep the trains moving on time, while Grace was more of a creative partner. This may be why it felt like she genuinely cared that I had managed to procure enough of my own client base to pay off my school loans (a BA in neuroscience and visual arts, followed by a MArch degree), leave my corporate architecture job, convert a garage in Cobble Hill into an open-floor studio, and become the principal at my own firm.

It felt like an accomplishment to have done that without a financial assist from my father. He'd certainly helped support me while I was growing up, but once I left home, it was understood I would do it on my own. I wasn't a martyr, but it was important to me to be self-made, and it was important to my mother. It was how she'd raised me. *Too much money causes trouble,* she used to say. And my father respected that this was how she (and later I) wanted to do it.

Grace certainly knew this, which was probably why she leaned in and gave me a smile, happy to see me on the rewarding end of a long road.

"We've started exploring a property on the Nayarit Peninsula," she said. "Has your father mentioned?"

"I don't think so, no."

"There are some geological complications, but it's quite special. We want to integrate the landscape, really lean into sustainability and health. Not just giving a nod to it but taking a page from a resort your father just visited in Asia. Creating a wellness clinic, having a medical director on staff. Obviously that will all start with the property design . . ."

I smiled. It didn't feel like a coincidence that Grace was raising this a few weeks after my father came to a trade talk I gave about the impact of built environments on health solutions and longevity. That was what my father did—he saw an opening to involve me, and he wanted to step into it.

"Anyway," she continued, "your father was hoping that might hold some interest for you?"

I could feel the air shift, Sam suddenly tuning in. "Grace, you know Nora here isn't interested in our little company . . ."

I looked over at Sam. "True," I said. "I am, however, interested in speaking for myself."

Then I turned back to Grace. This was a conversation I'd had with my father on many occasions, the answer never shifting from a hard and fast no. But I appreciated it all the same. I was grateful my father took pride in my work, in how I approached it. Even if I wanted to stay away from his.

"I'm fully committed at the moment," I said.

"You sure? We'd all really love to do this with you."

"I am. But thank you for asking."

Grace nodded, happy to drop it, especially because it was my father's mission to make me feel included, not hers. Also, because he was now motioning for her to come and join him and Uncle Joe at the other end of the table.

"I'll be back," she said.

And, with a squeeze to my shoulder, she was up and out of her seat, leaving me alone with Sam.

"Your own shop, huh?" he said. "Congratulations."

The way he lingered on *congratulations* felt loaded, like he meant the opposite.

I forced a smile and busied myself smoothing out my dress. I'd come straight to the dinner from a client meeting, so I was still wearing my work clothes: a button-down dress and structured loafers, a corduroy blazer. My long hair pulled back in a loose bun. I could feel Sam's judgment in the way he was eyeing me (in his suede jacket and Chelsea boots), like he'd decided I was somehow too dressy and not dressy enough.

I met his gaze, unbothered. My mother had modeled for me early on that the quickest route to unhappiness was to pay too much attention to anyone's disapproval, particularly someone that you barely knew.

"Thank you," I said.

"Dad said you were up for a big commission in Red Hook?" Sam said. "An art gallery or something?"

It was a primary school. I'd been working on it for the last two and a half years—collaborating with a team of engineers, educators, and neuroscientists. The school was right off the water, with large windows and open classrooms, everything centered on natural light and fresh air, on spaces for running and free movement. *The Record* had recently featured it in a cover story on buildings at the forefront of neuroarchitecture and education. And the response to my work on it—the positive reception—was a main reason why I had the freedom to become the principal at my own firm.

"Something like that," I said.

"How much money will you bring in a year?" he asked.

"Excuse me?"

Sam kept his eyes on me. "I'm just wondering, from a business point of view."

"Well, from a business point of view," I said. "That's not really any of your business."

"Until you take Dad up on his offer . . ."

I looked out the window at Tommy—as if he was going to save me. But he had his back turned to me, rendering him completely oblivious to my stare. As if he would be showing up for me, in this instance, if he was paying attention.

I turned back to Sam, ready to ask him what I'd ever done to make him think I had any interest in following that path. In his job. In his life. In any of it. But then I reminded myself it wasn't about me. Like everything Sam seemed to be concerned about, it was about himself.

"It's cool with me if you do want to come in," Sam said. "Contrary to what you might think, I'm not against you."

"Why would you be against me? You barely know me."

He picked up his tumbler of bourbon, tilted it in my direction. "That, right there, is reason number one."

~

"There is just no way, he didn't just *fall*," Sam says now.

We've moved into the kitchen, the kitchen Morgan wants to strip down—despite its floor-to-ceiling windows that look out into the yard, its newly pitched ceilings, a playful hunter-green Bertazzoni range.

The center island separates us. Like an agreed-upon safety zone. Or an impenetrable moat.

Sam stands at one end of the island and I lean against the other end. Neither of us sits down on the countertop stools, keeping open an easier path to leave. Morgan has left already. She is on her way back into Manhattan and a cocktail at Gramercy Tavern with her wedding planner. At this moment, for many reasons, I envy her.

"So what do you think happened exactly?"

"That he was helped," he says. "Over the edge."

"Like pushed? Intentionally?"

"That's usually how pushing works."

I turn away from him. My father's cottage, Windbreak, was his retreat, his private place. It wasn't unusual that he'd been there alone that night. He was often alone there. And there had been a joint investigation with local law enforcement and the internal Noone Properties security team. Their findings were in line: It was a rainy night. The cliff's edge was slick. There wasn't anything notable to suggest foul play or self-harm. He simply slipped.

"I was told there was an investigation," I say.

"Yeah. There was." Sam shrugs, like he is unimpressed by this. By that investigation. By any of its conclusions. "And it must have been really thorough to be put to bed less than a month later."

I take my brother in, his jaw clenched, his shoulders too tight. Sam was a ball player while he was growing up, an ace pitcher. And when I see him focused like this, intense and determined, it takes me back to that version of him. To the photograph of Sam on the pitcher's mound on my father's desk. To Sam's game face. His devotion. His talent.

Sam was the starting pitcher for Vanderbilt the year they won their D1 championship. Shortly after graduation, he was drafted in the second round by the Minnesota Twins. But on his way to practice the second week, a midwestern rainstorm surprised him, as did a student driver—whose driving academy car plowed straight into

Sam's Jeep. Sam's wrist went through his windshield and was punctured in two places. His MLB career over before it started.

"Look, Sam, I get that you're concerned here . . ."

"Doesn't sound like you do."

"Well, do you have any evidence at all that someone else was there with him that night?"

"No," he says. "But that doesn't mean anything. You know how Dad was about privacy. There was limited security at Windbreak, except by the front gate. And just because someone didn't come through the front gate doesn't mean they didn't get in there another way. I can think of several."

"Sure. But . . . who would even want to do this?"

"Do you remember our father?" he says.

It's a joke and it's not. Even staying far removed from my father's business affairs, I knew enough to know that he had a particular way of doing things, which made him respected by some, but disliked by others. Professionally. And personally. His supporters called him exacting, his critics exhausting. A famous story was that the day before he was set to open a property in Napa Valley, just outside of St. Helena, my father did his final tour of the grounds and was unhappy. There was a new construction project on Highway 29 that you could hear from the main pool. So he pushed back the opening by six months (until said construction would be completed), turned over the entire staff, and personally rebooked every opening-weekend guest at other luxury hotels in Napa Valley, footing the bill himself. Also, of course, he offered a complimentary weekend stay at the hotel as soon as he did open the doors. Once the pool was quiet.

Sam walks around the island and reaches into his messenger bag. He pulls out a blue folder, places it on the countertop in front of me. There's a thick pile of papers inside. He motions for me to open it.

"What's this?"

"The most recent copy of Dad's will, among other things. Did you know he changed it earlier this year?"

I shake my head. I didn't.

"I don't know what it said before he made the alterations or why he made the changes. None of the lawyers will tell me anything, obviously."

I look up at him, processing what he's suggesting.

"Is there something weird in there now?"

"Not on the face of it," he says. "No."

"Then I don't follow you."

"My working theory is that there may have been something weird in there before he decided to change it."

"That's quite a theory. What does Tommy think about this?"

"At the moment, I'm not so interested in what Tommy thinks about anything."

I clock the edge in his tone. "What's that mean?"

He shakes his head, ignoring the question. "You've got to admit the timing is odd," he says. "Dad changes his will for the first time in decades and then he just dies not too long after . . ."

I look down at the blue folder. I'm unwilling to open it just yet, as if doing so will make Sam think I'm agreeing with him. I don't want to make any sudden moves that put us on the same side of this, a side he seems to be clinging to for air.

"How do you even know this?" I ask instead. "About the lawyers?"

"I have access to his calendar. Dad and Uncle Joe had eight meetings with Dad's wills and estates team over the course of several weeks. That much time? That had to have been . . . a reimagining."

He looks like this proves something, but all I can think is that a series of meetings with lawyers and an altered will (a will that could have been altered for a variety of reasons) sounds less like evidence of a murder plot and more like a grieving son reaching wildly for answers. A grieving son who is also a corporate heir.

"Look, Nora, before you go thinking that I'm stirring up trouble or trying to settle some personal score . . ."

I put my hands up in surrender, even though this is exactly what I was thinking.

"I wasn't," I say.

"Sure you were," he says. "But, just so you know, there is no score for me to settle. If anything, opening this whole thing up will only cause problems."

"How's that?"

"Dad walked us through what he was planning. It was copacetic. No party fouls. We got equal shares. Me and Tommy . . ."

Tommy, who is two minutes older than Sam but has always behaved as though it is closer to ten years. He earned a JD/MBA straight out of college, married his long-term girlfriend, and rose to the top ranks at Noone Properties, all before his thirtieth birthday. Tommy, who, my father would joke, came out looking more like my twin than like Sam's. The two of us have the same dark hair and eyes, same long legs and athletic build. It must have somehow come from our father's side of the family, even though you'd think both of us looked more like our mothers. But the resemblance is undeniable—something identical weaving through our facial structure—the turnup around our mouths, our cheekbones. Though any other similarities, at least those that are readily apparent to me, end there.

Not that Sam and I are any more similar. Sam, who is standing in front of me now. Sam who, since that car accident, has been (how did my father put it?) *seeking*. He coached baseball at a boarding school in Connecticut, moved to Bristol for an assistant job at ESPN, wound his way back to New York City and our father's company, working alongside Tommy.

For reasons I'm not unsympathetic to, the look that he is wearing now—suspicious, unhappy—isn't that far off from how his face has looked the other times that I've seen him since his baseball career ended.

What isn't clear to me, just yet, is why he is so beside himself. Is it really because he thinks something happened to our father? Or is he searching for something else?

"The point is," Sam says, "he left me and Tommy in charge."

He shrugs. And I can see he is surprised that our father left the company to him as well as Tommy. A little surprised, and a little proud. He shouldn't be. My father would never have picked one son over the other. That's not who he was. If I were the least bit interested, he would have figured out a way to include all of us.

"That's great, Sam," I say.

"Sure. I mean, he's keeping Uncle Joe in the top job for consistency," he says. "It's a logical choice, but Uncle Joe is just in there for a finite period. Fourteen months. Just to keep investors calm, keep the operations steady. This was all specified by Dad. Then Tommy and I will run it together."

"So what's the problem? Isn't that what you want?"

"Ask me when Dad discussed this all with us? His plans for the company, the details . . ."

"When?"

"Eight days before he died."

I must wear my surprise on my face because Sam leans into it. "Strange, isn't it?" he says.

"Or a coincidence."

"A pretty strange coincidence."

I meet his eyes. "Sam, I just . . ."

"You just what?"

"I get that this is really tough. It's tough for me too. But just because you have a feeling . . ."

"It's more than a feeling," he says. "If you want to try and push back on the timing with the will stuff, chalk it up to a coincidence, fine. I can't prove it's more than that yet. But that doesn't change the fact that Dad had been acting weird."

"Define 'weird.'"

"Distracted, absent. Coming into the office less. You know how close to the vest Dad held everything, but he wasn't himself."

He looks at me like that seals it. But all it seals for me is that my brother has convinced himself that something was going on with our father. Something that, if he's right, I knew nothing about. It nearly breaks something open in me to think that I didn't know. To think *why* I didn't know. And I start to feel it, a drumbeat pulsing in my head, the skin growing tighter and hotter behind my ears.

"You still haven't said one thing that contradicts what happened on the cliff that night," I say.

He nods. "Except for the one thing I don't need to say to you."

I look away, the drumbeat getting louder. Windbreak was my father's favorite place. It was his private refuge. He knew it like the back of his hand. And rainy night or not, too much bourbon to drink or not, moonless sky or not, would he really forget where the rocks started? Where they ended?

"Would you just do me a favor?" Sam says. "I'm flying out to Windbreak tomorrow to look around. To meet with the caretaker and the local police. See what I can figure out about what exactly happened that night."

"What's the favor?"

"Come with me."

I laugh out loud, before I can stop myself. "To California? No. You've got to be kidding."

"I'm not."

He isn't. And I start to double-down on my rejection of this plan when I see it in his eyes, those familiar eyes: his supreme discomfort to be standing here in front of me, asking me to be there for him. It stops me cold, partially because it's the first time I've seen that color on him—the first time he's been vulnerable with me. But also because of how it alters his face: the lines around the eyes creasing, his brow tightening up. Suddenly, like a magic trick, it feels like I'm standing in front of my father.

I open the folder, flipping through that thick pile of papers inside, neatly paper clipped and labeled. Color coded.

"The will's reading was two weeks ago," Sam says. "If you called anyone back, you would know he left it to you."

I look up. "Left me what?"

"Windbreak."

I try not to react, my face heating up and turning red. One of my last conversations with my father comes hurtling back. He called to ask me to come out to Windbreak with him. I didn't often go to Windbreak with my father, only a handful of times while I was growing up, a handful as an adult.

It was the place where he went to recharge, where he often went alone. So I was surprised to get the phone call from him. A little less surprised when he said: *I could use your opinion on renovating it. I'm looking to make some changes.* But I put him off. I said I was too busy with work. And I was busy. But, if I were being honest with myself, it hadn't been just about work. I was mad. I hadn't wanted to give that to him.

I feel a pulling in my chest, my breath trying to quell it.

"Sam . . ."

"If you're right, if this is totally crazy, we can be on the red-eye back tomorrow night."

He thumbs the folder, turns to the first page. He points to the single piece of paper, on which the itinerary is written down.

"Would you just think about it?" he asks.

I stare at the information: airport, flight number, the flight time in bold. **10:08 AM.** Tomorrow.

I close the folder, ready to say no.

But when I look back up, my brother is gone.

# Sheet Music

I get on the subway, decide to head home.

As I squeeze onto the corner bench, I pull out the blue folder. I start scanning the documents. There's a copy of my father's will inside, the deed for Windbreak, the full-page obituary that ran about my father in the *New York Times*. All the documents that, because there was no funeral, I haven't had to deal with yet. My father had wanted to be cremated, his ashes strewn across Windbreak, down into the ocean below. My uncle Joe was in charge of making that happen.

I pull out the obituary (the one document I've read before), focusing on the photograph of my father. He is standing with his arms crossed, on top of a lush hill, the San Ysidro mountains behind him. The caption beneath the photograph reads: **Liam Samuel Noone, founder of Noone Properties & Resorts, photographed at his flagship hotel, The Ranch.**

An asterisk next to my father's name explains that Noone is pronounced like *noon* (the time of day) and not pronounced like *no one*. Though I know my father liked that people got the pronunciation wrong sometimes. No one Properties, he would joke, could not be a more perfect place for someone to escape.

I zero in on the photograph. My father looks strong, intense, and virile against the mountainscape backdrop. I'm not surprised that this is the photograph the newspaper used.

For one thing, The Ranch was the first property my father built after taking over at Hayes. And this photograph leans into the mythical quality of how my father's rags-to-riches rise is often described: Liam Noone—Brooklyn born, the only child of Irish and Russian immigrants, his father a plumber and his mother, his father's bookkeeper. He was the first person in his family to go to college, let alone to attend Yale University, where he graduated first in his class, earning his MBA at Columbia, where he finished in the top three. He took a job out of business school as director of operations at Hayes Hotels, a family-run hotel chain, which had five properties along the eastern seaboard. An odd choice, one might think, to sign on to such a small operation. An odd choice to accept a position that was far less lucrative than entry level at any of the big consulting firms or fancy investment banks courting top students to join their ranks.

But when Walter Hayes died, he left the company to my father ("the most exacting young executive he'd worked with in forty-eight years"), and my father went on to turn the small hotel chain into the most sought-after luxury boutique hotel and resort empire in North America, with thirty five-star properties, eighteen more under development. A billion-dollar empire. He turned himself into an extremely wealthy man in the process. A mostly anonymous wealthy man who never wanted to be the face of the brand, letting his properties speak for themselves. Each of the properties had its own special story—its own mythical creation that made people long to stay there. Bucket-list properties that, Liam Noone worked tirelessly to ensure, always overdelivered.

I turn to the final paragraph, which focuses on his personal life, highlighting that my father was survived by his children: a daughter from his first marriage, two sons from his second. There is no mention of his wives (or that they are now all ex-wives), which would be how my father wanted it.

My father was married three times, but he never really got divorced. Even after he and my mother ended their marriage, he was a regular fixture in our home. He worked hard to maintain a good relationship with me and insisted it should disrupt my life as little as possible. It wasn't just about me, though. My father wanted to disrupt his life—all of his lives—as little as possible too: the one with my mother and me that he was trying to preserve; his life with his new family; and, then, the even newer family. It was as if he could only figure out a way for his worlds to never intersect; then he could get to pretend he was solely living inside each of them.

I wasn't mad at him for this when I was growing up, especially because I had a great childhood with my mother in Croton-on-Hudson. I loved our farmhouse and my friends at school—and the history of our small, sweet town, including the pride everyone took in the downtown "dummy light," the oldest traffic light in America. And I didn't have any desire to spend my time shuttling to my father's New York City penthouse and a stepmother who didn't have any interest in my being there.

But even though I loved my father deeply, there is a limit to how much time you can spend with someone who compartmentalizes his life like that. We had our Friday nights together—and if I had a school play, or an art show, he rarely missed it. But he spent much of the rest of the time with the other families and in the other worlds he occupied. Worlds he also needed to tend to, worlds that I knew almost nothing about.

This is one of the reasons why I'm stunned at how hard a time I'm having on the other side of his death. I'm not surprised that it's painful, of course, but it's staggering how deeply whipped I feel by the loss of him.

It doesn't help that my father and I had been somewhat estranged since my mother's death last year. After losing her, I started pulling away from him. Maybe part of that was that she died so suddenly—a shocking bicycle accident during her usual evening ride home. A trucker who failed to turn on his headlights. And, like that, I was without her.

My most important person. My mother used to say that what you did first thing in the morning was what was most significant to you. While I was growing up, the first thing we did every morning was spend time together. Real time, uninterrupted time. We'd get up with the sun still rising and take a walk into town, head to the bakery when it opened for fresh bread and hot chocolate, sit by the river and talk. We kept up our morning ritual even after I left home for college—my phone ringing every morning at 8:00 a.m., wherever we both were in the world, so we could talk on my way to class, and then on my way to work, so we could have a coffee together, if a virtual one. So she could provide me with her daily reminder that nothing mattered to her more than I did.

How can I explain the way her loss has broken me open? I've spent the last fourteen months looking at my phone at 8:00 a.m. every morning, willing it to ring again.

In the aftermath, I've felt a twisted, long overdue loyalty to her—especially when it came to my father. I couldn't seem to help it, even knowing my mother never harbored any anger toward him herself.

My own anger may not seem to make a lot of sense, then. Part of it was that he tried to take on a more daily role in my life (something he'd never had), which only exasperated my feeling that the wrong person was doing it. The other part was a strange side effect of my grief—the unmitigated grief I felt since losing my mother.

It had suddenly felt wrong to allow my father to occupy any emotional terrain in her absence. So I left the space empty, digging into that parental void on my own. Hurtling myself toward a simple, impossible mission: I could keep her as close as when she was alive.

Now that my father is gone too, I can't deny that I was on the wrong mission. The distance I kept from him didn't bring her back any more than it softened the pain of losing him now.

Where does that leave me, though? What good is knowing that you were wrong when there is no one left to hear you say that you're sorry?

The subway lurches forward, then stops completely, the lights going out.

An irritated murmur fills the car, but I feel relieved that, as my eyes fill with tears, no one else can see.

~

When I get off the subway, it's started to snow.

I live so far out in Brooklyn that my subway stop is aboveground, snowflakes starting to stick to my coat—to my skin—as soon as I step outside.

I love everything about my neighborhood, even how long it takes to get here. It's an area of Flatbush called Ditmas Park. It is historic Brooklyn—more small town than major city—with quiet streets, dogwood trees, old Victorian houses. A professor of mine in architecture school lived in one of those houses and rented me a room on a sliding scale. When her husband ended up taking a job in Northern California and she moved out west to join him, she let me lease the whole house until I could put together enough money to buy it from her.

My house is a mint-green Victorian, complete with its original staircase and stained-glass windows, its parquet floors. Pocket doors. Boxed vegetable gardens in the backyard.

I feel a surge of relief as my block of Marlborough Road comes into view, the respite of my home in striking distance.

But tonight, instead of heading that way, I follow the Christmas lights on Cortelyou Road into the heart of Ditmas Park's restaurants and bars—and my favorite local restaurant, Sheet Music, the name (and the small wooden sign hanging above the door) a relic from when it was a guitar shop.

Now its chef serves wood-fired pizza and elevated farm-to-table comfort food in a space I designed with him. The two of us reimagined the main room together, working to incorporate contemporary details—plaster walls, a stainless-steel canopy over a central dining counter, vintage chairs—while maintaining its former life as a music store, highlighting the tin ceilings and the baby grand piano, brown and lush, in the restaurant's far corner.

The restaurant was (and is) a passion project of mine.

This makes more sense when you know the chef is also my fiancé, Jack.

I take the side gate and walk around back to the service entrance, peeking into the dining room as I walk past. It's bustling and full, music seeping out through the windows, the lights low and inviting.

It's Friday night, which—at least in our little corner of the world—is the busiest night of the week: first dates (and last dates), after-work cocktails, parents wanting a New York City nightcap before disappearing into their family weekends.

I pull open the back door and step into the steamy kitchen, laying eyes on Jack at his station. He is wearing his chef whites and a San Francisco Giants baseball cap, his handsome face (my favorite face) sweaty and focused.

I breathe easier just at the sight of him, my heartbeat picking up.

It's the same weird combination of elation and calmness that comes over me whenever I see him at the end of a long day, taking in his skin and his hands and that face. Even now. Even still.

Jack is a year and change into being my fiancé, but he started off as my boyfriend more than twenty-five years ago; though, admittedly, boyfriend is overstating what we were to each other. He sat in front of me in eighth grade woodshop. I don't remember actively clocking that he was cute, even though he was really cute: tall and lanky with curly hair and dark eyes.

What I remember about him, though, was how he carried himself. Even if I didn't know how to name it, I could feel how comfortable he was in his own skin. He was sure of himself in a way that most eighth grade boys weren't. In a way that, I'd come to learn, a lot of grown men weren't.

He made it clear in how he spoke. His voice was gentle and kind and fleshy, like he belonged on the radio as opposed to sitting on a wooden bench in last period. Like he was only going to speak if he was certain that what he was saying was true.

It made me like being around him. It made me want to be around him more.

I think this is why (though I'm not sure we really ever know why) I did something completely out of character for my eighth grade self. I tapped him on the shoulder and asked him if he wanted to come get some ice cream with me after class. Does that count as asking someone on a date? It was certainly the closest I'd ever come in my thirteen years on the planet.

Jack, to his credit, didn't make it the least bit weird, even though that was the first time in his thirteen years anyone had asked.

*Sure . . .* he said, as though his cheeks weren't turning red. *I like ice cream.*

---

That afternoon, we biked to the A&P and ate our cookies and cream waffle cones by the river. It was one of a handful of outings before his family moved out west to Mill Valley, a small town just north of San Francisco.

We didn't see each other again until we were adults. I was on a first date at a much-discussed restaurant near Madison Square Park with a patent lawyer who also happened to be one of the restaurant's investors. After our meal, he tried to impress me by taking me into the kitchen to meet the chef.

Jack was the chef.

"Hey, Nora," he said, as if it had been twenty minutes since we last laid eyes on each other, as opposed to more than twenty years. The next day he found me online and sent a short message. *Nice seeing you again. Let me know if you want to get some ice cream.*

Now, I stand back and watch Jack work. He drizzles some Saba oil onto the crust of his signature pie, which he makes with this incredible strawberry sofrito sauce: a savory mix of garden-grown strawberries and San Marzano tomatoes, balsamic vinegar, onions, and pine nuts. He marinates the sauce for hours until it comes out tasting like the juiciest, richest, tangiest tomato sauce you've ever had.

It put Sheet Music on the foodie map less than two years after the restaurant's soft opening, the pizza topping several notable food critics' lists of must-try dishes.

Jack sends the strawberry pizza out for service. Then he looks up and spies me standing there and breaks into a smile. The smile that he reserves for just me: intimate and carnal and focused. How do I explain it? It always makes me feel like he can't believe I'm his, two and a half years in, twenty-five years in. In the same way I can't believe he's mine.

I walk over, and he kisses me hello, his warm hand cupping the back of my neck, his breath against my lips. Steadying me. The way only he steadies me.

"I didn't know you were coming in," he says.

I close my eyes as I sink into his skin, take him in.

"You okay?" he asks.

"Maybe."

He laughs. "Maybe isn't great."

"Sam Noone came to see me today."

He pulls back and looks at me, confused. "Your brother?" he says. "What did he want?"

"Just to catch up, get a coffee . . . You know, tell me that he thinks someone may have killed our father."

"What?"

I nod.

"Come with me," he says.

He gently steers me toward his office, motioning to his chef de cuisine, Kayla, that he'll be back. I lock eyes with her as we pass and try to give her an apologetic smile. The last thing she needs is me interrupting their dinner service. She turns back to her work, not even feigning a smile. She has been annoyed with me since Jack's good friend from culinary school, Becker, asked him to come and run her restaurant—a two-star Michelin restaurant in Northern California—while she is on maternity leave. It is a position that, if he'd taken it, would have left Kayla in charge of Sheet Music while he was gone.

Even though I encouraged Jack to go, Kayla blames me that he decided against it.

I think of how absent I've been lately. And I wonder if she isn't wrong.

Jack and I fall into lockstep as we walk into his small office. He closes the door behind us and turns to face me.

"What did he say exactly?"

"He's convinced someone pushed him over the edge . . ."

He looks at me like that's insane. It's probably not all that differently from how I was looking at Sam a couple of hours ago. I wait for it to make me feel better—to climb into the comfort of this all being a far-fetched idea.

"Is there any reason to believe that?" he asks.

"Not really," I say. "I mean, even if there are some threads I could pull at, my first instinct is that Sam has another agenda here. That this is a money play for him in some way. Or a power grab. Or I don't know."

"So why do you look like that?"

I shake my head. "I just also keep coming back to something else."

"Which is?"

"Why did he choose to tell me?"

Jack takes this in. And I can see that he knows the answer as well as I do. My brother may not know me well, but he knows me well enough to know that I'd have a hard time just letting this go. Maybe I've always been like that to a certain degree, but the technical aspect of my job necessitates an intense focus on such sexy details as safety and energy performance and egress. And now I'm unable to ignore it—whether I'm at work or not. I can't shake a lingering suspicion when something feels off.

"He wants me to go with him tomorrow," I say.

"Where?"

"To Windbreak."

"Seriously?"

"He wants us to take a look around. See if his concerns punch through."

"To California?" he says.

His tone mirrors how I'm feeling: this is all a little extreme, for me to fly across the country on a hunch. To fly across the country on someone else's hunch, someone who I barely know, whose motives are still unclear.

"I know it's insane . . ."

He pauses, considers. "I didn't say that."

Then he looks at me, that look he gives me when he's waiting for me to catch up to what he already knows I need to do. The only other person in my life who was able to do that, to know what I needed almost before I did, was my mother. With her it felt like safety—to be seen and understood like that. With Jack, it has always felt that way too. At least it used to. But since losing my father, my connection to Jack (its tenderness, its depth) has felt like something else. Something closer to a threat.

"I'll go with you," he says. "If you need to do this, I'll come."

"I wouldn't ask you to do that."

I see something pop in Jack's eyes, the sting of it, the surprise. "Well, you don't have to ask," he says.

I look down, not saying anything. What is there to say? I know he senses what I haven't wanted to talk with him about: since my father died, I have kept Jack at a distance. I have kept almost everyone at a distance. Closeness, especially closeness to Jack, stings too much. Like my most visceral reminder of what I've lost. Of what I stand to lose.

Even if Jack gets it, the distance is like its own kind of injury—to him and to me—especially considering that historically and effortlessly, Jack has been the person I most want to reach for.

So far, he has refused to punish me for it. He has tried to give me ample room to do what I'm doing. To grieve.

He takes my hand and kisses my palm, soft and quick. The safety of his touch, of him, rises up to comfort me, in spite of myself.

"I'll be home later," he says. "Get some rest."

Then he is opening the office door and heading back to work and away from me. I call out after him.

"Jack," I say. "Wait."

He is just outside the office door. He must hear me. I know he hears me.

But he doesn't turn back, probably because he already knows that if he does, I have nothing else to say.

~

At midnight, I can't sleep.

Jack is still at the restaurant. I get out of bed and head downstairs to my small home office, roll open the window, the cold flow of air moving me all the way to wide-awake.

I take a seat at my drawing table, ready to get to work. I have a proposal due for a project in West Chelsea—a children's bookstore that two retired book editors are opening near the Highline.

I'm hoping the quiet of the house will help me focus, but I spot the blue folder on the edge of the table and I'm back in my conversation with Sam. I'm circling back through it—trying to make it click into place—when my phone starts buzzing.

I look down to see a familiar name splash across my screen, a text coming in from ELLIOT.

Can you talk?

I push the phone across my table, try to push away the guilt that comes with it.

I tell myself Elliot could just be reaching out about Austin. I tell myself it could even be Austin texting me himself—even though I know Austin is not texting, not after midnight.

Austin Abrams: eight-year-old piano prodigy, world-class brownie baker, one of my favorite people on the planet. Elliot's son.

Elliot and I started dating four years ago, shortly after he separated from Austin's mother. He moved into the same West Village apartment building as my father. Elliot hadn't yet gotten Austin a piano for the new apartment, so Austin would do his practice sessions on the old upright in the apartment building lobby after he got home from school, after Elliot got home from the hospital.

My father heard him playing one evening and invited Austin and Elliot to use the Steinway grand piano in his apartment instead. They accepted his offer, happily.

And one night, when I went to meet my father for an early dinner, Elliot answered the door. Six-foot-six Elliot in his hoodie and wire-rim glasses, sweet Austin walking up to the door right behind him, the four-foot-four version of his father. Sporting a matching hoodie and glasses.

It was easy between us from the jump—easy, if not too intense. I was inundated at my new firm and Elliot was focused on handling his medical practice (he's a pediatric cardiologist) while navigating his new co-parenting role. I'd joke that we were half dating, half ships passing in the night. That joke hit a nerve, though. One reason he was getting divorced was that his wife felt Elliot was never able to leave the hospital at the hospital. *She'd tell me that I was always twenty-five percent absent,* he said.

I didn't feel that from him, but it's possible I was too busy to notice. I was actually so focused on my own work that I decided we should take a step back. Not long after that, Austin's mother decided she wanted another chance to make the marriage work, and I was quick to extricate myself entirely. I wanted nothing to do with keeping their family apart.

Austin wanted me in his life still—a decision that Elliot and I were happy to support—but I stayed in their lives in the gentlest of ways. I'd take Austin for an occasional hot chocolate after school on the days when Elliot was staying at the hospital late; and I'd try to attend his piano recitals, occasionally with my father.

I was careful to keep the lines clean, even before I started dating Jack. And I was even more careful after Austin's mother and Elliot separated for good.

It wasn't hard to keep them clean.

That is, until my father died. And Elliot started reaching out.

His presence in my life again feels like a balm. Is it just that he knew my father well? That he and my father adored each other?

Is there an innocent comfort in that? It doesn't feel so innocent at 12:08 a.m. It doesn't feel so innocent when, these days, it feels easier to talk to him than it does to talk to Jack.

That's probably because Jack is the opposite of twenty-five percent absent. He is wholly there. Talking to Jack is too much like looking in the mirror. He sees everything about me. Since losing my father, I see the reflection of it in Jack's face: the weight behind my eyes, in my skin. I'm a grown woman, but I'm also someone's child, looking for the parents to whom she didn't get to say goodbye.

I pick the phone back up. My fingers hover over Elliot's name, debating whether to reply. Whether to answer his request to talk. It's just a phone call. We're just talking. I repeat that part to myself, like an anthem.

And, still, what kind of anthem do you tell yourself in a whisper?

My phone starts buzzing before I hit reply. An incoming call, the ID coming up UNKNOWN NUMBER.

I nearly drop the phone. My first thought is that it's Elliot calling from the hospital landline. But my second thought fires in before I can stop it. Someone else is hurt. Since the loss of my parents, whenever an unknown call comes up on the caller ID, especially late at night, I'm sure it's going to be someone else I love in the type of trouble I can't save them from.

I click accept.

"Did you decide?" Sam's voice jolts me.

"What the hell, Sam? Why are you calling so late?"

"Same reason you're picking up, probably," he says. "Can't sleep."

I close my eyes, irritated, trying to slow my heartbeat. I force myself to take a few deep breaths, to find my center.

"You scared the crap out of me."

He ignores this. "Did you look through the documents yet?"

"Some of them."

"And?"

I reach for the blue folder and open it back up. The obituary, the will, the rest of it.

I flip to the Windbreak deed, pull it out. My father's signature stares back at me, stamped and dated, from more than three decades ago. The first home my father ever bought for himself. His favorite place in the world.

"Hello?" Sam says.

I hear the creak of my porch door opening, Jack pushing past the screen, keying our front lock, home safely. I don't call out to Jack to let him know I'm downstairs, to let him know I'm still awake.

I don't say anything to Sam for a moment, either. I rub my eyes, a wave of exhaustion coming over me. Grief is exhausting. No one talks about that. Or, at least, no one told me. No one told me just how exhausting it feels to carry it around with you. And it uses the same muscle as love. Because with real love you have to show up and give. You have to show up and be given to. And it's not so much that I've forgotten how. It's that it's all added up to be so heavy.

"What are you thinking?" Sam says.

I shake my head as though he can see me. And I start to say it will be a wild goose chase, that this seems like nothing to me. I want to believe it's nothing. But I feel a rush of something else. Maybe it's just guilt that I pulled away from my father. Maybe it's the need to be somewhere other than where I am.

But it might be something else—something closer to instinct, a deep-felt instinct, that my brother may not be entirely wrong. Did it take him showing up at the brownstone to see it? Maybe. Or maybe his showing up at the brownstone has finally encouraged me to say it out loud.

"I'm thinking Dad has taken quite a few night walks around Windbreak to screw one up now," I say.

"So . . . you'll come with me?"

I'm silent. We are both silent, for what feels like a long time. Then he breaks it, sounding not at all like himself.

"Nora . . . " he says. Like a prayer. "Please."

This is when I agree.

## An Early Departure

I don't see Sam at the gate.

I board the plane without him and settle myself into the window seat. Sam has gotten us business class tickets. This is something I don't normally treat myself to, Jack and I choosing to invest our earnings back into my firm, into his restaurant. I sit back and stare out the window, watch the flurries that are starting to pick up, water plinking on the glass. After my mostly sleepless night, it's all I can do not to doze off. I down the rest of my coffee and reach into my messenger bag, pulling out the blue folder. I want to share with Sam what I learned about Windbreak. At three in the morning. At five.

My father had two different architects draw up plans to expand on Windbreak's original footprint. The first time was more than two decades ago, when he was still married to Sam and Tommy's mother, Sylvia. It doesn't surprise me that Sylvia's plans involved razing the house and building a ten-thousand-square-foot Mediterranean palace in its place, a four-thousand-foot guesthouse by its side. Everything my former stepmother did was ostentatious, large. I'm also not surprised they didn't move forward with doing any of it. After marrying my father, Sylvia stopped working, but she remained wedded to New York City and her society events and her very active social life. While she probably liked the idea of a West Coast estate in theory, Sylvia has been to Windbreak even fewer times than I have.

What did surprise me was that my father also had a set of design plans from a little less than a year ago. Instead of razing the bungalow, the plans called for updating it: pitching the ceilings in my father's bedroom, expanding the galley kitchen so it was a place to gather. The design choices were simple and elegant, much closer to how I would choose to renovate the house myself. But I have no idea what (or who) motivated my father to consider renovating the house recently. What motivated him to stop.

Which brings me back to that recent conversation with my father. He wanted me to fly with him to Windbreak. He wanted my opinion on it, all over again. *I'm looking to make some changes.* Was he planning to have me reenvision a version of the most recent plans? Or was he going to ask me to start with him all over again? Either way, why now?

"I wanted the window."

I look up to see Sam standing above me in the aisle, wearing jeans and a Minnesota Twins baseball cap. He is struggling to catch his breath, his forehead dripping with sweat.

He throws his backpack into the overhead compartment and drops down into the aisle seat.

"I almost missed the flight . . ." he says.

"Nice to know this is important to you."

"It is important. I'm just not used to flying commercial. And I forgot about, you know, leaving enough time for security."

"You're kidding, right?"

"I thought about flying us in the company jet, but I wanted you to know I'm a regular guy."

"A regular guy doesn't say those words in a sentence."

He buckles himself in. Then he motions to the flight attendant, who is holding a tray of orange juice and champagne.

"Can I trouble you for one of those? Thanks . . ." He picks a glass of champagne off the tray. "I'll also take a whiskey when you have a chance. Straight up, please."

Sam takes a large pull of the champagne. I stare at him.

"Why are you looking at me like that?" he says.

"It's ten a.m."

"Which makes it early for a lecture," he says. "Besides, if it's all the same, I could use some latitude. I'm going through a breakup."

I look at him, surprised. "You and Morgan broke up? Since yesterday?"

"Who said I was talking about Morgan?"

Sam downs the rest of the glass as I look at him in disbelief. I seriously consider whether it is still possible to get off this plane.

"You know," Sam says, "I can feel your judgment."

"I'm not trying to hide it."

This is when the captain comes over the loudspeaker and announces the snow is coming down a bit harder. And I think I'm about to have a get-out-of-jail-free card. That the next thing the captain is going to say is that we are grounded because of the weather. But, no, he says while we may hit a few bumps, we'll be on our way soon. Boarding completed. The plane door closed and locked.

I sit back, take a deep breath in.

"Anyway," Sam says. "It's not what you think."

"I think that it's none of my business."

"So maybe it is what you think."

"Let's just stick to talking about Dad, okay?"

"Fine by me."

I stare down at the Windbreak information that I have analyzed and tabulated, the property map and the design plans ready to be further dissected.

"There are a bunch of things we should get clear on before we talk to the police," I say. "I also have some questions about the perimeter. And we should loop in Tommy too, don't you think?"

"Why?"

"It affects him, for starters. And maybe he'll have some insight."

"No. He won't."

He shakes his head, shutting it down.

"You know that's the second time you've responded like that when I've brought up Tommy," I say. "What is going on with you two?"

"Nothing worth getting into."

He puts his arm over his forehead, wipes at the sweat there. And I notice that he's wearing a brace on his wrist, a thick black brace. On that wrist. The one that he broke, the one that ended his baseball career.

He shrugs. "It always acts up in the cold. Alcohol will help."

"I don't think that's how alcohol works."

He keeps his arm on his face, lowering it over his eyes, a makeshift sleep mask. "Can we pause on the chitchat? I'm just not in a great place at the moment."

"You're aware that you're the one that wanted to be doing this?"

"I am," he says.

"You sure about that?"

"I will rally."

I turn toward the window as the plane jerks forward, then back, and then we are heading away from the gate and toward the runway. The plane picking up speed, about to leave the ground behind.

"You let me know when," I say.

~

It takes us just over ninety minutes to drive up the coast to Windbreak from LAX, Sam curling our rental car along the Pacific Coast

Highway and the 101, roadside signs starting to appear for Carpinteria.

I look out the window as Sam takes the exit into town, climbing over the railroad tracks until we are driving down Padaro Lane. The afternoon sun disappears beneath the tree shade, the light slipping through the fog and the dome of branches, the world around me entering a permanent kind of shimmery dusk.

And it happens, like it always seems to happen when I turn onto this road—I am six years old again, seeing it for the first time.

My father took me here on his own, my parents already at the beginning of their end. And he was nervous—I could feel that he was nervous. He wanted to make sure I was comfortable and happy. The whole drive from the airport he'd talked about how we were going to drop our bags and head straight down to the beach, straight into the ocean. But the clouds started setting in as we got closer to Carpinteria, and by the time we got to Padaro Lane, there was heaping rain and crushing thunder. So we raced into the house, drenched, and waited for it all to stop.

After the rain let up, it was too late to swim. But my father took me out to the cliffside and we drank milkshakes and ate tomato sandwiches and watched the sun set, a silvery-orange hue.

*Maybe not the best first impression, Nora-Nu,* he'd said, kissing me on the forehead, calling me what he always called me. *But she's showing up now.*

Then we took those creaky steps down to the beach and the ocean some eighty feet below, my father not letting go of my hand the entire time. Not on the way down, not on the way back up. My hand in his, safely. And I asked him if we could move there. He loved to tell me, every time after, that I asked him that. Does he remember what he said in response? Why did he say it? *Windbreak doesn't just belong to me.*

"We're here," Sam says.

Sam's voice pulls me from the memory, as he turns down a driveway, a large gate greeting us. We pull in front of it and Sam reaches out the window to tap out the alarm code onto the keypad.

The gate creaks open and the property comes into view behind it. The driveway taking us over the stones, toward the expansive lawn, the open sky and ocean beyond it.

And the house itself. This cottage, proud and hopeful, holding its own against the expanse, the light in the trees, all that showing off. This small, perfect cottage: two bay windows circling the front door, a wraparound porch, the rocking bench perched on the corner, oceanside, taking in the bluffs.

"It gets you, huh?" Sam says.

I nod, feeling uneasy.

He pauses, looking straight ahead. "So you think you'll keep it?"

I turn and look at him. "What?"

"I'm just asking," he says. "'Cause if you sell it, it's worth a lot of money. The land alone is worth eight figures . . ."

"I'm not thinking about that, Sam."

"No reason to be testy. Dad knew you didn't want any part of the company, and you'd never take any money from him, so maybe this is his way of trying to make it, I don't know, even."

I turn away from him, my skin suddenly on fire, my nerves heightened. The last time I was here was a little over two years ago. The last time I was sitting on that rocking bench, Jack was sitting there with me. It was the only time Jack had come to visit Windbreak. My father handed him a glass of wine, kissed me on the top of my head.

A hazy and warm recollection. Jack's hand resting on my knee, my father's smile.

My voice catches in my throat. "The red-eye leaves at eleven fifteen tonight," I say. "I'd like to be on it."

"Can I put the car in park before you make an exit plan? We can always stay at Uncle Joe's place, if we need more time. Or we can stay here."

"Why would we need more time?"

"Once again, I'm going to need to actually get out of the car before I know how to answer that."

Sam kills the ignition. And two men walk out of the front door to greet us. The one on the left I recognize. His name is Clark, and he has been taking care of Windbreak since before my father even bought it. It's been years since I've seen him in person, but he hasn't seemed to age. He is still strong, tall and wiry, in his jeans and work boots. His skin tanned and uncreased, his smile keeping his face young.

The other man I don't know. He is linebacker large and burly in a too-tight suit, his hair buzz-cut short, his skin red and ruddy. He is also much younger than Clark, probably close to Sam's age.

Close to his chest, he holds a clipboard. I can see, even from here, that it's covered with police department decals.

Sam motions to him. "That's Detective O'Brien," Sam says. "He's our liaison at the police department."

"So, he ran the investigation?"

He opens the car door. "Apparently not well."

~

"You took a long flight for me to tell you what the report lays out," Detective O'Brien says. "We're confident we don't have a lot of unanswered questions . . ."

Clark has gone back inside and we are walking the property with Detective O'Brien. Or rather, O'Brien is walking several paces ahead of us. He moves quickly, not stopping as he looks down at his clipboard and the police department's incident report. A report that is tucked into my blue folder.

"The fall happened between approximately eight fifteen and eight thirty p.m.," he says.

He keeps walking toward the southwest edge of the property. We all know, without him saying it out loud, that he's moving in the direction that the police department ascertained our father was walking that night. In the direction of the spot where he fell.

"Considering that it was a rainy night, we are lucky that there were people on the beach to corroborate."

"I don't know if *lucky* is the word I'd use," Sam says.

Detective O'Brien turns back, offers a small smirk.

"There were three pedestrians on the beach. A couple was walking their dog and approaching the accident site from the west," he says. "And a jogger, who circled back from Loon Point . . ."

He motions up the beach as we arrive at the edge of the property, the grass ending, rocky stones leading to the small stone palisades, the edge of the cliffside just beyond it.

"Their witness statements locked in a tight timeline."

I look down to see a yellow stake in the ground, so inconsequential it could signify anything—plants, a rosebush, where you lost your father.

I step past the stake and grind my sneakers into the rocky edge, slippery even when dry like this. And I can imagine it so easily: two steps too many and you are clinging to that cliffside. But why would he stand so close? He wouldn't, unless he didn't realize he was so close, a drink in his hand, a trippy look over the edge, and suddenly he was plummeting down the eighty feet to the beach below, the rocks catching him almost before he knew what was happening.

"Our conjecture is that your father fell from right near here," he says. "And that he was killed on impact . . ."

Killed on impact. The words feel harsh and clinical coming out of his mouth.

"How did you determine that?" I ask.

"Excuse me?"

"That he died on impact?"

"No one could survive that fall," he says, as though that answers the question. As though that addresses my concerns.

But it's becoming more and more clear that Detective O'Brien doesn't have a lot of interest in our concerns—nor does he care that we are grieving. Maybe he even thinks what I thought of Sam when he showed up at the brownstone yesterday. That whatever we are here about, it's not about what we are saying it is.

I try to take a different tack to make him less defensive, to move him closer to our side. Shouldn't we all be on the same side here?

"Detective, you're certainly much more well-versed on all of this than I am, so I really do appreciate you taking the time to go over it again," I say. "But . . . could we back up a bit? It feels to me like we are still missing large pieces of this puzzle."

"What puzzle?"

"We don't think he was here alone that night," Sam says, less diplomatically.

"I can assure you that he was," he says.

Detective O'Brien looks back and forth between us, like that seals it.

"Okay. Why's that?" I ask.

"Noone Property's internal security confirmed early on that it was a last-minute change in his itinerary for your father to be out here," he says. "He was supposed to be at an event in New York. No one on his team was informed about his impending arrival at Windbreak. The property's caretaker just reconfirmed that he wasn't even made aware."

That seems off. Because, at least the handful of times when I've been here, Clark is always the person who opens the house for my father.

Sam looks at him, confused. "Clark is always informed," he says.

"Apparently not this time," O'Brien says.

Then he flips to a different page on his clipboard.

"My team ran out your father's entire day. A driver picked up your father from the Santa Barbara airport and drove him directly to Windbreak. They keyed into the property at twelve fifteen. Your father was the only one on property from twelve fifteen until the time of his death."

"Except for the driver," Sam says.

"The driver keyed out at twelve thirty-two," he says, his tone tightening. "The limousine company showed us his records for the rest of the day . . ."

"I wasn't suggesting it was the driver," Sam says.

"What are you suggesting?"

"You said my father was the only person on property," Sam says. "And right away that's not accurate."

Detective O'Brien gives Sam a warning look. I put my hand on Sam's arm, trying to regulate his tone. But I'm feeling heated myself. Even if I don't want to admit it, these explanations are raising more questions for me than answers.

I look over the palisades, the massive cliffside, the ocean and the sand swirling below, and try to picture his fall. My father would be the first to know how to do it, if he started tipping toward the edge. How to catch himself, steady himself, move quickly to safety.

"I spent a little time looking over property maps last night," I say. "Am I correct that there are no cameras along the perimeter?"

"Yep, that's right." Detective O'Brien nods. "There is an alarm system in the house, linked directly to the precinct. But the only camera is by the front gate."

"Isn't that unusual?" I ask. "My experience in working on properties of this size is that most have some sort of security on the grounds themselves. There are over a hundred yards of bluff front, alone . . ."

"Well, that's a question for the alarm company. But it's my understanding that your father refused to even consider a guard by the gate, so the keypad to enter and exit is pretty much all there is in terms of perimeter security."

I look left, into the distance at the neighboring property—the closest property, which is hard to even see from here. I don't think I've ever met the family who lives there. The only neighbor of my father's that I've met lives farther up the road. Benjamin King. A real estate investor of some kind. He and my father went to college together and he was the reason my father even knew about Windbreak. My father loved telling the story about how he saw Windbreak for the first time when he was sitting on Ben King's deck, discussing a business proposition.

But I've never heard my father say much about his next-door neighbor, one way or the other. There is a stone wall separating the two large plots of land—theirs nearly consumed by a Tudor mansion, large and ponderous, big enough to swallow three of my father's cottages.

"Did you speak with the family next door?" I ask. "Do they have cameras on their property that we could access?"

"We did access them," he says. "We watched down the footage for the whole night and unfortunately, the cameras are only pointed so far as the wall that separates the property. We have no sighting of your father at all." He pauses. "I can confirm that no one scaled the wall."

"In the footage you saw," Sam says.

"Again, my team watched the entire evening's footage." He turns to his clipboard, starts flipping pages. "Actually, we watched down the afternoon as well."

"Did you check the day before?" I ask.

"We have no indication of anyone else on the property the day before your father's arrival."

"So no," Sam says.

I scan the rest of the cliffside, eyeing the antique gate leading to the large set of wooden stairs, rickety and old, winding into the cliff-side, eighty feet down to the rocky beach below.

"Someone could have entered this way . . ." I say. "They could have taken the steps from the beach."

"Only if they knew the code to the door. Which would've had to be someone your father knew."

"So maybe it was someone he knew," I say.

"Why would someone he knew enter from the beach and climb up dozens of stairs in the dark of night, just to enter the property?"

Sam points at him, smiles. "That right there," he says. "That's the first good question you've asked."

Detective O'Brien doesn't like this and gets busy looking down at his clipboard again.

I walk over to the break in the palisades and down to the landing where the gate is, set into the cliff itself. I pull on the gate's rusty knob. There is a small lock over the opening, a keypad to set it free.

"What if they did know the code? From my father or some other way. Is there any electronic catalog of who entered that way?"

"No. It's just a keypad, a manual lock. It's not connected to the rest of the security system."

I look up at the detective and Sam on the cliff's edge. "Why?" I say. "That doesn't seem particularly safe."

Detective O'Brien offers a tight smile, failing to hide his increasing irritation. "That's a question for your father," he says. "It was his decision. As I said, it's my understanding that privacy was of the utmost importance to him."

"Did you at least look into who had access to the code?" I say. "It doesn't seem like a bad idea to run out the scenarios as to who could have entered this way. Check their alibis . . ."

"Only if you believe that there is real evidence of foul play," he says. "Which I do not."

"Well maybe you should consider doing it now," Sam says. "So we can all be that sure."

O'Brien raises his eyebrows, like this is (next to continuing this conversation) the last thing he intends to do. And while I'm not at all convinced that anyone entered from these stairs, that look is the final nail in convincing me that his only concern here is keeping the case closed. Which is why I decide to press.

"Could you tell us a little more about the pedestrians, Detective?" I ask. "The three people who found my father? The couple and the jogger."

O'Brien flips through his clipboard, lands on his witness reports. "The couple, Meredith and Nick Cooper, were house-sitting for the Velasquez family at 2082. They'd been there for the last several months while the Velasquez family was at their home up in Ross," he says. "And they were doing their regular evening walk with their golden retriever when your father fell. Nick was the person who contacted 911."

"And the jogger?"

Detective O'Brien pauses, as if not wanting to share what he is about to. "He was no longer there by the time the police arrived."

Sam notes it at the same time I do. He meets my eyes.

"What do you mean no longer there?" Sam asks.

"Meredith, the wife, used to be a volunteer EMT, so once she determined that your father hadn't survived impact, they decided she and her husband would wait for the police to arrive. They didn't need his help."

"You don't think that's suspicious?" Sam says.

"I think people choose to live here because they want privacy. And your father was clearly no longer alive, so it wasn't like there was anything to do. He probably didn't want to be involved."

*Or he was involved,* I think before I can stop myself. I walk back up the landing, holding his gaze.

"But the Coopers didn't recognize the jogger?"

"No, they didn't recognize him, but again they aren't homeowners. They are just house-sitting, so . . ."

"For several months, though, yes?" Sam says. "You just said they had been staying here for several months."

He nods reluctantly, and I know he recognizes what Sam is suggesting, even if he doesn't want to see it himself. Something about that doesn't track. If the Coopers walk their dog every night and this man jogs with any frequency, you would think they'd have run into each other before that night. Or since that night. It's a fairly safe bet that people living on this small strip of beach would run into each other more than once.

And then there is this: Why is this the first time we are hearing that one of three people on the scene, who apparently wasn't recognized by the other two, left before he could be interviewed?

"I thought you said that you obtained witness statements from all of the witnesses?" I say.

"That may be what you heard."

"That's what we both heard," Sam says. "Because that's what you said."

Detective O'Brien sighs. He actually sighs. "Look, guys, I lost my father last year. I get that this is all painful," he says. "But I learned early in my training, when you hear hoofbeats, think horses, not zebras."

"Sure. And I get why you'd want that to be the case," Sam says. "If a horse turns out to be anything other than a horse, then someone didn't do their job very well. And this neighborhood, on your watch, doesn't get to be as safe as property values need it to be."

"That's ridiculous," Detective O'Brien says.

"Maybe. But what sounds ridiculous, to me, is everyone suggesting that a potential victim forgot how to walk the line on his own property," Sam says. "Not to mention that one of three people there that night apparently is still unaccounted for. Plus, you know, we still have no information on anything that happened to our father from the time a driver dropped him off at noon until he fell eighty feet to his death that night."

I can see Sam clenching his fingers, clenching them right over the brace. So I step in beside him, in case I need to step between them.

"But, please, feel free to enlighten us," he says. "Which way is the horse?"

# Most Likely to Succeed

After a tense goodbye, Detective O'Brien leaves.

Sam and I walk back toward the house, moving at a steady clip.

"We need to find the jogger," he says.

I scan the police report, searching for any information about him—any information we have about the Coopers.

"We've got the Coopers' contact information on the police report," I say. "I'll start there. See what they can tell me about him."

Sam holds the screen door open. And I step ahead of him, up onto the back porch.

"I'm going to search Dad's office," he says. "I want to push down on why he changed his plans. According to his calendar, the event in New York was for Inez. Dad would have wanted to be there for that."

Inez Reya. She was wife number three (ex-wife number three), and certainly my preferred stepmother for the brief period that she was. She created a holistic skin care line that Noone Properties featured in most of their spas. This was how my father met her. It was his shortest marriage (less than three years) but it became one of his most important friendships. My father stayed incredibly close to Inez and her now wife, Elizabeth. And their daughter, Luna.

If Inez had a launch event, my father would want to show up to support her. Why did he decide he had to be at Windbreak instead?

Sam walks into the house, disappearing down the hall toward our father's office. I walk into the kitchen, the galley kitchen, a blast of light and familiar smells greeting me—the potted sage on the windowsills, coconut soap, sandalwood candles on the island.

I love the feel of the kitchen, which, like the rest of the house, is relaxed, and low-tech: a vintage oven, a farmhouse sink, not even a dishwasher. I lock in on the drying rack next to the sink. It almost does me in, the stupid empty drying rack taking me back to that last visit here. Jack asleep. My father turning the record player on but low, just the two of us, washing and drying that night's dishes together.

I run my finger over the rack and lean against the counter, centering myself. Then I pull out the Coopers' contact number. I call it, but I'm greeted with an out-of-country ringtone. I click off and send an email instead, hoping that a note will find its way to them quicker.

I leave the kitchen and head through the rest of the house. I pass by the two bedrooms (the second of which my father used as his office), the one full bathroom, the tiny powder room. All the walls are painted a soft white, the furnishings spare and thoughtful.

The clean beach air feels like it is running through all of it, especially in the room I enter last. My favorite room, the living room, which is more like a makeshift library, complete with tall white bookshelves surrounding a bay window, the walls adorned with wild bird–splattered wallpaper that doesn't exactly feel like my father, but which I love. And which somehow fits more than anything else here.

For me, a project always starts with a central image. Something that identifies what a space or a property most organically can be. In how I approach my work, this is a fundamental principle: How am I going to take that image and build out from it? Build out from the feeling of it to craft something that isn't only beautiful, but also that utilizes the right materials and design elements to create something healing, something hopeful.

The whole of this house, the loving force that swings out from it, seems to have started with someone imagining what this room could be.

I walk over to the bookshelves, filled with so many gorgeous books stacked in every direction. There are only two shelves not overflowing with books, two shelves that are tightly filled with framed photographs and a variety of other personal items, scrapbooks and a couple of yearbooks, old journals, old playbills.

I lean in and start leafing through some of the playbills. I can't remember ever going to a play with my father, and yet he must have two dozen playbills here that he's chosen to hold on to: *The Real Thing, Lost in Yonkers, King Lear.*

Then I turn to the photographs. Many of them I recognize—photographs of me and my mother that she had framed at her house too. Several are of Sylvia and my brothers, of Inez and Elizabeth and their little girl, Luna. One is with a past president.

The other shelf has photographs and framed newspaper clippings of my father at work. Some are with my brothers. Some are with Grace and Uncle Joe. There are photographs of the team in the New York office, clippings from hotel openings in Aspen, Whitefish, Cabo San Lucas. My father smiling happily, completely in his element with his sons; and with Grace and Joe, both of whom had remained by his side for decades, from the early days of Noone Properties until Grace passed away earlier this year—a heart attack taking her too young. Which left my father and Joe to run the business together. One trusted advisor left.

It makes me wonder how that shifted the dynamic between my uncle Joe and my father. Though, in fairness, I didn't really keep up with how the dynamics had worked before. My mother rarely talked about my father's company, and I followed her lead. *You only need to remember two things about Noone Properties*, she'd said. *It happened after me. And it has nothing to do with you.*

Of course, that is revisionist history. My parents may not have been together by the time my father had turned Noone into the empire that it now is, but they were still married when he took over at Hayes. They were married for the early part of that empire-building, for those early years of his meteoric rise. They had actually met during his second year working there, my father still fairly fresh out of business school.

My mother was a music teacher and a session musician at that point. On occasion, though, like the night they met, she would sing with her friend's wedding band at the Hayes Hotel in Watch Hill, Rhode Island.

My father was spending several months on property, overseeing a renovation there. She saw him sitting at the hotel bar during her dinner break, my mother feeling fierce in her gold jumpsuit. She was the one who approached him. She took the barstool beside him and asked him if he wanted to buy her a drink.

My mother said he intrigued her: this too-serious young guy with his mop of blond hair who seemed out of place in a family-focused hotel. My father felt like she didn't belong there, either. She belonged on a movie set. She belonged on a world stage. He said one of the things he liked most about my mother was that she was so comfortable in her own skin that people just wanted to be around her—wherever she was.

He was correct about that. My mother was confident in a way you could only be when you really knew yourself. When you really knew what you wanted. And, at least then, she wanted to get to know him. She also didn't want to change her life. She loved her old farmhouse in Croton. She loved walking to work at the high school and only going into the city for studio sessions, or the occasional night out.

So my father sublet his West Village apartment and moved in with her. He started doing the hour-plus commute to Midtown Manhattan each morning and back every night, not begrudging her that it added two hours to his day.

And my mother didn't begrudge him when their marriage started to show strain and he started coming home less, staying at his West Village apartment again.

She didn't begrudge him when shortly after Walter Hayes died and left him the company, my father started spending longer days at the office in Manhattan, which led to even more nights spent in that West Village apartment, and (eventually, as they grew further apart) to a new friend, the travel expert on a popular morning show. The new friend named Sylvia.

I spent almost no time at my father and Sylvia's place while I was growing up. Sylvia had little interest in having a stepdaughter around—a point she made clear by purchasing a penthouse apartment for her and my father's growing family and conveniently not designating a bedroom for me. One of the few times I visited them, I overheard my father insisting that I have my own space to decorate in a way that made me feel comfortable, to which Sylvia replied, without a hint of irony: *There are Frette sheets in the guest room. If those aren't comfortable, I can't help her.*

Even if Sylvia had been welcoming, my father would have siloed his different families anyway. He was more comfortable focusing on each of us separately rather than figuring out the implications inherent in merging all of us. He liked to come up to visit me in Croton most Friday evenings, so the three of us could have dinner together.

He often came up for dinner, even when I was older and I chose to spend most free nights with my friends instead of with him.

He and my mother would take walks by the river or drive to Cold Spring to get an early supper, just the two of them. Sometimes, they'd just sit on the porch and catch up.

It wasn't romantic between them. My mother started dating another musician, Julian, shortly after she and my father separated. From day one, she was completely devoted to him. They were devoted to each other. She'd often say to me, *I was meant to meet your father so we could have you. I was meant to meet Julian for me.* As for my father, he was the one who left their marriage in the first place.

I pick up a photograph of the three of us at my college graduation—my mother in the middle of my father and me—our arms wrapped around each other, all of us laughing. I zero in on their faces, easy with each other, relaxed. They'd been divorced for over a decade at that point, but you wouldn't know it from looking at them. You would only see how close they seemed.

So how do you explain it? My father's desire to keep my mother close, long after it was about me. How could I begin to understand his need to start new lives but never to walk away from the old ones?

*Oh, for Pete's sake, my love,* my mother used to say when I'd ask. *It's like you don't know your father at all.*

# *Fifty-One Years Ago*

The first time Liam met Cory, she was coming out of his bedroom.

"Hi there," she said.

She was wearing a green wrap dress, her curly hair running halfway down her back. The shock of her standing there—this beautiful girl in his bedroom doorway—like she belonged there, made him step back.

"Can I help you?" he asked.

"I don't know, can you?"

She smiled at him, her eyes shining. It wasn't just that she was beautiful, though she was beautiful. But it was more than that when she looked at him with those eyes. She was so familiar to him. So present. Liam had never seen her before, and suddenly he felt like he'd never *not* seen her.

"I'm Cory," she said.

"Liam."

She held out her hand, and he took it just as his cousin Joe walked out of his bedroom too.

"Hey, bud," Joe said. "This is Cory."

"I heard."

"She just transferred to Midwood . . ."

Liam nodded, keeping his eyes tight on Cory. He didn't even look over at Joe—Joe who had recently transferred to Midwood and moved in with Liam's family. He'd moved, more specifically, into the top bunk in Liam's room after running into some trouble at his own high school in Vinegar Hill. His father wasn't in the picture to help out. And his mother (Liam's mother's sister) decided Joe needed a change. Needed a good influence, needed someone with his head on straight. Needed someone like Liam.

Cory was still holding his hand.

"Where'd you transfer from?" Liam asked her.

"Immaculate Heart, unfortunately."

"Like . . . unfortunately you went to Immaculate Heart? Or unfortunately you're stuck at Midwood now?"

Cory tilted her head. "What's wrong with Midwood?"

"How long do you have?"

"Not long actually. I was on my way out."

Liam cleared his throat. "Is Cory short for something?" he said. "That's a guy's name, isn't it?"

"Wow, you're the first person to ever point that out," she said. Sarcastic, but not angry. "It's short for Cordelia. Which I like less."

"Cordelia. Like *King Lear*?"

She nodded. "Exactly," she said. "My mother's a lit professor at Brooklyn College."

This surprised him. "What does your father do?"

"Most days? Drink."

But she smiled. She smiled that smile again, Liam working hard to hold her gaze. Like she could disappear if he didn't. Cory was taking her hand back, pulling her hair off her face. What a feeling this was, standing this close to her. Brand-new, for him. He wanted to be exactly where he was.

"I've seen you before," she said.

"What do you mean?"

"At the library. After school."

It didn't seem possible that she'd been in his vicinity and he'd missed her. But the way he'd been studying, he guessed it was possible. What did the guidance counselor say about Liam? That, in her thirty years at the school, she had never seen a student as driven as Liam was. She meant it as a compliment, but she also meant it as the opposite.

As if hearing Liam's thoughts, Cory leaned toward him.

"You were extremely focused."

"I wasn't that focused."

"Never apologize for focusing," she said. "Joe says you're going to Yale next year?"

That's when they looked up and realized Joe had left. He'd gone downstairs or back inside the room. He'd gone somewhere away from them.

"How about you?"

"I'm a sophomore so . . . I have a little time."

"But you're going with Joe?"

"Maybe. I don't know."

He nodded. Joe was good-looking. Too good-looking, really. He was already six foot two with shaggy hair and a strong jaw and chiseled muscles and all the rest of it. That's part of the reason why he got in trouble. That's part of the reason he didn't think he needed to try hard. Liam wasn't bad looking, either. Maybe not as tall or as broad, but he had Joe's jaw and he had really nice eyes, kind eyes. And he had a couple of years on him, so there was that. But he wasn't Joe.

"You should know," Liam said, "Joe's got a lot of girlfriends."

"You have at least one yourself."

He looked at her confused. "How do you know that?"

"She was at the library with you," Cory said. "She was trying to get you to stop focusing."

Liam felt his skin heat up, his cheeks turning red. He and Christina had been dating for the better part of two years. She was planning on working at her father's dress shop after graduation. She was putting pressure on him to think about getting engaged. But that was the last thing he wanted. He had one foot out the door of this house, of this street lined with its identical homes, of this provincial slice of Brooklyn a world away from New York City. Everything about being here made him feel trapped. The broken television his parents couldn't afford to fix, the moveable tub his father soaked his frozen shoulder in, his classmates seemingly all too happy to raise kids on these same streets where they grew up. Rinse and repeat.

He wanted none of that. The reason the guidance counselor said Liam was so driven was that he walked into her office the first week of his freshman year and laid it out for her. He would do anything that was needed to get himself to somewhere better. To get himself to a completely different life.

"You guys staying together after graduat—"

"No." He answered before she even finished asking. "Definitely not."

She laughed. "Didn't mean to hit a nerve there."

"You didn't," he said. "I'm just not taking anything with me from here."

She smiled, but she started to walk past him, toward the stairs. "That sounds like a dare . . ."

He turned around. "Where are you going?"

"I've got to go back to school. There's a meeting tonight for the literary magazine. Not a lot of outlets at Midwood for writers, so . . ."

*Jabberwocky*—that was the name of the school's literary magazine, wasn't it? Liam wasn't sure. He wasn't sure he'd ever even picked it up.

"What do you like to write?"

"Oh, you know. Short stories. Plays. Poetry. All sorts of things."

"What are you writing now?"

"That's a longer conversation."

He wanted to say, *Let's have it.* He wanted to hear all about her writing and anything else she was willing to tell him. It was unnerving.

"Nice meeting you, though," she said. "Liam."

His name had a finality coming out of her mouth that he didn't like. He stared at her, unsure what to say. She was almost at the staircase.

"Just . . . would you . . . can you wait a second?" he said, his words jumping over themselves, fast and furious. And, if he was being honest, a little desperate.

He didn't sound anything like himself—at least the self he'd always thought he was, calm and collected at all times. Suddenly, the real him could be summed up by one thing: he didn't want her to leave.

She shrugged. "I don't want to be late."

"Fuck late," he said.

She laughed, took him in again.

"Okay," she said. "Maybe."

And, like magic, Cordelia started to walk back toward him.

"Do you need some help?" he says.

I jump back at the sound of his voice, startled. I am so focused on the photograph of my parents that I don't hear the footsteps. I don't hear anyone behind me.

I turn to see Clark, Windbreak's caretaker, standing in the doorway.

"Didn't mean to scare you there," he says.

"No, no . . . you didn't. I didn't hear you. Sorry. I'm just, you know . . ."

"A little on edge?" he says.

I nod. "A bit."

He points toward the office. "I just was talking to Sam," he says. "Sounds like Detective O'Brien wasn't much help."

"Have you had a lot of interaction with him?"

"Tried to avoid it," he says. Then he smiles, puts his hands in his pockets. "You looking for something in particular?"

I place the photograph back on the shelf, still holding on my father's face. "Yes. And I have no idea what yet."

"Well, I'll hang out for a bit, in case it comes to you."

"Thanks, Clark."

"For whatever it's worth, I have been on edge as well. I feel bad I wasn't here to open the house that day. He didn't let me know."

"Why do you think?"

"I don't know. If had to guess? He knew I was taking my grandkids camping and maybe he didn't want to bother us. Didn't want me to feel obligated. You know how he was . . ."

I wonder, not for the first time in the last few days, if that's true.

"Do you think there's any possibility that someone else was here with him that night? I mean, that would explain him not letting you know too."

He pauses, considers. "Sure, it's possible . . . I don't think they got anyone coming through the front gate, right? Not that that's necessarily definite. There are other ways in and out of this place. Of any place if you work at it hard enough."

I nod.

"That's not a whole lot more than you already know, I guess. But, like I said, I was out of town."

And he shrugs. But he hesitates. He hesitates like there is something more to say.

But before I can press it, Sam comes running into the room, holding a large manila envelope.

"We need to go," he says.

"Now?"

"Yes, now."

He is so riled up that his face is turning red.

"I'll give you two some privacy . . ." Clark says.

He exits, happy to extricate himself, and I turn back to Sam. "We were in the middle."

He ignores this. "Have you heard of Cece Salinger?"

"Cece Salinger. Like the hotel magnate?"

He nods. "Exactly."

"Why?"

Instead of answering, he is already slamming down the hall. He is already heading toward the front door.

I call out after him. "Sam, where are we going?"

"Uncle Joe," he says.

# There's One Way into Hope, One Way Back Out

I drive.

Sam is too worked up, his words tumbling out on top of one another, coming out too quickly. Like he isn't only trying to explain the situation to me. Like he is also trying to get hold of it himself.

"Cece and Dad go way back," he says. "She started building out her hotel business when Dad was taking over Hayes, so in a weird way they came up together. They were on these parallel tracks. But also totally different. I mean very different, obviously—"

I pick up speed as I merge onto the highway, heading toward Santa Barbara. "How do you mean?"

"I mean we're small in comparison," he says. "She has more than a hundred hotels all over the world. Larger hotels, but really nicely done. Their main competition is Four Seasons, the Ritz. With a nod to local architecture, uniform service. The opposite of how we do things. Of how Dad did things . . ."

"I'm familiar with the largest hotel chain in the country, Sam."

"Well, you may not be familiar with the fact that I almost went to work for her."

"What? When was that?"

"Hotels are a core business for Cece, but they're also just a piece of the Salinger Group portfolio," he says. "She's across a bunch of sectors.

Entertainment, book publishing, sports. Including this sports marketing firm called PNG. After I got injured, someone at PNG reached out to me. Not uncommon to recruit old athletes, so I didn't think much of it. I didn't think about any connection to us, to Dad, until I saw his reaction when I told him I was thinking of taking a job there."

"Which was?"

"Not great. Apparently he and Cece have a long history."

Sam opens the window and motions for me to take the exit for La Cumbre Road. "He told you not to take the job?"

"You know Dad. He wasn't going to tell me not to take the job, but he told me not to take the job."

"What was the deal with them?"

"Cece had tried to break into the luxury boutique market for a long time, exclusive properties, privacy driven. Small footprint," he said. "Apparently, she'd been after Dad for years to sell her Noone Properties. She wanted to go into the boutique market wholesale that way, use his branding, all of it. Because Dad had figured out how to scale it. That's not easy to do. Which is probably why Cece made some pretty generous acquisition offers."

"So?"

"So he always turned her down," he says.

"I'm not following."

"Unfortunately, that makes two of us."

~

Hope Ranch is a stunning coastal community just west of Santa Barbara proper, just south of the Pacific Ocean. It's hilly and serene. Beautiful homes blending in with the oaks, equestrian trails crisscrossing the roadways.

We wind our way down Las Palmas and up Via Esperanza until we pull up to Joe's house. It's a gorgeous old Spanish hacienda, lined with weeping willows, horse stables, and a circular cobblestone driveway—which is alive with activity. Several trucks are parked there, movers unloading flower arrangements and boxes of dinnerware and furniture rentals.

"What the hell is all this?" Sam asks.

He steps out onto the cobblestones, closing the passenger-side door before I've even put the car in park.

I turn off the ignition, jump out after him. "Sam, just wait a second. Pull it together," I say. "We don't need this to escalate."

He looks at me and nods like he hears me. I can even see him trying to take a breath in. But then our Uncle Joe opens the big oak door. That's all it takes—seeing him in that doorway—and Sam's face turns red again.

"What the fuck, Joe?"

"Or go ahead and escalate it," I say under my breath.

Uncle Joe weaves past the staff and trucks and walks toward us. He is in a wet suit. Even in his late sixties, he looks twenty years younger than he is: his wet hair still thick, his skin tan from several decades in the California sunshine, his frame strong and lean.

My father would often joke that Joe got the looks in the family, but it always felt like my father was trying to give Uncle Joe any leg up that he could. He didn't like that Joe was often unfavorably compared to him while they were growing up. Joe was considered to be more of a troublemaker, less motivated, less brilliant. My father would swat away the comparisons. He was fiercely loyal to Joe in that way. In all ways. From my vantage point, my father and Uncle Joe had that loyalty in common.

He smiles at us. "Sorry for the chaos."

Sam stares him down. "He was going to sell the company to Cece? How long was he keeping this from us?"

"Hello to you too, Sam."

Then Joe turns toward me. "I didn't know I was getting you."

He leans down to give me a hug hello, which is more like a back pat and somewhat awkward. It's also out of character, but I know why he does it. We haven't seen each other since I lost my father. Since we both lost him. So I reach up to offer him a hug back.

"How you holding up, kid?"

"Okay. You?"

He shrugs. "Certainly have had better months."

Sam looks between us, aggravated. "We all have. Where can we talk?"

Joe eyes the movers and staff circling around. "This way," he says.

We follow him into the house, which is lovely—complete with its original oak floors, high vaulted ceilings, and a U-shape courtyard. But it's even more chaotic inside than it was outside. A woman is on a headset directing staff. People are milling through every room.

"What's all this?" I ask.

"Your cousin's engagement party."

Sam looks confused. "That's this weekend?"

He nods. "It sure is. I think you replied that you were going to be in Australia for work. How's your trip going?"

Then he turns to me.

"Don't look at me," I say. "I didn't even get an invitation."

"And if you had?"

It's a fair point. My cousin Diana is Joe's only daughter and ten years younger than I am. I didn't even realize that Diana was getting married, let alone that they were celebrating her engagement this weekend. I haven't spent much time with her. Not long after Uncle Joe went to work with my father, he came out to California to manage Noone Properties' West Coast expansion. Joe met Diana's mother, who was born and raised in Santa Barbara. They bought this house and made a life here. A world away from my life in Croton.

Diana's mother took off when Diana was really young, which left Joe to raise her on his own. He has done so lovingly. A bachelor since, but a completely devoted father. I know from my own father that Joe has been something of a serial monogamist over the years, but that too hasn't been a part of his life I've seen firsthand.

Joe leads us out to the courtyard, which is a quiet respite. Beautiful succulent plants line the perimeter, a firepit lit up in the center.

He motions to the chairs surrounding the firepit. We all take a seat, Sam tossing the manila envelope onto the table.

"What's happening with the Salinger Group, Joe?" Sam asks. "Why did I find deal terms for a sale of Noone Properties?"

"Cece was after Noone for years. That can't be news to you."

"What's news to me is that Dad would even consider it, let alone get lawyers involved in drafting possible acquisition plans. These are signed and dated earlier this year."

"It didn't get as far as you'd think."

Sam points at the manila envelope, like a certain kind of proof. "Really? 'Cause this seems pretty fucking far."

"Okay. Let's calm down."

"How did no one tell me?"

"Because there was nothing to tell. Your father and I discussed it and he wanted me to run out whether a sale was worth pursuing, so that's what I did."

"And?" Sam says.

"And he ultimately decided it wasn't what he wanted to do," Joe says. "He changed his mind—"

"No. This went further than that."

"Until it didn't, Sam," Uncle Joe says. His tone sharp.

Then, as if hearing himself, Joe takes a deep breath and stands up, heads to the serving cart. He reaches for a pitcher of lemonade, pours three glasses.

Joe turns, hands me a glass. "How did he get you involved in this little mission anyway?"

"That's not exactly what I'm here about."

"No?"

"Sam actually came to me with some concerns about Dad . . ."

I feel Sam's eyes drilling into me, and I look over at him. He shakes his head no, quickly. I don't know how to challenge him on *why* we can't talk to Joe about our father's last night, at least not in front of Joe, so I drop the point, change tack.

I clear my throat. "Did Dad seem off to you? The last few months?"

"What do you mean by 'off'?"

"Distracted," Sam says. "Distant."

Uncle Joe shakes his head. "I didn't get that," he says.

"Oh, come on," Sam says. "Something was going on with him."

Joe sits back down. He looks down, as though he is actually considering what Sam is suggesting, like he is trying to remember anything he may have missed about what my father was struggling with, what maybe he hadn't wanted to see.

But I can see it, beneath his neutral stare. His Adam's apple, the vein in his neck, pulsing. Like he is having trouble staying calm himself. Like he is stalling until he can figure out what he's willing to say.

"I've got to say, Sam," Joe says. "I think you are seeing something in hindsight that wasn't there."

"Really?" Sam says.

"Really."

"Then you're not telling the truth."

Joe puts his drink down, leans forward toward Sam, toward both of us.

"Guys, can we just let this lie, please? Whatever you've convinced yourself was going on with him, why does it matter now? The company's yours and Tommy's now, Sammy. All's well that ends well. And your father loved you . . ." He looks over at me. "He loved you all very much. I love you too. It was never about punishing you."

"What the hell does that mean?" Sam asks.

"It means stop making something out of nothing. I know you're in pain. I'm in pain too. And I'm not going to pretend that I always understood your father's choices. But the priority for your father was that you guys were going to be taken care of."

"What choices, Joe?" Sam says.

"I'm talking generally."

"Can you be less general?" I ask. "What choices didn't you understand?"

Joe shakes his head. "I'm not going to excavate the past with you. It has nothing to do with anything."

"So Dad's history with Cece didn't play into this somehow?"

Something flashes in Joe's face, his jaw tensing, before he pushes back against it. "That wasn't what this was about."

"You sure about that?" Sam says.

Joe stands up, done with this conversation. "The engagement party is tomorrow night. Come if you like. You're both welcome."

He starts to walk away, but I'm going over it in my head, his choice of words, his careful phrasing: he just said that the sale wasn't about our father's history with Cece. And I hear what he refused to flat out say in the silence. He didn't say that Cece and my father didn't have a relationship. He didn't say there wasn't a history there to factor in.

"So what was this about?" I call out after him.

He turns back. "What's that?"

"For Dad. What was it about?"

Joe shakes his head. But I see it in his face, the sadness there. It's gone as quick as it came, but it's there all the same. That tiny part of him seems to want to just say it, whatever it is that he knows.

"Something else," he says.

## *Fifty Years Ago*

"I don't want to be apart," Liam said.

"Well, I would hope not," she said.

It was the night before he was leaving for college. They were in Cory's bedroom, lying on the floor—her hand on his stomach, her head against his bare chest, against his heart. Her bed was covered with books. They hadn't even waited to move them. The floor was good enough for them, being alone good enough for them. Her mother was teaching a night class at the college. Her father was out with friends. They had at least a couple of hours more. They had right now.

"I'm serious about this, Cory . . ."

"I thought you weren't taking anything with you from Midwood."

"Things change."

"Not that much they don't," she said.

"New Haven isn't that far."

"For someone who has been planning his escape from Midwood for his whole life, you maybe should have thought of that."

"Cory—"

She sat up and reached for her dress. It was its own small injury, how easily she moved away. How cold the air felt without her.

"You told me yourself that you can't wait to leave this place behind. If we stay together, you'll resent me. I have no desire to be something or someone you resent."

"I'd never resent you."

She turned around to face him. "So maybe that's just an excuse. Maybe I just don't like you very much."

"I'm serious."

She pulled her dress over her head, Liam sitting up so he could zip it for her. "So am I," she said. "I know how this goes if we try to stay together."

"What do you know?"

"I know you. And this time tomorrow night you're going to be in a different state, sharing a dorm room with Charles Theodore Hearst III, who can't wait to introduce you to the guys he went to boarding school with in Maine. And isn't that funny, he likes football too. And you should come with the guys to Mory's for a beer. The Whiffenpoofs are singing later, and there's this girl he thinks you may like—"

"You think I'm that easily swayed."

"I just refuse to be something else that makes you feel trapped," she said. "Or to put myself in a position of being someone you feel like you have to lie to. I want to be the person you never lie to."

"I can make you that deal."

"Except you're going to want to go to the Cape for fall break or on a road trip with your roommate for Christmas. You're going to want to do all sorts of things that have nothing to do with coming home to me . . . which will make you feel badly and then you will lie about that, so I don't feel badly too. I'm not interested in any of that."

"I have no intention of lying to you about anything," he said. And he meant it.

"Great," she said. "So that's settled."

He tilted his head, looked up at her. "I don't think we just agreed to the same thing."

"Can we not spend the night this way? You understand what I'm telling you even if you don't want to understand what I'm telling you."

He didn't say anything. What was there to say? She saw right through him. She saw right through most people. She'd figured out how to do that, early on. She'd learned it as a coping mechanism, as a way to survive in her house. It was one of the reasons arguing with her was so difficult. She was wiser than he was. She knew better. But what good was her knowing better, if that meant he was going to lose her?

"You're my favorite person," he said. "That isn't going to change."

"Then we have nothing to worry about, do we?"

She straightened her dress and stood up. He looked up at her. He had never known anyone like her. He suspected, even in this moment, that he would never know anyone like her again.

"Let's go downstairs and I'll put on some pasta. I need sustenance if you want to continue pretending tomorrow is going to go another way."

"New Hampshire," he said.

"What?"

"Charles Hearst III went to boarding school in New Hampshire. Not Maine."

"See?" she said. "We're already growing apart."

"What if I want more?"

She bent down, looked into his eyes. "Well, on the day that I believe you're capable of that, maybe we'll be more."

# Three Lies & the Truth . . .

"Tell me he wasn't being super cagey," Sam says.

Sam is driving us out of Hope Ranch and toward the 101, toward Los Angeles, toward the red-eye that will take me home.

"Seriously," he says.. "Look me in the eye and tell me there isn't something going on here."

"You came at him pretty hard, Sam."

"So?"

"So that would make anyone defensive. Who knows how much of it was that he was just reacting?" I ask.

"How much of it do *you* think was him just reacting?"

I turn toward Sam, more suspicious than I'm willing to let him know. I could see it when I looked at Uncle Joe and we were pressing him. He was keeping something from us, protecting it fiercely. The question is: Was it the thing that could help explain what had been going on with our father?

"Why didn't you want me to talk to him about the night Dad died? Isn't that what we are supposed to be doing here?"

"That is what we're doing here," Sam says. "But we can't be telling anyone about that. Not even Joe. Not until we know he wasn't involved."

"Wow. Just when I think you're not entirely crazy."

"I'm not saying it's likely."

"Oh, I'm glad you don't think it's likely that our uncle pushed our father off a cliff."

I look out the window, refusing to engage with this level of insanity. Whatever Joe was keeping from us, it didn't necessarily mean there was a nefarious decision behind it. There were much simpler explanations. Maybe our father didn't want Sam to know certain things about his past. He certainly kept the compartments separate when he was alive. He certainly fought to keep all sorts of things private. What if there was a reason for that? Beyond what we know?

Maybe Joe was being loyal to our father in ensuring we don't get to know, even now.

"You can call it whatever you want," he says. "I'm telling you that Joe has his own agenda here. He knows that Dad was having a hard time these last couple of months. Anyone who was spending time with Dad knew it."

His words hit me, catching in my throat. I hate that I can't properly speak to how my father was doing in his last few months, not in the way I normally would be able to, not in the way I should be able to speak to it.

"Did you notice how agitated Uncle Joe got when you mentioned Dad's history with Cece?" I ask. "Were you just fishing or do you have any actual evidence they were involved?"

"Rumor is that they had a thing a long time ago."

That stops me. "Like how long?"

"Like forever ago. Like when they were in college or something . . . I don't know exactly. It was only a rumor."

I think about Uncle Joe's face even when Cece's name came up, like Sam was tripping into a secret Joe wanted to pretend didn't exist. Thinking of his face, it feels like it could be more than a rumor.

I pull out my phone and do a search for Cece Salinger, but my coverage is spotty, images of her not fully loading.

"Salinger Group's headquarters is in Century City," Sam says.

I look up from my phone. "In Los Angeles?"

He nods. "It's worth a shot to try and talk to Cece, don't you think?" he says. "We could try and talk to her on the way to the airport."

I don't answer him, which is the only answer he needs.

Sam checks the rearview, the highway in the distance. "At the very least, maybe she can enlighten us. She has no reason to lie about what happened."

"We don't know that."

"There's reason number two," he says.

~

We are on the 101, passing the Summerland exit, when Jack calls.

"Hey. I'm just checking in before the dinner rush," he says. "You doing okay?"

"Yeah, we're heading back to Los Angeles . . ."

I look over at Sam, who is speeding down the highway. He must feel my eyes because he turns to me too.

"Who is that?" Sam asks.

Sam and Jack haven't met. I assume my father has told him I'm in a relationship, but I don't want to get into any details of my personal life with him, so I just shake my head, not answering him.

"What time do you land?" Jack asks.

"A little before six."

"I'll have the coffee on."

I start to smile, that making me feel sad and happy at once. My desire to head home to Jack laced with the discomfort I feel in my body, in my chest, at the promise of that very thing.

Sam's phone buzzes, a text coming through.

"Shit," Sam says and holds up the phone for me to see.

"Hey Jack, I'll call you back, okay? I love you . . ." Then I click off and take Sam's phone from him. "What's the problem?"

"My office just texted," Sam says. "Cece's not in L.A. But she's willing to talk with us if you're up for taking a little ride."

"Where, exactly?"

"Santa Ynez."

"Santa Ynez?"

He pulls off the highway and plugs Cece's address into the GPS. "We can probably be there at about five fifteen."

It's a little before 4:00 p.m. That's at least an eighty-minute drive in the opposite direction of Los Angeles, of LAX, of the red-eye home. I start doing the math in my head—the amount of time we'd have for this conversation with Cece in order for me to make that flight, in order for me to be there for that cup of coffee.

"We're going to need to talk quickly."

Sam turns the car around. "In my limited experience," he says, "Cece Salinger doesn't talk any other way."

## Los Alamos, Nowhere Near New Mexico

We head north, driving through the heart of Santa Ynez Valley.

Signs on the side of the highway start to greet us, then vineyards, welcoming us to California's Central Coast. It's untouched wine country: more rustic than Napa Valley or Sonoma, with small-batch vineyards, sweet roadside restaurants, the river flowing west toward the Pacific.

Sam heads up 154, the mostly one-lane highway keeping us locked behind trucks and slow cars, the late afternoon wind. We work our way through, heading past Los Olivos, the signs leading us north toward Los Alamos.

Los Alamos. As soon as I see the signs, I remember it immediately.

Last year, Jack and I were in Northern California for his friend's wedding, and we rented an Airstream and drove down the coast afterward. We camped out every night, Jack making us these incredible dinners around a small campfire. The two of us took long walks on the beach, Jack humoring my eight-hour architectural pilgrimage to the Poly Canyon Structure Labs, another to the Salk Institute.

We spent a lot of time making plans in the loose and unhurried way you get to when you are with the person you love the most. We discussed things as light and easy as Jack joining me for an upcoming Nashville work conference; things more involved like details about a potential winter wedding, both of us agreeing there was nowhere we wanted to have it more than at my mother's house. Eight minutes from where we met in eighth grade.

It was a great trip. The last trip I took before my mother died. The last trip I took while it felt comfortable and uncomplicated to plan anything. And before winding our way down to San Diego, we stopped in Los Alamos to see a chef friend of Jack's who had just moved there from Los Angeles, a happy expat, eager to tap into the Valley's burgeoning restaurant scene.

Now, with the downtown five miles away, Sam turns onto Alisos Canyon Road, a long winding road that takes us past an equine center, stables and vineyards. Sam drives us farther down the road, the numbers going up until we hit Cece's address—and a private driveway that takes us up a mountain pass.

At first, it all seems desolate and dusty, an isolated rural road. But then we are heading deeper up into the mountains, enraptured in the kind of hilly, ridged terrain where the sky hits the empty earth on a brilliant angle, turning everything a soft yellow, turning the world into the gentlest version of itself.

We turn left at the top of the mountain pass and head under a steel arch, toward a small guardhouse, Cece's gorgeous ranch house (all glass and reclaimed wood, enormous steel doors) on the hillside just beyond it. Sam's phone buzzes.

He looks down, pumps the breaks. "Fuck."

"What?"

"Cece just canceled."

"No, really?"

He shakes his head, reading from the phone. "'A family situation came up that needs her attention. She sends her apologies.' You've got to be kidding me."

He pauses, and I think he is going to turn around. But then, as if rethinking it, Sam looks straight ahead, puts the car back in drive, and pulls up toward the guardhouse.

"What are you doing?" I whisper as he lowers the window, the guard stepping out. He buttons his sport jacket as he approaches the driver-side window.

"Good evening," he says. "How can I help you?"

Sam pulls out his license, hands it over. "Sam Noone," he says. "Cece is expecting me."

The guard looks at his license, hands it back. "You should have been notified. Ms. Salinger was pulled into a dinner in town."

"Oh, is that so? Not a lot of service up here."

"Apologies for that."

"Thing is, to be honest with you, we just drove quite a long way, and it's a bit of a family emergency. Maybe someone could buzz her and ask if there's a place where we could just park the car and crank up the radio until she gets back from her dinner? We really just need a minute of her time."

"That wouldn't be possible."

Sam smiles at him. "Well, it would be possible."

"*Sam* . . ." I say.

He turns and looks at me. "What? It's entirely possible."

I put my hand on Sam's arm, leaning across him, making eye contact with the guard, forcing a smile.

"Can we just ask you one thing and we'll get out of your way?" I say. "When you say Cece is having dinner in town, do you mean the town of Los Alamos?"

"That is the town here, yes."

The guard tilts his head and looks at me, like I've asked the dumbest question he's heard in recent memory. Then he points down the driveway, to a turnabout, that will take us back in the direction we came.

"You're going to need to reverse and turn the car around right over there, thanks."

"Sure, sorry to bother you."

He heads back into the guardhouse, Sam turning toward me. "What the hell was that? I was getting somewhere."

"You were getting nowhere, to be clear," I say. "And that was me confirming Los Alamos, because I've been there. It's not a big town, one main strip. There can't be more than four or five restaurants on those few blocks."

"And?"

"And I'm guessing, if we want to find someone eating dinner there, it won't be impossible."

Sam starts backing up, his arm on my seat's back, his eyes on the rear window.

"That's your plan?"

"Well, my preferred plan is for you to drive us straight back to LAX because apparently Cece Salinger has no intention of speaking to us, but I figured you'd think this is better than nothing."

"She could be eating at someone's house. She could be in her house and the guard's lying entirely."

"True," I say. "You want to head back to LAX, then?"

I don't need to toggle through my calendar, or study my notes file, to know what I'll find there. I have hours of weekend work to get done tomorrow in preparation for a busy week. I have a pitch to ready for a large commission—a drug rehabilitation clinic in Jackson Hole, Wyoming. I have Jack. Jack whose love and worry I can feel, even from this far away.

Sam heads back down the mountain pass, stealing a glance in my direction. "Okay but I want you to admit it . . ."

"Admit what?"

He turns back onto the main road, heads in the direction of the downtown. "We were never going home tonight."

~

Downtown Los Alamos is similar to how I remember it.

The entire business district is essentially one long strip running the length of Bell Street: quiet, gentle, and yet it has a surprising energy. People head in and out of restaurants. Families eat nighttime ice cream on benches. A lone guitarist plays Bob Dylan, the sound rising along the lantern-lit main drag.

There are several establishments already closed for the day—a bakery, a lunch spot—but Sam pulls into a parking spot in front of Charlie's Restaurant, a line of eager diners waiting outside the front door.

We pop out of the car and head inside, scanning the full restaurant and the side patio. From Sam's face, I can see that none of them are Cece.

We head down the street on foot, stopping in Full of Life Flatbread, a pizza restaurant that smells so good my stomach rolls, a small wine bar across the street from it. And, a few doors down from there, Babi's Beer Emporium.

No Cece, not anywhere.

"Well, this is working out great," Sam says.

"Patience," I say.

We cross Centennial Street, the open establishments getting fewer and farther between, when I see a small restaurant on the corner. Bell's Restaurant. It's lovely—with a garden in the back, a wide blue door, a window in the middle of it showing off the elegant interiors: antique tables and Windsor chairs, an open kitchen complete with copper pots and wine bottles and plants.

I'm peeking through the window when Sam bangs on it.

"Holy shit," he says.

"Your fist was like an inch from my face."

"That's her."

He points to a woman sitting at the corner table, closest to the kitchen. She is typing on her laptop—two people sitting across from her, their backs to us.

She is stop-and-stare gorgeous with this sleek silver hair, large eyes contained behind thick black glasses—and so impossibly elegant in a white button-down shirt and jeans, cowboy boots. She looks less like a hotel mogul and more like a Ralph Lauren model.

She wraps her hair around one of her shoulders, continues keying her laptop.

"Let's do this," Sam says.

Then he pulls the blue door open. And we walk past the entry table, flush with flowers and books, and head straight to her table.

She must feel us looking at her. Because she looks up as we approach and then she sees Sam. A look of recognition comes over her face.

"Hey, Cece."

"Sam . . ."

Then she turns and meets my eyes, looking me up and down.

"I'll be damned," she says. "The daughter."

"Did we get our signals crossed?" Sam asks. "We thought we were meeting you up at the house."

Instead of answering him, she keeps her eyes focused on me, in a way that feels a bit too familiar. I hold her gaze, Sam motioning toward the table.

"Okay for us to sit?" he says.

"It's not really the best time, Sam. We have a bit of a fire drill at work."

"Really? Because your office said it was a family matter."

She turns and gives him a smile, like she is enjoying this—her discrepancies, his discomfort. Or maybe what she's enjoying is that my brother is calling her out.

"Sometimes it's everything at once, isn't it?"

"Sometimes," he says. "We can be fast."

She rubs her hands together, as if considering how she wants to handle this. Then she turns to her colleagues.

"Can you give us a few minutes?"

They stand up to leave and Sam and I each take a seat across from her. Cece reaches for the wine bottle in the middle of the table. She uncorks it herself, a waiter appearing with fresh glasses, Cece pouring for each of us.

She slides one of the glasses toward me. "You know . . . we almost met last year, you and I," she says.

"Is that right?"

She nods. "It is. I'm a big fan of your work. I know quite a bit about you."

I don't respond, trying to stay neutral, when what I want to say is *Really? Because my father told me nothing about you.*

"I was very impressed with your build-out on Joanna Harrington's property in Taos," she said. "She's an old friend."

Joanna Harrington owns a large family ranch just outside of Taos, New Mexico. I helped her reimagine the property as a community-focused equestrian center.

"I was so impressed with your work for Joanna that when I moved here, I wanted to hire you to do my house," Cece continues. "I even had Joanna inquire about your availability. You had none apparently."

She offers a smile.

"Sorry about that."

"Don't be. When I mentioned it to your father, he put the kibosh on all that anyway. You know how he was about holding firm to his boundaries."

Holding firm to his boundaries. That was certainly one way to put it. And yet, I feel as though she is baiting me—isn't she baiting me a little? Isn't that the purpose of this anecdote? She wants me to know what she understands about my father, disarming me with that familiarity. With their familiarity.

"Sam hasn't actually filled me in on all of this," I say. "How do you and my father know each other?"

"I grew up not too far from him. We went to school together," she says. "I'm close with your uncle Joe too."

*Too.*

She looks back and forth between us. "I feel like I owe you guys an apology for the runaround tonight," she says. "To be honest with you, your uncle Joe called and I decided it was best not to get in the middle of anything."

"We weren't aware that there were opposite sides," Sam says. "So thank you for that further clarification—"

"I wouldn't say opposite sides."

"What would you say?" Sam asks.

"For starters, I'd say that it's a little hard to even look at you, Sam," she says. "Too much like your father."

Sam flinches. And I recognize it immediately on his face, how it feels to hear that, now that our father's gone. That twist of pride and sadness—the grief switch being turned on. It's exactly what happens to me when someone comments on how much I remind them of my mother.

I jump in, feeling something that surprises me—something like protectiveness.

"Look, Cece, we don't want to take up your time—"

"You just want to take up my time?"

I force a smile. "We found documentation at Windbreak that suggested our father was going to sell you the company," I say.

She takes a sip of her wine. "Until he wasn't."

"My understanding was that he had no intention of ever selling the company," Sam says. "We're just looking for any insight into what changed there?"

"Well, I'm not sure I can be all that helpful on that front. I would never aim to guess what motivated your father to do anything. But it was my understanding from what I was told that he was done running the company and I happened to reach out at the right moment. After reaching out at many wrong moments."

"So why did the sale fall apart?" Sam asks.

"I assumed it was that he decided to leave it to you and your brother."

"He said that?"

"He didn't say much of anything to me, quite honestly. I mostly dealt with your uncle Joe."

"Why was that?" I ask.

She turns back to me. "How do you mean?"

"If you and our father go so way back—"

"We all go way back. And Joe and I are quite close. Our kids grew up together. My husband still has a house down the street from him. Ex-husband, I should say . . . Still getting used to that."

Ex-husband. I try to keep my face neutral, but I clock that. Apparently, Sam does too. I see him look at me out of the corner of his eye.

"It was recent?" he says.

"What was recent?"

"Your separation."

"Which time?"

She smiles at him, as if she knows what he is trying to factor in. Did the end of her relationship fit into this? Did it have anything to do with the end of our father's most recent marriage?

"You must have been curious, though," I say.

"Excuse me?"

"From what my brother here tells me, you and my father were pretty far down the line on the sale," I say. "A vague idea as to why it fell apart was enough for you to let it go?"

She takes me in, clearly not liking the question. Maybe because it's coming from me and maybe because she doesn't want to answer, whoever it's coming from.

"In my experience, when someone pulls away, they don't usually know why. And I try to avoid unreliable narrators."

She picks up the wine bottle, pours herself and Sam what's left. "I'm going to need to invite my associates back in soon, so do you want to tell me why you're really here before I do?"

Sam starts to speak, but Cece stops him.

"Not you." She points the wine bottle in my direction. "You."

"Sorry?"

"From what your father has told me about you, his company is the last thing you would drive ninety miles to hear about. So while I appreciate the guessing game as to why he chose to pull out of our agreement at the eleventh hour, I'd like to know what's going on here."

"We have some concerns about our father's fall," I say. "About the night he died."

"What does that mean?"

"*Nora,*" Sam says.

Cece puts up her hand to quiet Sam.

"What does that mean?"

I don't look at Sam. I don't let him stop me. "We're trying to figure out if maybe he wasn't alone that night."

She looks confused until it must click, something washing over her face. Something like fear. Or is it anger?

"You think that someone hurt him?"

Sam puts his hands up. "No. Absolutely not. No one's jumping to that," he says, even though he is the exact person who has been jumping the fastest to that.

"What does any of that have to do with his decision to sell Noone Properties?"

"I guess that's what we're asking you."

But Cece isn't exactly listening to what Sam is saying. She is shaking her head, as if considering it—what one thing could possibly have to do with the other.

And she looks genuinely upset. She looks so upset that I realize this is precisely why I asked her the question. To see if she was as surprised by this being a possibility as I was.

"We have something of a complicated history, your father and I, but I've always cared for him. A great deal . . ."

She looks up—her eyes pained and glossy.

"We hadn't spoken in several months. And I stand by what I said about why Joe took the lead. But it was somewhat unlike your father that he wouldn't want to reach out in some way, to *acknowledge* the deal, but Joe and your father had a specific dynamic so that was between them."

She pauses, almost as though she is torn about saying what she feels compelled to say. She closes her mouth, as if deciding against it. Then, she leans forward and does it despite herself.

“But in the spirit of things that we shouldn’t be offering up, your father did reach out to me. He didn’t leave a voice message, so I don’t know exactly why. It may have been nothing, but he did call me. Twice.”

Sam sits up. “When was this?”

“The night he died.”

## *Forty-Eight Years Ago*

"Liam?" she said.

He knew who it was before he even turned around. He knew it from the sound of her voice, quiet beneath the snow and the wind and the loud street. He knew it from how the air shifted, making room for her again, giving all the room to her, even if Cory wanted to pretend it was a question.

This was his first Christmas going home. He'd avoided going back to Midwood for the holidays. He'd avoided going home for more than two years. The only exception had been at the end of his sophomore year, when he had to come back for Joe's high school graduation. Which, of course, was Cory's graduation too. He saw her standing there in her graduation gown, her floral dress peeking out beneath the lapels, her curls in a matching hair clip. She'd looked beautiful and happy and sure of herself.

He'd walked the other way, wanting to be generous to her—to not make that day about them. But that wasn't the only reason. It was also about protecting himself. He knew what would happen if they met face-to-face. Exactly what was happening now in front of the damn liquor store on Avenue J. His unraveling.

She was wrapped in a thick scarf and a beanie, her curls long and wild around her shoulders. Snowflakes dotted her black coat, dotted the wine bottles sticking out of her paper bag. And it was as if not a second had passed, not one, looking at her again. Where had he been that mattered more than this?

"Cory," he said.

"How are you?"

"Fine. Good."

He was neither thing. If you had asked him yesterday, he would have insisted he was better than good. He was thriving at school in ways he could calculate (his grades, his classwork, his extracurriculars) and ways he couldn't (his daily sunrise run from his residential college to the library where he couldn't believe he got to study, where he couldn't believe he belonged).

Looking at Cory again, that all disappeared. Everything disappeared. There was only her.

"How about you?" he asked.

"Oh, you know."

She forced a smile, offered a shrug. She'd made it so easy for him to disengage from her. He'd tried calling at first, those early weeks of college, and she never came to the phone. And while he imagined taking the train home from New Haven and showing up at her front door, he never did it. And then he started to get busier and stopped imagining doing it. He eventually did his best to not allow himself to think about her at all.

"Joe told me you're at Brooklyn College," he said. "How's that going?"

"I love it."

"What happened to Wellesley?"

"What do you mean?"

"I thought there was that professor there you wanted to study with."

"Well, Brooklyn College gave me a full ride and I can commute from home, so it made more sense . . ."

He nodded.

She tilted her head, took him in. "Does that disappoint you?"

"Why would it disappoint me?"

"Because I know you," she says. "And you think I should have gone farther than across the street."

"Brooklyn College is a good school."

"Nothing to do with anything in your mind."

He looked away from her. This wasn't going how he wanted. What did he want? If he was being honest, he wanted to take her hand, like he had any right. He wanted to lean in and feel her cold breath. He wanted to put his arm around her and get her inside out of the wind and the snow. Like she needed him to do those things.

"Picking up last-minute supplies?" she asked.

"Sorry?"

She motioned toward the wine store. "Joe told me you guys are having a Christmas party tonight. He invited me."

"Yeah. Really our folks are, and it's not going to be much of a party. Just a few of their friends . . ."

"Don't worry, I'm not coming."

"I wasn't worried."

"I don't think that's entirely true."

She smiled—her real smile. And it nearly killed him. Two years. Four months. Eighteen days. Wasn't that supposed to ease what he felt when he looked at her? When he took in that smile?

"You should come," he said. "I'd like you to. We can sneak up to the roof. Drink hot toddies."

She nodded. She didn't acknowledge the weakness of his invitation by responding. Two years, four months, eighteen days.

"It was good to see you, Liam. Take care."

She hoisted her wine bag higher in her arms and turned to walk down Avenue J in the direction of her house. He didn't say it was good to see you too. Because what he wanted to say was something else entirely. Which was that it was awful to see her. It was awful to remember how wrong it felt to not see her every day.

He watched her retreating, the angles of her hair and her back, still within reach. Let her go. Let her go. He turned and opened the door to the wine store, the forced heat and peppermint candles and holiday music making him want to vomit. The bell above the door. Let her fucking go.

This is when he heard her voice for the second time.

"I may be open to another offer though," she said.

The relief he felt. The amount of fucking relief. He turned around. She was standing right outside the doorway.

"What did you have in mind?" he asked.

She shrugged. "I don't want to go to your party and I don't want to go to my house, but pretty much anything else will do."

He let the door to the wine store close behind them. The heat gone. The cold night air and her skin and arms and face inches from him.

He took the paper bag out of her arms to carry it for her. He put his free hand on the small of her back.

"Then let's do anything else," he said.

# Old Friends Are the Best Friends

"She's awful," Sam says.

"She didn't seem awful."

He shakes his head. "That's what makes her so awful."

We are walking back to the car, the sky dark and starlit, the main street now quiet and mostly emptied out. Sam is upset, too upset to be rational. So I take the keys out of his hands, work it through in my mind. Why would our father have called Cece that night? Could he have been rethinking the sale? Possibly. But it feels more likely to me that he would have reactivated that interest through other channels, more official channels. Uncle Joe.

No, it was something else. Two missed nighttime calls. No message. If I'm guessing, it was something more personal.

"She has an agenda here, I'm telling you," Sam says.

"What does that mean, Sam?"

"There's something she doesn't want us to know."

I pull my sweater more tightly around myself and consider what he's saying. "I don't disagree with you on that," I say. "Cece was being evasive."

"Thank you."

"But when I said we had concerns about what happened to him that night, she looked worried, Sam. She looked worried about him in a way that made me wonder—"

"How deep they went?"

I nod. I picture Cece's beautiful face, her confidence, her strength. It wasn't a leap to picture my father being enraptured by all of it. It wasn't a leap to picture my father being enraptured by her.

"Something like that."

He looks down and opens the passenger-side door. I get in on the driver's side, key the ignition, turn the headlights on. I feel it bubbling up—the possibility that's been coming at me all day, a possibility that would explain why our father went to Windbreak unannounced. Why he tripped and fell over the edge of a landscape he knew too well.

"You don't think Dad hurt himself, do you?" I say before I can stop myself.

Sam gives me a look. "Like jumped? No way."

"I know Detective O'Brien says that they ruled out self-harm. But I'm not convinced by anything he said."

"That I agree on—"

"Look, I'm just saying we should talk it through. You're the one who keeps telling me he wasn't himself. And he's finalizing his will. And now we hear that he's making weird phone calls. Don't we have to at least consider it?"

Sam gets quiet, and I can see him turning the idea over in his head. All the details could add up to point that way, especially after today. The canceled sale, Uncle Joe's defiance, the calls to Cece. The disconnected calls to her, which may be the weirdest puzzle piece yet.

As an architect, I often think in terms of puzzle pieces. I've learned, over time, that a requirement of the job is to find a simple and elegant solution that addresses all the complexities inherent in any project. That makes all the disparate pieces fit together. When I find that right answer, I can almost hear it all click into place, the whole picture coming into a unifying focus. This is the way I'm supposed to go.

But this answer isn't clicking. Our father was wired for problem-solving—it was what made him so good at his job. He always said that he and I had that in common. Which made it feel clearer to me: even if he was facing something that felt insurmountable to him, he would be too stubborn to give in to it. He wouldn't give in to anything, not until he believed that he had managed to come out the other side.

Plus, there was the other thing that would push him away from doing anything to hurt himself, no matter what was going on. His children. And if he couldn't fight against his sadness (if he couldn't overcome what ailed him), he would leave us notes, he would leave us an explanation, he would leave instructions. He wouldn't just leave.

"No," Sam says, getting there too. "No way. I don't believe it. That's not what this is."

I'm glad that he's gotten there too. I'm relieved that, whatever this is, we agree it's not anything self-inflicted.

But before that can bring too much relief, I realize something else. I realize that the possibility has been swirling around in me because it's moving me closer to it: What's hitting me hard. What I do think is more than possible. What I believe now to be true. In someone I knew less well, I'd ascribe his strange behavior to depression, to being unsettled. But I knew that with my father it wasn't as simple as that.

My father was up against something that maybe, for the first time, he couldn't find his way through.

# The Late-Night Special at the Holiday Inn

We settle on going to The Ranch.

Neither of us wants to go back to Windbreak or to Uncle Joe's. And it's too far, and too late, to start the 140-mile drive all the way back to Los Angeles.

It's a little after nine when we turn onto The Ranch's long cobblestone road. I drive past the guardhouse and head around to the circular drive that houses reception, where I spy the nondescript WELCOME sign by the front door.

Sam pops out to get the room keys. I stay behind the wheel and stare at the stone main house, lantern-lit and quaint. Nothing about it suggests what lies just beyond it: forty-eight vine-covered cottages, surrounded by mountain trails and gardens, graciously spaced over a five-hundred-acre estate.

After my father rebranded Hayes as Noone Properties and Resorts, he opened The Ranch. It was his first new property and the way he announced the shift in the company's mission. They were no longer a small, regional hotel chain. This West Coast hotel, his flagship property, stood as the model for what he wanted all his hotels to deliver: luxury comfort and seminal design. Even more than that, he was rebranding the idea of what a small hotel could be. Each hotel would not only stand on its own, holding on to the specificity found in individual hotel ownership, but also adhere to global standards not historically seen in small properties, offering as many amenities as hotels three times their size.

And he was going to do it while providing the thing even the most luxurious large hotel couldn't—complete and total privacy. No property would have more than fifty rooms, each hotel revolving around the singular principle of total retreat and sanctuary, but the type of retreat where all your needs were anticipated and cared for. The way my father described it to me (one of the few times we talked about it): He wanted to provide the opportunity to disappear from your life for a while. Or, you know, to become someone else entirely.

I would love, at this very moment, to be here for that kind of a visit. Apparently, I don't get to stay at The Ranch under those conditions. Despite how seminal this hotel was to my father's work life (or maybe because of it), I've only been here twice before—once with my parents, shortly before they told me they were separating; the next time for my father's wedding to his second wife, Sylvia. For entirely different reasons, but in equal measure, each of those visits created the same kind of dread as I was feeling now.

"We're all set," Sam says, walking back to the car.

Sam called on the way and the receptionist had our keys waiting. There is only one cottage available for us to share. We're lucky it has two bedrooms. We're lucky, really, that the hotel has anything vacant at all, even if the reason they do is that the cottage we are staying in had a short-circuit earlier in the week and is still without electricity.

Sam hands me the map, and we head on foot toward our cottage, white lights strung through the oak trees, orange magnolias lining the trails. The nighttime air, soft and bright, centering me.

"Under different circumstances this is a vacation I could really use," he says.

Then he keys the front door. And races to pick the better bedroom.

I stand in the foyer, take in the living room. The electricity may be out, but someone has lit the fireplace in the living area, placing candles around the room, so we aren't walking into the pitch-dark. And it's hard not to feel like I've walked into a kind of refuge—the comforting smell of that fire, those soft lights.

It's different from the other cottage I remember staying in when I was a child—different from the cottage I stayed in a few years later attending Sylvia and my father's wedding. And yet it carries a similar cozy and rustic feel, that nod to the Arts and Crafts Movement, full of the thoughtful fixtures and antiques that make it feel more like a home than a room frequently visited.

I get it, being here as an adult. I get why people would want to disappear here for a while.

I text Jack to let him know where I am—that I'm not making that red-eye after all. Then I drop my phone on the end table and head into the bathroom to take a shower, put on fresh clothes for the first time in eighteen hours.

When I come back into the living room, Sam is sitting by the fire, wearing a jersey and track shorts, the brace visible on his wrist. Maybe it's that combination, but he looks like the little-boy version of himself about to head out to a Little League game, his baseball bag too big for his body.

I sit down on the couch across from him and he looks over, nods in my direction.

"Nothing from the Coopers yet," he says.

"Is that a question?"

He shakes his head. "Not really. I looked through your phone while you were in the shower."

"I'm choosing to ignore that."

I lean back on the soft cushions, crossing my legs beneath myself, when I notice the covered trays on the coffee table between us.

"What's all this?"

"I ordered dinner while you were in the shower," he says.

He pulls the lids off the trays.

"Lettuce and tomato sandwiches, and beer."

I look down at the tray of sandwiches, unable to hide my surprise. They're just like the sandwiches my father used to make for me—for me and for Sam, the few times Sam and I had been at our father's apartment at the same time. It may sound like a weird sandwich, but I relished it when I was a kid, at least the way my father would make it (which, incidentally, was the way my grandmother made it for him): thick tomato slices on griddled rustic bread, crisp romaine lettuce, mayonnaise, and flaky salt.

"This was my favorite growing up."

"I know, that's why I ordered it," he said. "I'm just drinking the beer."

It's so kind—so kind and so surprising—that he knows that I liked it, let alone ordered it for me, that I'm not sure what to do.

"I can't believe you remembered that."

"How could I forget? You and Dad both liking the dumbest sandwich in the world," he says. "You're missing half of it. Where's the bacon? Where's the turkey?"

I smile at him. "Dad always said that Grandma couldn't afford that," I say. "So he got really good at making a sandwich without."

"That's a nice story," Sam says. "You're still missing a cheeseburger."

I reach for a sandwich and lean in to take a bite, closing my eyes to properly savor it. The first piece of joy in this crazy day. This perfect sandwich: an ideal mix of crispy, tangy, and sweet. No other food item need apply.

Sam reaches for a handful of onion-fries that room service had included. Then he cracks open a beer and sits back.

"So I was just thinking," he says. "You see any point in trying to talk to Joe again tomorrow?"

"I don't think we'll get anywhere different with him," I say. "Whatever he knows, he's not looking to share."

"Yeah, I think that's true," he says.

I'm still trying to make sense of why that is. Is Uncle Joe trying to protect my father? Or is he trying to protect himself? It's disorienting to be wondering that about my dad's closest friend, his constant. There was no one else my father was as close to, certainly professionally, with maybe the exception of Grace, or perhaps my father's general counsel. His face comes to my mind before his name does: ice-blue eyes, slicked back hair. He hadn't been working with my father for as long as Grace and Joe, but he had been there for a long time, nevertheless. He had certainly been there long enough to have access to things we don't.

Jonathan. That's his name. I'm guessing that attorney-client privilege would end any conversations with him before they started, but it feels like Grace would have been a different story.

"I've thought about Grace a bunch since she's passed," I say. "And I don't know. I wish she were here. I'm not saying she would have any insight necessarily, but I bet she would help us if she could . . ."

"I think you're giving her a lot of credit there. I liked Grace, but she wasn't exactly forthcoming, either."

"That's not the read I got on her."

"Well, as much as I hate to discount the four times you met her, I doubt she would talk to us, even if she were here."

That strikes me as off base. It might not have been often, but I certainly saw Grace several times over the years. And she'd always been open with me. But before I decide whether to argue, my phone starts to buzz. I pick it off the table, Sam's fiancée, Morgan, coming up on the caller ID.

I hold the phone up so Sam can see the screen—can see for himself that it's Morgan calling.

"Don't pick up," he says. "She's just trying to reach me."

"How do you know?"

"'Cause I've sent her to voicemail like eight times already."

"I refuse to be in the middle of whatever's going on with you two."

"Hence why I said don't pick up."

I click the volume off and put my phone back on the end table, watch as Sam cracks open a second beer.

"What's going on, Sam?"

"What do you mean?"

"Who is the other woman?"

"Morgan."

"No. The other woman."

"Morgan is the other woman," he says.

I look at him confused. "I'm not following."

"I was with someone else for a long time before Morgan and I started dating. Taylor, that was her name. *Is* her name. We broke up about nine months ago . . ."

"What happened?"

"She apparently had doubts about whether I could commit."

"So you got engaged to Morgan to prove that you could commit?"

"Well, when you say it that way . . ."

I know he's trying to make light of this, but I can see that he doesn't feel light. I don't, either. I feel heavy. All these questions about my father are gnawing at me in the way things tend to gnaw at you right before you figure out that they're worse than you thought.

Sam opens another beer, hands it to me. I take a long sip.

"Dad said that you're getting married too?"

"I am."

"And you're happy about it?"

"Very," I say.

It relaxes me, how instinctively my answer shoots out of me. I shouldn't need it to relax me, but it's a nice reminder that my inherent certainty about Jack is holding steady.

"Whatever happened to the guy you were with before? The one with a kid. He was a veterinarian, wasn't he?"

"A pediatric cardiologist."

"Dogs, kids. Both close to the ground."

I give him a smile.

"Elliot, right? He seemed . . . proud of himself."

They had met once. Accidentally. Sam walking into my father's apartment as Elliot and I were walking out.

"Why the questions about him?"

"He called while you were in the shower." He holds up two fingers. "Twice."

"It's not what you think."

He shrugs. "All I think is that he called twice."

I don't want to think about Elliot calling twice. I don't want to lean into what I know to be true: Elliot shouldn't be calling me, and certainly not the way he's been calling me, at all. I move the food out of the way so I can sit down on the edge of the table, his side of the table. So I can meet him at eye level.

"Sam, it's really not my business," I say. "Your relationship with

Morgan. But nine months is pretty short to be dating, engaged, and moving to Brooklyn."

"What's that expression? When you know, you know."

"Do you know? Because I'm pretty sure you just said the opposite."

"What I said is you probably shouldn't pick up the phone," he says. Then he clears his throat and takes another sip of his beer. "But, for the record, I wouldn't mind if you did . . ."

"Did what?"

"Make it your business," he says. "It's starting to feel like I could use the assist."

It's so earnest that it catches me off guard. I don't know if this is all new since losing our father (his emotions raw and elevated) or if he'd been like this all along. Either way, it feels like something has shifted in him, a seismic shift, where now he is doing exactly the opposite of what I'd historically known him to do. He is reaching toward me.

My desire to meet him there, to offer something like protection, comes in fierce and quick.

I lean toward him. "Were you hoping this conversation was going to the place where we realize that we're in the same boat?"

"Which boat is that?"

"The sinking one."

He laughs. "I guess so."

He pulls the Velcro on his brace, taking it off, and rotating his free fingers, stretching them out. Holding that palm tight.

"You know, it wouldn't have been the worst thing for me to have been around more when we were growing up," I say. "I wish Dad hadn't felt the need to . . ."

"Keep us apart?"

I nod. He knows as well as I do that this was the best way my father knew how to be there for us. It was easier for him to focus on each of us, separately, rather than do the more complicated work of trying to merge us all together—even though it meant that in trying to keep everyone happy, he often was letting someone down. This part I've known and mostly accepted, because I understood that in always insisting on only putting forth his best self for each of us, the person he was probably letting down the most was himself.

But here's this other part that I'm starting to suspect: Maybe not merging his children's lives together was about something else too. Maybe he thought that if we all left our respective corners, we would have started talking. And it would have revealed something he wasn't ready to look at—or something that he didn't want his children to look at. The version of himself he needed to keep private.

"I think that was more about him than about us," I say. "But it doesn't make it better."

He looks up at me, holds my gaze. "So when do we get to the part where you tell me what to do?"

"I can't tell you what to do, Sam."

"Well. Then maybe it's okay Dad kept us apart."

~

A little after 2:00 a.m., I get out of bed.

I take my blanket and go sit on the small deck, the moon bright tonight, the sky so cloudless that I can see all the way out over the hills, down to the Pacific Ocean, glistening in the distance.

I take a photograph on my phone, focusing in on the shimmer coming in off that distant ocean. The blue lines skimming the bottom half of the frame.

My professor in graduate school, the one whose house I now own, taught a workshop that focused on neuroarchitecture. She opened the first lesson in a way that sits with me still, by talking about how buildings can make people sicker. Or they can make them better. And she wrote a question on the blackboard—a question that she always asks herself early in the conception stage to ensure she is doing the latter: Where does the joy come in?

For me, that axis always centers around light (or an angle of light) that I try to honor in the construction of any space. I had nothing to do with constructing this space, of course, but for a moment it brings me joy to imagine that it was built around this very seat, this very view, for a moment where someone needed it.

Because this is what I keep thinking: What happens if you lose your own axis? Since my parents died, that's how it feels. That the axis on which I spun—like a certain angle of light, like a prayer—is gone. I can't find it. I'm not even sure it still exists.

I think of Sam's question to me about Jack. I think of my steadying and true answer. Yes, I want to marry him. I want to be with him and keep loving him. But what if that's true and there's still nothing I can do about the other part? The part that keeps me isolated from him—all my grief, all its ache—erecting an invisible wall that I can't seem to climb over. Toward him. Toward *us*.

I look down at my phone and focus in on the photograph, the stream of light—the soft and gentle beauty.

Jack is probably already up, heading to the restaurant to start his morning prep. I want to call him. I want to finish our conversation from earlier. But how am I? He'll want to hear a real answer. *I'm fine. I'm lonely. I'm worried, every time I hear your voice, how and when I'll lose you too.*

So, I don't call. I shoot off a text with the photograph attached.

Then I shut off my phone and decide to move.

---

~

I walk the property. It's eerily silent, even considering it's the middle of the night. No other person is anywhere in sight. I pass by the landscape gardens and citrus groves, circle a lily pond, lanterns in gnarled oaks lighting my way. I end up back in the reception area. The only cottage lit up.

The overnight receptionist is behind the front desk in a button-down shirt and trousers. He nods in my direction as I walk through the living area. The room low-lit and quiet. A fire going strong in the stone fireplace.

There are framed photographs covering the wall above that fireplace. Framed articles about the property. Each of my father's properties has this kind of area designated to the history of the property, leaning into a mythical story behind what makes the property specific, what makes it singular.

I start to read through the articles here, focusing in on a cover story in the *Santa Barbara News-Press*, announcing the sale of The Ranch to my father. He had bought the land from citrus farmers who harvested an average of 500,000 lemons and oranges a year. He was turning it into a boutique hotel. He was promising to preserve almost all the acreage.

I move farther down the wall and spot the one photograph of me at six years old, my father carrying me on his shoulders, standing not too far from this exact spot. The first time I was ever here, the time shortly before my parents split up. My mother was not in the photograph. Maybe she already knew. Maybe they both already knew what was coming.

"You look the same," he says.

I turn to see the night receptionist coming out from behind his desk and walking toward me.

"Sorry?" I say.

He motions to the wall, to that photograph of me. "You look the same as you did when you were little," he says.

"You think?"

I turn and look at the photograph. Then I look back at him as he comes over to stand beside me, his hands in his pockets.

"Your father would talk to me about you. You and your brothers. He'd come over after he had dinner in the cellar and we'd play cards."

"What kind?"

"Gin rummy. Poker occasionally, but only for pretzels."

I smile at him. How strange—and how nice—to know this now. To imagine my father sitting here in the middle of the night.

"What's your name?" I ask.

"Carmen."

"You've worked here for a long time?"

"A long time, yeah." He motions toward the photograph. "He was a pretty good guy to work for, your father."

"I don't hear that often."

"Sure, he was tough. I've seen a lot of guys get sacked over the years for not taking their jobs seriously," he says. "But he let you know that up front. And he didn't think he was above it, either. I remember one night when we were playing cards, the toilet in here overflowed. And the plumber was taking a long time to get here, too long for your father, and so he just went in there and snaked the damn thing himself. Came out covered in toilet water, smelling a little like shit. Had to borrow a shirt so we could finish the game."

I let out a small laugh. "That's disgusting."

"Yeah, well. He came up that way, right? And from where I stand, he was real generous. And decent. You had to work hard to earn his respect, but once you earned it, he would do anything for you."

"How do you mean?"

"My wife had a tough pregnancy a few years back. He gave me nine months off, paid. So I could be home with the babies."

He pulls out his phone, starts scrolling through his photographs. "They just turned three," he says. "But they were so small at first, three and a half pounds. And he just kept promising me it was all going to turn out okay. He would show me photographs of your brothers. How small they were. What they turned into."

Then he holds out his own phone, anxious to show me his twins—his girls—and how big and strong they are now.

I take his phone and look at the photographs of his girls, who are so cute—beyond so cute—and so happy. I start flipping through to see other photographs of them. Other pieces of his history.

I think of my father standing here, showing him my brothers. His own history. We all want to show that, don't we? Like proof. We helped them survive. They will survive.

Which is when I realize.

I start to shake, his phone still in my hand.

"What's wrong?" he asks. Because I must be wearing it all over my face—my rising concern.

"Maybe nothing," I say.

But I hand him back his phone and say a fast goodbye, running quickly back to the cottage.

In the living room, I find a flashlight in the coat closet and check the police report to make sure I'm correct.

Then I go straight into Sam's room and shake him awake. "Where's his cell phone?" I ask.

He rubs his eyes. "What? What are you talking about?"

I hold up the police report.

"They recovered his wallet and his glasses and a pen from his front pocket. But no phone," I say. "Why wasn't he carrying his phone?"

"Yeah, I don't know . . ."

"He called Cece that night, right? We know that much. We know he had it with him. Did you see it anywhere at Windbreak?"

"No . . . I didn't see it in his office," he says. "We can ask Clark to double-check, but I don't think it was there."

"It's possible that it got swept away on the beach," I say. "Or it hit the cliff during the fall."

He sits up, considering. "Or someone took it."

I look back down at the police report, then up at my brother. I feel it moving forward, that thing that's been coming at me, moving into the light. That thing I need to see clearly to get us somewhere better.

"Maybe you're not entirely wrong," I say.

"Of course I'm not. About what?"

"You keep saying Dad wouldn't sell the company," I say. "That he would never wake up one day and suddenly want to sell—"

"This doesn't sound like the part I was right about."

I ignore him.

"We've been looking at this from the wrong angle," I say.

"Okay . . ."

"What if it wasn't his choice? What if, for some reason, Dad was compelled to sell the company?"

He shakes his head, confused. "Compelled how?" he says. "The company was doing great. It is doing great."

"Still, isn't it possible there was something going on that you didn't know about? That made him need to get out all of a sudden? It would help explain it. Dad's absence. Why he was so off."

He looks at me. "Like what?"

"I don't know yet. All I know is trying to talk about him, to all these people, it feels like we can't trust them."

"Careful there, you're starting to sound like me."

"Well, Uncle Joe, Cece, Detective O'Brien. It feels like they're all pushing their own agenda, like they're sharing just a small piece of a puzzle that they don't want us to solve. That's the one thing I'm sure of." I pause. "Trying to talk to them isn't going to get us to the bottom of this."

"Okay. So who should we be talking to?"

I think of Carmen. I think of the photographs of my father on the wall. He was always presenting himself in the same way—smart and eager and solid. The best version of himself. That's the only version of himself that he showed me—in the pieces, the compartments, he'd allow me to see him. But what didn't he want to show me? What didn't he want to share with any of his children? And why?

"Nora? Who should we be talking to?"

"Dad," I say.

# — Part II —

Architecture appears for the first time when the sunlight hits a wall. The sunlight did not know what it was before it hit a wall.

—Louis Kahn

# Not All Road Trips Lead You Home

Somewhere over Colorado, we make a plan.

I spread my father's will and the police report on our tray tables, Sam powering up his laptop. He shifts the computer screen so I can see too.

"There's a lot of shared files at the company, so I have some access even remotely. See? The calendars and scheduling are all shared. That's how I knew about the meetings with the lawyers . . ." He motions toward a date on his screen. "And here's Inez's event from last month . . ."

"So all of Dad's commitments were shared on here?" I ask.

"Not all, but a lot of them were. Certainly anything that conflicted with something important that was happening at Noone," he says. "His desktop might have a more complete inventory."

I motion to Sam's laptop. "Did Dad also have a laptop?"

"Yep. Everyone on the executive team does."

"Would that be at the office?"

"Should be," he says. "It certainly wasn't at Windbreak. I combed through that office. Now Clark has too."

He clicks through to his most recent iMessages. Clark has sent along several photographs he's taken of our father's Windbreak office, as well as a detailed inventory of what's still in his desk, on the shelves. He's confirmed for us what we suspected: our father's cell phone isn't at Windbreak, either.

"So, let's assume we can't find his actual phone," I say. "Where would we be most likely to find the backup to his phone? Was there a company server? Could it be downloaded on his work computer?"

Sam shakes his head. "I don't know. If it were on the company network, I should have access on here and I don't."

"Who would have access?"

"To his personal laptop? Uncle Joe, probably. Though he's a dead end as you saw."

I nod, trying to go through it in my mind—my father's inner circle, his trusted advisors: Joe, who isn't talking, at least to us; Grace, who is no longer here. Which is when I hit on my father's general counsel again. Jonathan hadn't been working with my father for as long as Grace and Joe, but he had certainly been there long enough to have access to things we don't.

"What about Jonathan?"

Sam shakes his head. "Steel box."

"Why? Attorney-client privilege?"

"For one thing. Also, every time I try to touch on anything about Dad, he keeps saying there is nothing to know that I don't already know . . ."

"Those are opposite statements."

"Exactly."

He shrugs, turns back to my computer.

"He's a lawyer, and he's good at it. If there was anything sensitive that he knows about, he's not offering it up. I mean, the day after Dad died, Jonathan had a new lock put on Dad's office door that only a few people can open."

"Isn't that extreme?"

"Jonathan's extreme. It's why he's good at his job."

I make a note on the police report about my father's cell phone, his computer.

"Could Tommy help ease things?" I ask.

"Why would Tommy be able to help ease things?"

"I don't know. They're both lawyers. Thought maybe they connected about that. How does Jonathan feel about Tommy?"

"How does anyone feel about Tommy?"

I turn and look at him. "Okay. I'm done with all of your veiled insinuations. What is going on with you two?"

"He's on-site upstate. We're finishing the build-out on a new property in Columbia County."

"That wasn't my question."

He doesn't answer me. He doesn't even look my way.

"Why are there so many secrets in this family?"

"I don't know," he says. "You do what came before."

"What does that mean?"

Sam turns back to his laptop. "None of this started with us," he says.

## *Forty-Three Years Ago*

"I don't want to talk about it anymore," Cory said. "There's nothing more to say."

"Why not?"

"You're working a hundred hours a week. You won't even miss me."

"I miss you right now. I miss you already."

They were walking around the Strand Bookstore, Cory searching through their new arrivals table. Cory browsing through books, trying to ignore him and this conversation Liam knew she didn't want to have.

She was right about how much he was working. He had been at Hayes for three months and had put in more hours than most people did in a year. No one understood him even taking the job in the first place.

He'd been a summer associate at Bain Consulting, and everyone assumed he'd accept a permanent position there and all the perks that came with it: a Midtown rental apartment, a six-figure starting salary. But Liam had been assigned to a project at Bain that moved the goalposts for him. He was brought in to analyze a large hotel group, three-star and four-star resorts around the globe, more than twelve hundred properties. He was supposed to be looking for opportunities to cut costs, to eliminate redundant staff positions, to recommend property changes across the portfolio so everything would run more efficiently. Efficiently as in cheaper. No particular interest in better.

This was when he fell in love with the business and his plan started to concretize. Even if he didn't know all the shapes and colors of it yet, Liam was going to do everything he could to create the opposite.

"Come on, Cory. You can't tell me that there are no good writing programs in New York," he said.

Cory picked up a copy of *The Hotel New Hampshire,* added it to the stack of books in her already full arms, including a fresh copy of *Barefoot in the Park*. She had given Liam her original copy, had given him a slew of Neil Simon plays. Neil Simon was one of her very favorites.

"University of Southern California has one of the best writing programs in the country," she said. "They're giving me a full ride, and I'll get to focus entirely on my writing. No waiting tables, no babysitting."

"You've mentioned."

"And it's just for a year," she said.

"Time is just a construct?"

"Why are you turning this into such a big deal?"

"Because. It won't just be a year."

"How do you know?"

"Because who would be dumb enough to let you go?"

She ignored this, continued looking through the books. He moved closer to her, wrapping his arms around her shoulders, pulling her closer to him.

"Cory . . ."

"Would you please get in line for the cashier while I finish up here?" she asked. "I really don't want us to be late for the movie. Indiana isn't waiting on us to save the Ark of the Covenant."

"What if we got married?"

"Married?"

She laughed. She laughed so loudly that the woman on the other side of the new arrivals table jumped back.

"Why is that so funny?"

"Sorry," she mouthed to the woman.

Then she leaned in closer to Liam. "Please. Marriage didn't save my parents. It wouldn't save us."

"What would save us?"

"Who says we need saving?"

"I want to be with you."

"You are with me. And I'm with you. In the ways that matter."

"Oh, for goodness sake. Here we go."

"Witnesses to each other's lives," she said. "That was the deal."

"I wish I had never shown you that poem—"

". . . Not something we push and pull from, no promises that someone may need to break. Just the people who know each other. Who love each other. Who see each other. Best friends. Lovers. Whatever title you give it or don't give it, just how we've always been. No way to lose each other."

"Why is marriage mutually exclusive with that?"

"It isn't. Not for all people. But for certain people I'm looking at, it would ruin it. You're not ready yet. You're not even close to ready to be in the kind of marriage I want. And in my limited experience—"

"You think you'll get less preachy with more experience?"

She gave him a smile. "I think you can try to lock up commitment in legal papers and promises. It is human nature to want that kind of security. And then it's human nature to fight against it. Because it is all those things and it's so much more. And we are lucky enough to have the more."

"You make this complicated," he said.

"You make this complicated," she said. "I just pay attention. If we are supposed to get married, that's for another day. If we tried to do it today, you know as well as I do, it wouldn't work."

"Why not?"

"For starters, I'm going to grad school three thousand miles away."

"Maybe."

"Definitely," she says. "But, putting that aside, I wouldn't get this anymore. All the good."

"What's the good?"

"You."

She looked at him with such love. Such understanding. That for a brief, shining moment, he believed her.

What did Cory like to say? Fidelity is who you tell your stories to. If he never stopped listening to hers, would she eventually trust that being here (with her) was the only thing he truly wanted? That it would never make him feel trapped. That it was, in fact, the thing that made him feel free.

"What if I told you I have a ring?"

"You have a ring?"

He nodded. He had it in his pocket. He often had it in his pocket. A simple band. Nothing to gawk at, but what he had to offer. His proof that he would know how to sustain it. To do his part to sustain them.

"I would tell you I don't need a ring. And, if you pushed me, I'd remind you that you'd be terrible to be married to."

"Thank you for that."

"You're welcome."

He kissed her neck, his hand cupping her head. "So . . . you'll think about it?"

She started to laugh, her cheek pressing into his face. "Ask me again when the right answer is yes."

"What if I don't want to wait that long?"

"Then you can go ahead and throw that ring of yours away."

# Eleventh Avenue Freak-Out

On the way to the taxi line at JFK, my phone buzzes with an incoming call.

A blocked number shows up on the screen. And I pick up to a voice I don't recognize.

"Nora? It's Meredith Cooper."

Meredith Cooper, who found my father on the beach. The EMT. The wife. I look up at Sam and put the phone on speaker, between us, so he can hear too.

"Meredith, I really appreciate the call back—"

"Sure, happy to help. But I should warn you. We are in Tuscany with very poor cell service so I may lose you."

Her voice is coming in crackly—and I'm missing every few words. I start to say thank you for trying to help our father, for being there even when no one could. But either she doesn't hear me through the poor connection, or she doesn't have time for that. Because she starts talking over me.

"I went over it with my husband," she says. "Both of us tried to recall anything specific about the jogger. We were focused on your father, to be honest. But we both remember that he was tall and Caucasian. He was wearing like these green cargo pants and a sweatshirt. Something like that."

Sam mouths, "For jogging?" Just as I have the same thought.

"And you had never seen him before?" I ask.

"No. Never. We were only there for a couple of months, but it's a small community . . ."

"You usually see the same people?"

"Well, we walked our dog pretty much the same time every night. People have their habits."

I lock eyes with Sam, who is staring back at me, like this proves something. At the very least, it proves that this man—who Detective O'Brien and the police haven't managed to track down—wasn't usually there at eight thirty at night.

"Do you think if you had a photograph, it could help?" I ask. "Would you potentially recognize him that way?"

"Maybe," she says. "I don't know. It was pretty dark out."

Sam mimes holding a phone to his own ear, mouths, "Dad's phone."

I nod at him, nod at the reminder.

"Can I ask you just one more thing?" I say. "Do you happen to remember seeing my father's cell phone?"

"No, I don't actually . . ." She pauses, considers. "I'm pretty sure it wasn't in his jacket pocket. When I tried to get to his chest, I think I would have felt it."

"That's helpful. Thank you. Sorry that's a weird question."

"Don't be. There aren't weird questions when you're grieving," she says.

That penetrates. The truth of it. And the kindness. Then while I sit there breathless, the connection cuts out, the line clicking off, and Meredith Cooper is gone.

~

The Starrett-Lehigh Building—home to Noone Properties—has always been one of my favorite buildings in West Chelsea.

It's a lauded building, particularly in neuroarchitecture circles, for its expressionistic design, which you rarely see in industrial buildings. The space creates a mood, an emotionality, pulling you in with horizonal ribbon windows, alternating between brick and concrete spandrels, large setbacks, incredible brickwork. All of the design choices move together to become the thing you can only feel when you walk inside. How, despite all the reasons a large New York City building shouldn't feel personal, this one has figured out how to comfortably hold you.

Noone Properties headquarters is on the two top floors. It has an open office plan with floor-to-ceiling windows looking out over the West Side Highway and the Hudson River just beyond it. The late-day sun, loose and white, coating that water gently.

We're sitting in our father's office, which is still intact, like he just walked out for the day. Not like it's been more than a month since he's stepped inside here. There's a large conference table in the middle of the room, an array of hotelier awards still framed on the walls, his desktop computer powered on. Sam and I hover in front of it.

Uncle Joe's East Coast assistant is pacing just outside the office door, short and fierce, and failing to hide that she wishes we would hurry this along. I don't blame her for that. From her refusal to stop peering at us through the glass, it feels safe to assume that Joe expects a full report on what we've done while we are here.

Sam keeps driving through the files on our father's desktop anyway. He is searching for anything related to Cece or the sale while we wait for Nate, the Noone Properties IT guy. Nate is supposed to be coming back in with answers about our father's cell phone, about what backups are in the cloud, the whereabouts of his missing laptop.

Sam shakes his head. "No paper trail in any of these emails," he says. "Not in any internal memos I'm finding, either."

He leans closer to the screen.

"Nothing really seems to have been downloaded from his phone. No messages have been shared, no personal photographs or texts I can find."

I'm not entirely surprised to hear this. From how Sam described the system, it seemed to me that anything we'd see on our father's desktop would have been on Sam's laptop.

"Okay, so this is not great . . ." Nate says.

I look up and see Nate walking back into the office, tapping on his tablet. He takes a seat across the desk from us.

"The last time your father's phone pinged on a cell tower was eighteen days ago in Santa Barbara, California."

Nate turns his tablet so we can see for ourselves.

Santa Barbara, California. That's close to Carpinteria, but not Carpinteria. Why was our father's phone there? And why was it findable eighteen days ago—almost two weeks after we lost him? If the phone had broken during our father's fall or had ended up in the ocean, it would have stopped being findable that night. That means it either survived the fall and someone removed it from him—or someone removed it from Windbreak.

Regardless, it seems, someone has it who shouldn't. Sam sits up, and I wonder if he realizes the same thing.

"So, if his phone was still online after he died, is there any way to access that activity?" I ask.

"Theoretically, assuming there was any. But that is going to involve law enforcement and warrants and all sorts of things above my pay grade."

"How about his laptop?" Sam says.

"Not on the premises," he says. "And I just confirmed with security that it's not in his New York apartment, either."

His laptop and his phone—the only two pieces of hardware that may be able to shed any light here—are the only two things missing from his seemingly completely intact office. That can't be a coincidence. It can't be a coincidence that anything of value (anything he deemed the most private) was nowhere to be found.

"Shouldn't they be backed up in the cloud somewhere?" I ask.

"They should be, yes," Nate says. "If you can go back in time and tell your father to authorize saving anything that way. Alternative storage opportunities were disengaged at his personal request."

"So you're saying his phone wasn't backed up anywhere?" Sam asks.

"I can't say that it's not backed up anywhere. But in terms of company storage, that is correct. For his phone and his laptop, he asked that all external storage and file sharing to the company network be suspended."

That seems intentional. It must be intentional, his wanting to keep certain things just for himself. Which is when I shift back to it: Sam on the plane with his company laptop, talking about the things he could and couldn't find on it. And I start to wonder if maybe it can be found a different way.

"Just for his own laptop?" I ask.

Nate meets my eyes. "What's that?"

"Was file sharing turned off just for his own personal computer or any other computer in the network?"

"It seems that laptops five through ten are all connected to the network. That includes Tommy's and yours, Sam." He looks up and nods in Sam's direction. Then he continues searching. "But, yes, actually, that's correct, it was not just your father's laptop where storage backup and file sharing were disabled from the company network."

"Who else's?" I ask.

"Okay . . . it was turned off for laptop issues one, two, three, and four," he says. "Laptop one was issued to your father. Two to Joe, three belonged to the general counsel, and four belonged to . . ."

I get there at the same time Sam does.

"Grace," Sam says.

I turn to Sam. "What if those computers were connected to each other? They could have access to his files."

Sam motions toward Nate. "Is Grace's laptop still in the company's possession?"

"No. Her laptop was delivered to her apartment along with all her personal belongings—"

"But that's not really characterized as personal, is it?" Sam says. "That's company property."

"Well, apparently your father wasn't particularly interested in making that distinction," he says. "But Terry would be more helpful on the specifics."

Sam turns back to me. "Terry was Grace's personal assistant. She retired after Grace passed away."

Nate taps on his device. "Says here Terry's in Burlington, Vermont. No email address, but I got a phone number and a physical address."

Sam stands up. "Would you text me her contact info? Thanks. Number and address."

I look up at him. "Please tell me we aren't going to Vermont."

"Depends on if she picks up," he says.

Sam starts walking to the door. Nate and I watch him go, and he looks back over at me.

"He's joking, right?" Nate asks.

My own phone buzzes, and I look down to see a text message from Elliot.

You okay?

I haven't called him back. Not Elliot, not Jack either, for that matter. I shoot Elliot a quick text that I'll call him a little later. But I owe Jack more than that kind of message. Jack, who I haven't spoken to except briefly in the car on the way to Santa Ynez. Twenty-four hours ago. A lifetime ago.

I sigh, stand up too. "I'm going with maybe," I say.

# All Roads Lead to Cece

Terry does pick up.

She is quick to confirm for us that all of Grace's belongings, devices included, were sent to her and her husband's apartment in Brooklyn.

Sam and I walk quickly down Tenth Avenue, heading toward the nearest subway.

"The question is," I say, "how much access do you think Dad gave her?"

"A lot more than me apparently," he says. "But as much as Uncle Joe? I don't know. I'd say he used to, for sure . . ."

"I hear a *but* there?"

Sam shakes his head. "Well, she had heart trouble a few years ago, and I think she had a heart attack. Before the one that . . . you know . . . killed her. It was minor, but she took a real step back from the company after that. She still helped Dad with some creative stuff and branding, but I don't know how involved she was in the day-to-day operation. Joe seemed to step in more, at least in a forward-facing way."

"Was there tension between them?"

"Joe and Grace? Not really, no."

"Not for who had Dad's ear the most?"

"Think you're confusing them with me and Tommy."

I suppress a smile.

"So in theory, if those computers were connected, she could have access to what no one seems to want to tell us about . . ."

"In theory. Sure."

We take a left, head toward the subway. The wind is picking up, that blustery early-evening cold.

"What's your relationship like with her husband?" I ask.

"We've met a handful of times. I barely have one."

"So this is going to go well?"

We hit the stairs, head into the subway. "Can't really go worse," he says.

~

Grace's apartment is located in a Beaux Arts building in Brooklyn Heights.

The building is something of a Brooklyn landmark. It's not too far from the promenade, with uninterrupted views of New York Harbor and the Manhattan skyline, yet in the heart of Brooklyn Heights' most famous brownstones.

I know these apartments well. Jack has a friend who lives on the fifth floor, and we were here for a dinner party a few months ago. I doubt the doorman recognizes me but he does give us a friendly hello and immediately sends us up to eight, not buzzing Grace's husband until we are already elevator bound.

When we step off the elevator, her husband is opening his apartment door, offering us a smile.

He looks familiar, which confuses me. I'm sure we haven't met before. I've met Grace's daughter, but he and I have never been introduced. He is not only familiar, but he is striking standing there in a pair of jeans and a flannel shirt, lean and strong and rugged, with these hazel eyes that bore into you. That are currently boring into me.

He shakes Sam's hand and ushers us inside to the foyer—which is when my confusion starts to lift. It feels less like we've walked into an apartment than into an artist's studio. Photography equipment fills the living room, and the walls are covered with beautiful photographs and portraits.

This is *why* he looks so familiar. It's not that I've met him in person or know him personally. But I know him, all the same. He is Paul Turner—the (well-known) editorial photographer. I had a friend in college who decorated her dorm room completely in his magazine covers. I've seen his photography exhibits at the International Center for Photography and the Brooklyn Museum. Prints of his work appear on the walls of several apartments I've worked on, including Jack's friend's apartment a few floors below this one.

I nod, working overtime to hide my confusion: Paul Turner was Grace's husband? It feels strange that I hadn't known that. At the same time, why would I have known that? Turner is a common last name. And it isn't like I was asking my father who his colleagues were married to.

"I don't think we've met before," he says to me now. "Paul Turner."

He gives me a smile and runs his fingers through his hair. And I clock it. He is wearing his wedding ring. Grace has been gone for the better part of a year now, and he is still wearing his ring.

I'm not sure if he sees me notice that, but he puts his hand in his back pocket.

I try to pivot in case he did notice. In case it made him feel badly, when noticing it made me feel the opposite. It felt like I was witnessing a gesture of something kind. Something like loyalty.

"It's nice to meet you," I say. "I don't think Grace mentioned to me that she lived in this building."

"Well, she didn't really. We lived over on Pierrepont. This used to be just my work studio. But I'm basically here since shortly after she passed away . . ." He pauses, as if considering that. "Eight months now."

"Fresh start," I say.

"Something like that."

He clears his throat, his voice catching even at the mention of her, and the last place I want to be is standing there in front of a grieving husband, still wearing his wedding ring, at the start of a night that shouldn't involve us.

"Look, I feel badly, guys, I know that I said it was okay to stop by, but my daughter is in town visiting and she just called, so I'm going to need to keep this real quick. She's five months pregnant. When she calls, I come."

"Sure . . ." Sam says. "We were just wondering if you still have Grace's office belongings here?"

"Like company files?"

"Terry mentioned that when her office was cleaned out, her work computer was sent to you."

He tilts his head, takes Sam in. "You mean her laptop?"

"Exactly," Sam says.

Paul looks back and forth between us. "Can I ask why?"

"Our father's cell phone is missing," I say. "That's the long and short answer. And Grace may have had access to whatever was on that phone. Family photographs, text messages, certain other communications that feel particularly valuable to us now that he's not . . . here."

"Why would her laptop have any of that?"

"Apparently, Grace often worked on her laptop at home, especially after she started coming into work less," Sam says. "And IT believes her laptop may have shared files that weren't on the company's mainframe."

"Well, if they weren't on the company's mainframe, wouldn't there have been a good reason for that?"

"Because it was personal," Sam says.

Paul shakes his head. "I'm confused," he says. "So are you looking for personal photographs? Or company data?"

"Point is," Sam says, "we aren't trying to cause any trouble for her or for you, obviously . . ."

"Why would this cause trouble for me?"

I'm quick to jump in, not liking the look he is giving Sam.

"I think, maybe, what Sam is trying to say is we aren't sure what her computer has on it. But we just want to see for ourselves what is there. We do realize that this is a bit of a strange ask . . ."

"Just a bit."

"That's not really the point," Sam says.

Paul crosses his arms over his chest, his tone growing more irritated. "If you're asking for access to my wife's personal property, it sure is."

"Actually," Sam says, "it's the company's computer, so I'm not sure why it's here in the first place."

"I'm just going to say, I think whatever this is, I'm going to pass on being involved in it, okay?"

"If you're hoping for compensation, we will gladly replace the computer."

Paul laughs. "I don't want your money."

"What do you want?"

"Well, right now, I want to say good night to you both, so I can hop on the subway and not keep my daughter waiting in the freezing cold."

I shoot Sam a look. This is going the wrong way and it's getting worse.

"I get it. We *both* get that. My brother is just concerned, we're actually both a little concerned, that something bad may have happened to our father. And we're having trouble getting answers from anyone about what was going on with him." I pause. "And Grace, I really thought the world of Grace, and I think if anyone would have known what was happening with him, it might have been her."

He softens, hearing that. "I get that. And that's probably true."

Then he gives me a small smile, something sad behind his eyes, letting me know he means it.

"Maybe you can just help us with one thing in particular, before you go," I say. "Did Grace ever mention Cece Salinger's interest in buying the company?"

He tries not to react, but I can see in his face that he is surprised by the question. "All roads lead to Cece, huh?"

"How do you mean?" I ask.

"That's a longer conversation than I have time for," he says. "But, yes, Grace mentioned that at some point. She mentioned Cece's interest, but my understanding is that your father wasn't interested. That was all settled a long time ago."

He meets my eyes. And I can see that this longer conversation is one he has no intention of having—tonight or any time. So what else did Grace know about Cece? From how he's looking at me, that suddenly feels like a question too.

"The truth is, I didn't hold on to most of her work files, devices, the rest of it. I didn't bring most of it with me from Pierrepont. It was easier not to have to face everything that reminded me of her."

I look around the foyer—the living room beyond it. There are family photographs on the mantel: photographs of their daughter, Jenny, of Grace holding her when she was a baby, of Paul and Grace's wedding. It doesn't look, at first glance, like what he's saying is true. But what do I know about what he feels like is true to him? Maybe this—this small number of photographs, whatever he has chosen to bring with him here—is just a fraction of it. A life together.

"I appreciate that your father's death is disorienting," he says. "It is for me too, truly, and I never even knew him all that well. But I doubt I even have the laptop. Like I told Tommy, Joe asked for most of her stuff shortly after the office sent it here, and I shipped it out to him—"

"Whoa," Sam stops him. "You spoke to Tommy about this? When was that exactly?"

Paul looks back and forth between us. "I'm pretty sure that's a conversation you need to have with your brother."

Paul's cell phone buzzes and JENNY comes up on his caller ID. His daughter. Grace's daughter. He looks back at us.

"Here's the thing," he says. "Grace worked hard and so she didn't talk much about her work when she was at home. Except to tell me two things. She cared about your father. She thought he was a good man despite whatever people said about him. She told me that."

I look at him, taking that in.

"Problem is the other thing she told me was not to trust his kids."

Then he walks back to the front door, holds it open, and waits for us to walk through it.

# If You're Going Down, Go All the Way Down . . .

"He definitely meant you guys, not me," I say.

We are in the elevator, heading back to the lobby, Sam already on his phone, trying to reach Tommy.

"Yeah, 'cause that's the point we should be focusing on . . ." he says. "Besides, Grace wouldn't have said that. He was just trying to get rid of us."

My instinct is that Sam is correct. But why was Paul so anxious to get rid of us? Was it just that he was late for his daughter—or was there something else he didn't want to tell us?

I hear the beep come through Sam's phone, connecting him to Tommy's voicemail. "Hey, why are you talking to Paul Turner?" Sam says into the phone. "What the fuck is going on, Tommy?"

He clicks off, shaking his head.

"Can you try and calm down?" I say.

"This is just like him. I'm working with all these people and none of them wants to tell me anything. Dad was keeping all sorts of secrets and now Uncle Joe is what? Stealing fucking laptops?"

"We don't know he has it."

"No, but I do know my brother. And if he is reaching out to Paul, it's because he's up to something."

The elevator door pops open and Sam starts moving through the lobby. I almost have to run to keep up.

"Did you talk to Tommy about Dad's accident?" I ask. "Maybe he ended up here the same way we did."

"No, I didn't talk to him about any of that. He would just have told me I was crazy. Besides, Tommy only cares about what affects Tommy. I know you probably think the same about me."

"That's a lot to throw at me."

"Bottom line is we need to talk to Tommy in person."

"Didn't you say he's upstate?"

He nods. "North of Hudson. But it's like a three-hour drive, tops."

"Oh, is that all?"

"If I drive, I can get us there closer to two," he says. "We should go first thing tomorrow."

"I'm not anxious for you to be driving me anywhere, to be honest."

Sam looks wild-eyed and exhausted. And, it seems to me, this mission is to the side of whatever we are trying to figure out. At least the part of it where he looks like he wants to tear Tommy's eyes out.

"Look, this is really between you two. My only interest here is what happened to Dad that night."

"Except that it's all related."

Is it? I start to do the math on what's going on, what we have found out for sure. Our father was going to sell his company to someone else, after a lifetime of not even considering selling it. Then, for reasons unknown, he walked it all the way back and decided to leave the company to his sons. And, eight days after that, he made two phone calls to an old lover and then fell off a cliff that he knew like the back of his hand.

If this was all related, who would have a reason be on the cliff with him that night? Who would have a reason if it wasn't?

"What's that look?" Sam says.

"Thought," I say. "I thought the same about you."

He looks at me, confused. "What are you talking about?"

"You said that Tommy is only ever out for helping Tommy, and that I probably think that about you," I say. "I did think that. I was wrong."

We step outside into the city streets and Sam gives me a quick nod. He tries to be casual about it, but I can see how much that matters to him.

Tomorrow is supposed to be the start of a new work week. I scheduled a conference call about a large commission in Sag Harbor. I have an on-site inspection and a long-planned lunch with an interior design firm I often collaborate with. I have work—days of work—piling up in a way I never allow to happen. And I have Jack. Most urgently Jack, who it has felt easier to have space from this weekend. As if easier is the goal, as if the goal isn't to figure out how to get back to it. To how we normally exist. How intimate and deep Jack and I naturally go.

But Sam's need is coming off him like a sound wave. Like an alarm. And I can't ignore it.

"You need to be waiting outside of my house at nine thirty tomorrow morning, you hear me? Or I'm done with this."

It deflates it, the pressure between his eyes, his energy shifting, a smile coming onto his face.

"I'll have the engine running," he says.

I start to turn onto Clark Street, toward the subway, when I hear Sam's voice.

"You ready to admit that I'm growing on you?"

"Good night, Sam."

"A little?" he calls out.

I shake my head, not turning around.

"Fine by me!" he says. "We'll leave it unsaid."

---

# In Ditmas Park, the Moon Turns Purple

The house is dark when I get home.

It's 10:00 p.m., Jack is still at the restaurant. Instead of going into the empty house, I pull my coat tight and take a seat on the front steps. The block is quiet this time of night, serene. The Ushers are walking their dog, but most of my neighbors are inside for the night—their windows lit up with late-night dinner and bedside lamps, the blue light of their televisions.

One of the last times my father came to see me in Ditmas Park, it was late at night, a little over a year ago, not too long after my mother died. I remember because it had been two months since she died. Two months exactly. I was still counting the days then. I'm still counting the days now.

My father was on his way back from an event in Midwood. Going back there was something he rarely did.

He had texted me to meet him at Sheet Music, but I was still working, so he said he would come to me instead and bring a little Sheet Music with him.

We sat on the steps and shared a strawberry sofrito pie and drank champagne out of coffee mugs.

"Are we celebrating something?" I asked.

"If I've learned anything it's that you don't need a reason for champagne," my father said.

I smiled at him.

"But if you'd like a reason, I was supposed to go to my high school reunion tonight." He shrugged. "And then I remembered I don't have to go anywhere anymore that I don't want to be."

I laughed. "That seems worthy of a celebration."

While we ate he asked me what I was working on, and I walked him through a commission in Connecticut. It was a memory care facility that I was building out with a geriatric specialist. Our goal was to create the type of coherent space that would aid orientation, alleviate confusion. We were leaning into a biophilic design concept to ensure all thirty occupants would be closely connected to nature and lots of natural light, a calming environment.

I thought I was boring him, but he kept asking more questions, wanting every detail. Pouring more champagne and asking more questions. It was his MO: He couldn't be prouder about what I was doing. He couldn't learn enough about what mattered to me.

But, that night, there was another layer to it. It felt like there was something my father wanted to tell me too. Something that he kept coming right up to the edge of saying. But he didn't.

I wondered if it had something to do with the distance I was keeping from him—if he was trying to figure out how to broach the topic. But that didn't seem like what it was. It seemed like it was good news he was trying to figure out how to share—something that was making him happy.

I didn't push him. Even if he didn't want to say it yet, whatever was bringing him joy just then, it was enough for him to be able to sit in it, with me. But I wish I had pushed. What I would give now to know exactly what had been going through his mind.

I pull my cell phone from my bag. And I click on his name before I let myself think about it.

Elliot answers on the first ring.

"Your ears must be burning," he says. "Austin was talking about you at dinner tonight."

"Really? What was he saying?"

"He wanted me to remind you about his piano recital on Tuesday."

I feel a twinge in my chest, thinking about Austin's last recital, last spring, his rhapsodic focus on his latest piece. My father was there with me, holding a big box of cookies on his lap. Proud.

"I'll be there," I say.

"So you're back?"

"I'm back."

"What were you doing in California?"

"That's a long story."

"I dropped Austin back at his mother's," he says. "I've got nothing but time."

I hear him adjust his position, his voice getting lower, like he's lying down. And I can picture him there, his arm behind his head, long legs hanging off the bed, his glasses beside him on the bedside table.

"Can I ask you something first?" I say. "Do you remember the last time you saw my father?"

"Where did that come from?"

"Part of the long story."

He pauses, considering. "We grabbed dinner probably five or six weeks ago."

I sit up, taller. It isn't weird that Elliot and my father saw each other that recently. They'd often run into each other in their building. And they stayed close. Shortly after Elliot and I ended things, my father made sure that their continued friendship was okay with me. I had no problem with it. When my father let someone in, the way he had let Elliot in, he didn't like to turn them out.

"Wait," I say. "So two weeks before he died?"

"Something like that. Why?"

"Do you remember what you talked about?"

"What we talked about?"

I try to get more specific, figure out what I want to know. "Did you talk about his work at all?"

"Not much. Nora, what's going on?"

"There are some things that aren't adding up about how he died, so I'm just trying . . . I'm pulling at every thread to see what I'm missing. Or what I missed."

"Okay . . ." I hear the concern in his voice. "Well, your father definitely asked about Austin," he says. "We talked a little about what was happening at the hospital. I think he asked about a patient of mine—"

"He didn't say that anything was upsetting him?"

"He didn't really talk much about himself. You know how your father was. He wanted to know what was going on with me."

That was true. My father did always like to focus on whoever he was with, especially the people he cared the most about. But, suddenly, I'm not sure that's the entire reason he tended to stay quiet. I doubt that I can explain that to Elliot or explain to him how it feels just beyond my grasp—what I'm missing about what was happening with my father, at the very end. How I'm increasingly certain that if I can figure that out, the rest of what I want to know about him will follow.

"Can I ask you something else? Do you have someone at the hospital who studies fall patterns? Like a pathologist who could look at an autopsy report and help me determine if someone fell or was pushed?"

"Okay, this conversation took a weird turn," he says.

"Hey there . . ."

Jack's voice jolts me, and I drop the phone. I turn to see him standing in our doorway, between the open door and the screen. His hair is rumpled, his feet bare. The house is dark behind him, Jack looking too much like a shadow from where I'm sitting on the porch steps.

"Holy shit," I say. "You scared me half to death."

"Didn't mean to. I come in peace."

I scoop up the phone and click off the call without saying goodbye. "I thought you were still at the restaurant," I say.

He walks onto the porch, sits down next to me on the front steps. "I cut out early," he says. "I wanted to be here when you got back."

I'm still working to catch my breath when the phone buzzes in my hand, ELLIOT coming up on the screen. I click decline as Jack looks at the phone in my hand and then back up at me. Not saying anything.

"Sorry," I say. "I'm just a little jumpy."

"I can see that."

He kisses my shoulder, moves closer to me. And I turn and take him in—his T-shirt wrinkled, his eyes glassy, pillow marks lining his face. My favorite face. I reach over and touch it.

"You fell asleep on the couch?" I ask.

"I think maybe."

"Just maybe?"

He leans into my fingers, giving me a smile. So happy, it seems, just to share that smile, for an honest moment of connection.

"How did it go?" he says. "At Windbreak?"

"Well. I'm starting to think that maybe Sam is right."

"Really?" he says.

I nod, something solidifying, now that I'm saying it out loud to him.

"I know you think that it's just my grief talking."

"I wouldn't say that . . ."

"What would you say?"

"I think that you're doing what you need to do. Figuring out what you need to figure out." He pauses, lowers his already low voice. "What are you figuring out?"

I'm figuring out that my father may have been hiding something. And I'm trying to understand how that coalesces with strange phone calls, on a phone that is now missing, and a mysterious jogger who could be in possession of it. And, you know, the rest of the story.

I'm figuring out that there is a reason I keep picturing the moment before my father went over the edge. In none of the scenarios do I think he was there alone.

I look at Jack and don't say any of that. I offer only the part I don't need to figure out. The part I know for sure.

"I was a pretty lousy daughter at the end," I say.

"Nora . . ." he says. Soft. Kind. He holds on to my gaze, as if promising me the opposite is true, and I fight the tears loading up in my eyes.

But he doesn't argue. He doesn't try to convince me that I'm wrong. Instead, he moves closer to me—his leg against my leg, his shoulder against mine, his hand reaching behind my back to hold my head, his fingers strong and steadying.

I can feel it. I can feel it beneath his fingers, pulsating, like a heartbeat. The soft little bug of a thing. This soft little bug that lives between us. A living, breathing reminder that we belong to each other.

I flinch against it, against the intensity of his touch, before I even know that I'm doing it. It's primal, something in me needing to shut that kind of closeness all the way down. Something in me shutting down.

Jack feels it and reacts, pulls his hand back, almost in an apology. This is when my phone buzzes again, ELLIOT coming up again on the caller ID.

I toss it in my bag, push it away from us. "I thought I shut that off," I say.

Jack offers a small laugh.

"No," he says. "Sure."

He moves back, away from me. But he holds my gaze for another moment, a short and terrible standoff. It's worse than if he just called me out. Aren't I begging him to call me out for the phone call, for the distancing, for what I'm giving away?

"Tell Elliot I say hello," he says.

Then he stands up and heads back inside.

# The Acres

When we hit the upper Hudson Valley, we are surrounded by farmland.

I tap out an email as we glide past creek bridges and post offices, American flags and steel trailers. Much of the landscape covered in old snow. I lower the window enough to let in just a little of that cold winter air, fresh and crisp, the sun streaming down despite it.

We've been making calls on the way out here, in the hopes of getting eyes we can trust on the police report and the autopsy. On Detective O'Brien's incomplete investigation. I didn't want to reach out to Elliot again, as if that would somehow remedy last night's conversation with Jack. As if that will help realign my loyalty. So, instead, I reached out to a neuroscientist with whom I often collaborate to see if she could put me in touch with an expert she trusted. She put me in touch with a neurocriminologist, who steered me toward two forensic pathologists.

As Sam drove, I emailed the two forensic pathologists all the information I have—the autopsy report and the police report, the Windbreak property map, and the geology report on the cliff itself. I forwarded Detective O'Brien's shaky investigative findings on which I hope they can shed an impartial light.

"Something's been bugging me since last night," I say.

Sam turns and looks over at me. "Just one thing?"

I give him a smile.

"Paul's reaction to Cece was pretty intense," I say. "It feels like it could be related to why Joe didn't want us talking to her."

"Meaning?"

"Uncle Joe was clearly worried she would tell us something we weren't supposed to know about Dad. And I keep thinking that maybe Grace, at some point, told Paul the same thing . . . We need to keep that in mind when we get to Tommy's."

"Why? What does that have to do with Tommy?"

"I think that should be the first thing we ask him."

Sam turns down a long gravel road still sporting a large sign for ROSE VALLEY APPLE ORCHARDS.

A much smaller wooden sign hangs beneath it, announcing itself in dark block letters. THE ACRES.

We drive past a working farm complete with an apple orchard and a large chicken coop, several hiking trails circling around it.

Sam pulls into a small roundabout, turning off the ignition. I step out of the car and take in the main entrance to the property with its beautiful gravel walkway and the enormous open-air porch house, a central meadow just beyond it.

The porch house is still midconstruction, but the bones are stunning: twenty-feet-high lofted oak rafters, wood-framed furniture, and large indoor trees, all organized around a central firepit.

But what's most spectacular is the vista—the expanse of that central meadow and the ridge—the property dotted with steel and wood cabins, in varying degrees of completion. I can see the amount of work they are putting into those cabins, clad in reclaimed wood, offset gabled roofs. And, even midconstruction, they're remarkable. They're rustic and gentle, not disturbing the land but very much a part of it.

I'm struck by the entire build-out for that reason. It isn't dissimilar to a project I worked on not too far from here in Woodstock, New

York. It's a family compound where the owners asked for a modern take on the eighteenth-century farmhouse on property. I created several vernacular buildings, a central communal firepit for family gatherings—a perfect and peaceful family retreat in the Catskill Mountains.

"Remind you of Woodstock?" Sam asks.

I turn toward him. "How did you know that?"

Sam hands me a hard hat. "Dad held up the photograph of your property in the *Record* at the first concept meeting. And he said, *something like this*."

I put the hard hat on, feeling his words in my chest. In my gut. My father's pride in me, in all of us, was immovable, even when we weren't in the room to witness it. If I had been in the room, would I have figured out how to tell him that he deserved credit for anything he liked about what I built? That I became the kind of architect I did in part from watching him work? He took joy in building meaningful spaces. He took joy in making things work and feel right. I don't think I'm the kind of artist I am without that influence. I never told him that. I gave that to my mother. Her attention to rhythm and to beauty. But it was him too. It was him. Suddenly, it feels like another injury that he'll never hear me say that.

Sam motions toward a larger (and completed) cabin toward the side of the meadow, and we walk that way.

"That's the Ridge House," he says. "Tommy's staying there."

"You're going to run out of time."

"For what?"

"To tell me what's going on with the two of you before we see him."

He shakes his head, like there's nothing to say. "Did I not mention that we haven't really spoken in about six weeks?"

I stare at him in disbelief. "No. You didn't."

He shrugs. "It's complicated. I don't think he was particularly happy to hear that Dad left both of us in charge. As opposed to just him."

"You told him that you were coming here, though, right?"

Sam walks up the front steps of the cabin, taking them two at a time.

"Not in so many words."

"In *any* words, Sam?"

Before he answers me, the front door swings open and Tommy's wife, Kira, is standing there. Beautiful Kira, who is also very pregnant.

She looks back and forth between us. "What the hell are you two doing here?"

I give Sam a look, which he ignores.

"For starters," Sam says, "your husband's a liar."

"Tell me something I don't know," Kira says.

Then she moves out of the doorway and lets us in.

"How are you feeling, Kira?" I ask.

"Like I have two four-pound babies inside of me. I thought twins were supposed to skip a generation."

"Not all the time," Sam says.

"You think?" she says.

She turns back toward me, looks me up and down. "It's been a while."

It's true. I haven't seen Kira since her and Tommy's wedding six years ago. I attended the ceremony but then snuck out before the reception. (Tommy and Sam's mother's chilly greeting that afternoon was enough to remind me that the ceremony was all that I was really wanted for.) They had been together since their senior year of college—Tommy and Kira—and the longest conversation we'd had was early on when Kira noticed that Tommy's mother harbored nearly as much disdain for me as she usually reserved for her. This was something Kira wasn't used to and couldn't understand. She was an artist, a young and successful designer, self-sufficient and in love with Tommy. How unfair that Sylvia wasn't welcoming. For a nanosecond, it made Kira interested in befriending me.

"You look different," she says now. "Are you pregnant too?"

That moment of her seeking friendship has long passed.

I force a smile. "I'm not, no."

"I guess you don't want kids."

"I wouldn't say that."

I don't elaborate. I'm not about to get into baby planning with my sister-in-law, especially in a moment that feels particularly complicated. Jack and I had been discussing how much we both want a baby. We were discussing a baby and my dreams for expanding the firm and Jack opening a second restaurant. We were discussing everything about the future. Until it started to feel like a jinx to me, to trust the days to lay out before me in that way, to trust them to keep turning up uninterrupted.

"Well, it was a nightmare to conceive these two," Kira says. "So if I can give you a little advice—"

"I'm good," I say.

"I would get on it sooner rather than later," she continues, ignoring me. "No offense, but the clock is ticking for you way more than it was for me."

Then she heads back into the main living area.

I smile at Sam. "She's charming."

Sam lets out a laugh. And we follow her into the other room, where she sits down in the window seat. The uninterrupted ridge is lit up behind her, its hills and trees jutting up against a cloudless hidden valley.

"It's freezing here. I can't handle it."

"Not a bad view, at least," I say.

She closes her eyes and wraps herself tightly in a blanket. "I couldn't care less."

It doesn't feel like it would go any better to compliment the interior design of this cabin and by extension what will be the zeitgeist of The Acres, which Kira is at least partially responsible for. She is the interior design director for Noone Properties, and this one has her signature all over it: reclaimed furniture, antique pieces, and botanical prints, everything bright and vivid and lush, like the ridge it's highlighting.

Kira cups her belly, sighs. "There are waters in the fridge. I have nothing else to offer you but ginger lollipops."

"We're just looking for Tommy," Sam says.

"They're trying to finish up out by the natural playground. Do you even know where that is, Sam?"

He laughs off her overt dig. Her insinuation that instead of Kira and Tommy being holed up here, it should be him. Or, at least, Sam should be there, sharing in the work. Maybe he should be. Either way, Sam is smart to let it lie. If she feels that way, it's being filtered through the person who would be reporting it that way: Tommy. He isn't going to convince her that she's wrong.

"Take a map with you."

"I've got a good idea where I'm going," he says. "Thanks, though."

"Don't be a fucking hero, Sam. Property map is in the crate on the porch. Spoiler alert, it's a hike."

Then she closes her eyes, apparently done with us. So, I walk back out of the cabin, Sam following.

He closes the door behind us. "Wow," Sam says. "That's the nicest she's been to me in a while. Worrying I'd get lost."

I smile. "Is that what that was?"

"Clearly. Plus, you know, the concern she was showing for you."

I look at him, confused.

"She's right. You're not getting younger."

My smile disappears. "Very funny."

"I'm just saying. Maybe you should patch things up with the veterinarian. You really like his kid . . ."

"Get the map," I say.

# Playgrounds Come in Different Shapes and Sizes

Kira isn't wrong. The property paths haven't been carved out yet and it isn't an easy hike, especially in the wind and the cold, walking through woodlands and over steep hills, until we find our way to the natural playground.

Despite the cold, we are both sweaty and breathless by the time we walk over the final hill and into the clearing, where there is a team of construction workers busy at work. There is a zipline being built into the trees, a rock-climbing wall embedded into a high bolder, an in-ground trampoline secured into the valley.

The trampoline is where we find Tommy. He is bouncing on it, in his puffy vest and jeans, talking to one of the construction workers.

From a distance it could look like he is enjoying himself. But, from what I know about him, Tommy doesn't believe in enjoying himself. He is probably trying to squeeze in a bit of exercise while he works. Because what Tommy believes in is achievement.

He looks up and sees us approaching him. And it's jarring, as it always is. His eyes, so much like mine, staring back at me. That face, just like my face.

"Well, I'll be damned. What are you doing here? And together?" he says. "I'd guess that Dad died, but that's already happened."

I shake my head, done with him already. "That's hilarious, Tommy," I say.

He offers a half-smile. "Just trying to break the ice," he says. "Kira texted that you two are on the warpath about something. Or did she get that wrong? Are you just here to check in on me? Offer your condolences?"

"Cut it out, Tommy," Sam says. "Why the fuck are you talking to Paul Turner about Cece Salinger?"

Tommy turns toward Sam. "Who told you that?"

"Who told me that?" Sam says. "That's what you have to say?"

Tommy stares at Sam, his smile disappearing. Then he steps off the trampoline and turns to me.

"We need somewhere private if you guys want to get into this," he says.

"Lead the way," Sam says.

Tommy motions toward the Airstream. And we follow him up the small stairs and inside. The cabin is hot and tight, a space heater going at full blast. Tommy pulls off his puffy vest, sweat pooling under each arm.

He grabs a kombucha and takes a seat behind his makeshift desk, leaving us to find room on the built-in couch, covered with boxes of files and endless cases of additional kombucha.

"Before you go losing your shit," he says, "it's not like Dad told me about any of this. I just found out he was planning to sell to her a couple of weeks ago."

"How?" Sam says.

"One of the lawyers was talking to Joe after the will reading and I overheard him say something about Salinger, so I started digging. I got the sale confirmed by a couple of people who are in-house with Cece."

"And you didn't think to tell me?"

"How do you want me to answer that?"

"By explaining why you didn't think to tell me, for starters."

Sam holds Tommy's eyes and I see it pass between them: this mix of anger and love and resentment. This quiet understanding that the two of them are always in it together and somehow, like now, the opposite of that.

"You're seriously going to give me a hard time? You've been totally fucking absent, man."

"Since Dad died?" Sam says. "I think that's understandable."

"It's been a lot worse since then, sure. But if we are going to be honest, then let's be honest," he says. "You're not exactly the partner around here you say you want to be."

"That's such bullshit," Sam says. "You just want to believe it should be you here without me."

"You know that isn't it," he says. "You're perfectly good at your job when you choose to be."

"Don't make me blush."

Tommy shakes his head, like the last thing he has time for is to convince Sam of what is true. And I certainly don't know if what Tommy is saying is accurate, but I can see how small it's making Sam feel. I feel a pull to lean in and make it stop.

"We don't need to get into all of this, Tommy," I say. "We are just trying to figure out what was going on with Dad."

"I literally don't even know what you are doing here," he says.

"Quite honestly, that makes two of us."

He looks at me and softens.

"There were things going on with Dad that we didn't know," I say. "That none of us knew . . ."

"Like the fact that he was involved with Cece?" Tommy asks.

*Like the fact he may have been murdered.*

I nod. "Among other things."

"Well, for what it's worth, Joe told me, categorically, that whatever happened with them happened a really long time ago."

"So . . . how did that end up with you reaching out to Paul Turner?" I ask.

He reaches into his desk and pulls out a copy of *Forbes* magazine—Cece Salinger on the cover, staring back at us, her arms folded across her chest.

He hands me the magazine, has one of the pages earmarked. "This was from five months ago," he says. "Page eighty-three."

I open the magazine to the earmarked page and am greeted with a large photograph of Cece walking through the small vineyard on her property in Los Alamos—the property Sam and I were turned away from two days ago.

I read the headers to each section. They focus on Cece's outsize success, on how she is rebranding the Salinger Group portfolio on the other side of her divorce, particularly as it relates to her lifestyle division.

I study the photograph and the bolded quote beneath it, which I read out loud: "'*Salinger's next chapter will be focused on building out her hospitality and resort portfolio, focusing on luxury-driven, private retreat experiences.*'"

"Just below that," Tommy says. "Right above the jump."

"'*While Salinger was hesitant to discuss her personal life in great depth, she did confirm she designed her new home for herself and her current partner, whom she coyly describes as an old friend. "But that's for another day," Salinger says, declining to discuss her personal life in any detail.*'"

"Sound familiar?" Tommy asks.

"Sounds like it could be Dad," Sam says.

"What does this have to do with Paul Turner?" I ask.

"One guess who the photographer for this profile was . . ."

I look up and meet Tommy's eyes.

He nods. And I add that piece of information to my growing list of things that aren't adding up, not on their face, living in that strange space between uncomfortable and weird.

"That's some coincidence," Sam says.

"He does a lot of work for the magazine, apparently. But still, I thought he might have insight into what was going on with Dad and Cece. And no vested interest in keeping it to himself."

"Did he confirm anything?" I ask.

"Not what I thought he would," he says. "He seemed to confirm that, from the little he knew, anything that had happened between Cece and Dad was ancient history. Paul seemed pretty confident that if she is involved with someone at the company, he didn't think it had anything to do with Dad."

Sam looks at him, confused. Which is when I put it together.

"You mean Cece and Uncle Joe?" I ask.

"That's where I went," Tommy says. I feel my jaw tighten, just as Sam's does.

"Paul said they were together?"

Tommy shakes his head. "It's what he didn't say when I put it out there."

"And what's that?" I ask.

"That I was wrong."

## *Thirty-Nine Years Ago*

"I very much like her," Cory said. "Rachel."

They were sitting in a sandwich shop near Liam's office in Midtown, sharing a slice of coconut cream pie, Cory's finger circling her coffee mug.

She was home, again. She had moved back to New York, back to Brooklyn. One year had turned into three and a half, just like he'd known it would. She wasn't even back now because she wanted to be here, but because her mother was sick and her father was useless and someone had to take care of them.

She was, apparently, the someone.

She loved graduate school. She loved the writing program and loved spending the day with people who wanted to talk about books and plays and poetry. She loved the apartment that she shared with two other graduate students. It was an old firehouse that had been converted into open-air lofts with enormous, pitched ceilings and a large bookshelf that ran the length of the living room. This was the first photograph she showed him: the photograph of that beautiful, endless white bookshelf that housed all her books, all her textbooks, all the used books she thrifted every weekend.

She was wearing it on her face—how miserable she felt to be back in her parents' house. What choice did she have? Her mother's pension wasn't enough. Her father was unemployed. Cory was three semesters shy of finishing her PhD and nowhere close to finishing a book. Teaching jobs would be fairly impossible to secure. As would any kind of jobs at New York publishers. They were impossible to acquire and low paying, at least when you were starting out.

She didn't have time to get into all that. She was interviewing for a job at the marketing company her friend Sally worked for. She was going to be a copywriter. They liked that they could tell clients she had a master's. And they would probably inflate it to tell clients that she had a PhD too. They were in marketing, after all. The bottom line was she'd make plenty of money to properly care for her parents. She would figure out the rest later.

Liam reached across the table, toward her. It was killing him to see her unhappy. But he didn't know how to fix it for her. She didn't want his fixes anyway. He wasn't an artist. He didn't have that compulsion. He knew that she had, in a way, been more comfortable discussing the situation with Rachel, even though Cory and Rachel had only just met. Rachel knew what it meant to move away from your art (or at least to move away from the idea that your art could also operate as your livelihood) and to try and build a different kind of life. That understanding was one of many reasons they had gotten along. That they'd genuinely gotten along. Somehow, for Liam, that made it harder.

Now Rachel had gone to catch the train back to Croton, and it was just the two of them. Just Cory and Liam. Cory kept looking away from him, her eyes focused on that damn mug, refusing to let him deeper in.

"I can call off the wedding," he said.

"Don't be ridiculous. She is lovely. I like her. And more importantly you like her. There's a reason you want to marry her."

"I didn't think you were coming back."

"Yet here I am."

"Cory . . ."

"Don't call me Cory," she said. "It makes me think of my father."

"What can I tell you? Old habits die hard."

She smiled in spite of herself.

"Let me help," he said. "With your parents."

"Already offered. Already rejected."

"You're very stubborn," he said.

"Maybe," she said. "Maybe that's true."

She shrugged and tried to play it off, but that wasn't possible between them. He knew, even if she wasn't going to say it, that it wasn't just the turn that things had taken for her. Maybe it was also something she couldn't exactly access. She was so used to him asking her to marry him that she never thought the day would come when he stopped asking. He didn't want to stop asking. How had they gotten here?

"I hate the reason you're back, I do, but—"

"But what?"

"I'm also glad you're back," he said. "I know that's selfish. I know that's the most selfish thing I can say."

"Just honest. Besides, I get it."

"You do?"

She met his eyes, finally. "We can't be apart this long again."

"No," he said. "No, we'll never do that again."

"But what will we do?"

He started to speak, but she shook her head and stopped him.

"Not for you to answer. Not what I'm looking for."

"So what are you looking for?"

He took her hand, her soft palm, wrapped it between both of his.

"Right now?" she said. "Some more pie."

# Detours Are the Only Way Home

"Cece and Joe," Sam says. "Fuck. Of course."

"It may start to explain some things," I say.

"It *may*?"

We are hiking back toward the main grounds and the car, the wind and the cold burning my cheeks, my skin.

Sam pulls out his phone, starts searching. "Cece Salinger and her husband of thirty-one years finalize their divorce."

He looks up at me.

"That was eight months ago. Timing lines up," he says. "Joe probably talked Dad into selling to his girlfriend—"

"When has someone talked Dad into anything?"

"The point is, it would also explain why Dad was off these past couple of months, especially if Uncle Joe kept the relationship from him. Pretty terrible betrayal after everything Dad tried to do for him."

I look at Sam, wondering which betrayal he is talking about: Joe convincing our father to sell the company to someone he was involved with? Or Joe being involved with Cece in the first place? Either way, it feels like a big jump—and maybe the wrong jump. Because even if Paul (and Tommy) are correct about Uncle Joe and Cece being involved, who says my father wasn't aware? What kind of deep history would my father have needed to have had with her for Uncle Joe to keep that from him?

We walk over another hill, the parking lot appearing in the distance. Sam holds out his hands for the keys.

"None of that tells us who was on the cliff with Dad that night," I say.

"Not yet. But if Joe and Cece kept this from Dad, you've got to ask yourself what they are keeping from us now."

"Except then why would Cece volunteer that she heard from Dad the night that he died? Wouldn't that encourage us to do exactly what we are doing? Ask more questions about her as opposed to fewer?"

He shakes his head, like I'm refusing to see what's right in front of me.

"Maybe she just knew we'd get here either way," he says.

"That doesn't follow, Sam. And it doesn't follow from what I felt when I looked at her."

"Which is?"

I think of the sadness I saw in her eyes that she had missed those calls. Especially when they were the last chance.

"She really cared about Dad."

"Both things can exist."

He opens the car door and gets in.

I don't want to rile Sam up further, so I get in the car too, closing the door behind myself. And I refrain from saying what I'm also thinking: *If both things do exist, how compromised did that leave our father?*

Sam puts his hands on the steering wheel, the ignition off.

"I'm not trying to play the game of who knew Dad better," he says. "I'm really not. But, working with him every day, I do think that Tommy and I understood something about Dad that maybe you didn't."

"Which is?"

"This company was everything to him."

"I don't think it's that simple."

"Well, it's not a lot more complicated," he says. "Everyone who was around him saw it. The joy when he was on a project site, his singular focus when there was a new property opening. Even when he was just in the office . . . All I'm saying is, you can feel it. When someone comes alive. That's when Dad would always feel the most alive."

I stare at Sam, feeling weird suddenly. Had I missed it entirely, what Sam had somehow been able to see?

Sam's hands are tight on the steering wheel. The car still in park.

"He's not wrong about the other thing, either," Sam says. "Tommy . . ."

"What other thing?"

"I haven't been myself lately," he says. "You want to know why?"

"If I say no, will it hurt your feelings?"

"Very funny. I have something I want to show you."

"No thank you."

"It's a bit of a detour if I'm being honest."

"This is getting worse."

Which is when he turns on the ignition and puts the car in drive.

~

We cross over the Hudson River and drive for a little over an hour until we hit the city of Kingston.

Upper Kingston. Which looks more than a little like it belongs in a movie set, especially with the winter lights, the holiday decorations still up.

Kingston was the first capital of New York State, and the architecture is locked into that history with this incredible mix of colonial stone cottages, colorful buildings, wrought iron balconies. The world of it so interesting and unique despite the fact that I was driven here against my will.

As soon as we pass through the town center, everything around us gets more rural again—shuttered farm stands, weeping willows, and RVs taking over the landscape.

Sam pulls over to the side of the road beside a wide-open farm, donning fruit orchards and tree-lined hilltops. A silver crest over the driveway entrance reads FITZGERALD-GROVE STONE FRUIT.

"Why are we stopping?" I ask.

Sam motions out the windshield. "This was originally where Dad wanted to build The Acres," he says. "The Fitzgerald farm."

"Okay . . ."

"Two hundred and eighty acres, the most beautiful sugar maple trees, three different kinds of orchard fruit. Apples, peaches, cherries. And when I tell you it's the best peach you've ever tasted, I'm not lying."

"What's happening right now?"

"I'm the one who found the farm. After months of looking at eighty farms up and down the Hudson Valley," he says, "I came up here to try and secure the sale of the property and the family wasn't particularly interested, which is typical at first, but most of the time they come around when they hear how Dad organizes his property buys. Eighty percent of the land is preserved, guaranteed. We keep a small working farm on-site, which they can manage if they want. And, of course, they can stay in their house. We build out five acres for them to have forever. So they aren't being asked to leave or relocate. Plus, they have more money than a lifetime of tending to the whole place could give them."

He pauses.

"Their daughter, who lived on property, she's a lawyer and she came around fairly quickly, but she had other siblings who just really weren't into it, so ultimately the family declined. But that's how we got to know each other."

"I'm not following."

"Taylor. I'm talking about Taylor. This is her family's farm."

I turn to look at him. "Your ex-girlfriend?"

"That's not even the craziest part. We'd met before that. Taylor and me. We met back when I was coaching baseball up at Hotchkiss. The school rules were that all the coaches also had to teach a class, so I was teaching this science elective on the psychology of sports. Which basically was me explaining to a bunch of juniors how to stay mentally tough on and off the field."

I smile at him.

"Anyway, Taylor's niece was in my class. Scholarship student, super bright. Taylor came up all the time to see her. And I don't know how to explain it exactly . . . I just . . . she had me from the start. But I wasn't going to be the creepy teacher hitting on one of my kids' aunts, so I didn't do anything about it. And then we met again, years later, in a completely different capacity. What are the odds of that?"

"I imagine not high."

"Exactly."

He heads toward the driveway.

"What are you doing?"

"I'm going to show you the property. It's gorgeous. There's a lake."

"Sam."

"It's really more like a pond."

"This is creepy."

"Why? Taylor and I are on great terms. And she's not here

anyway. She's at work. She's a family lawyer. Absolutely brilliant and so cool." He looks at the clock on his dashboard. "She's still in court."

He turns toward me, an idea springing into his eyes, like a piece of inspiration.

"You want to meet her?"

"Sam . . ."

"Let's meet her."

~

We head downtown, the snow kicking up again.

We drive past the Senate House and the Ulster County Courthouse, Sam pulling past the main drag—bread stores and bookstores and coffee shops—before turning onto a quieter road where he parks in front of a gray brick house, a small gold plaque reading FITZGERALD LAW LLC, which is my only indication that this is a law office.

Sam gets out of the car. "You want the best doughnut you've ever had?" he asks.

"What are we doing here?"

"She'll be out of court any minute. Hopefully I'll beat her back here. Just wait there in case."

He motions to the steps in front of the house.

"In the snow?"

"Don't be a baby. It's barely coming down."

Sam disappears down the street. And I get out of the car and have a seat on the steps, taking in the street around me. There is another law office, a church, a group of adorable kids biking by, out of school for the day.

I move onto a higher step, protected by the overhang, and start going through my phone messages. Jack left a short message and texted a few times. He told me he was on the way to the restaurant, checked in to see how it was going, asked what time I'd be home.

I'd really like to talk

That feels like a knife through my chest, knowing we need that and not wanting to need that.

I start to write back when I get an email alert. It's one of the two forensic pathologists. More accurately, it's his assistant, letting me know that his boss is testifying at a trial in Seattle through the end of the week. That he'll try to get back to me then.

Then, as quickly as he is gone, Sam is back, carrying a bag of fresh doughnuts and three orange drinks.

He takes a seat next to me, hands me a doughnut and one of the drinks. "Mango tea," he says. "Taylor dunks her doughnut in it."

"That sounds gross."

"Really?" he says. "Lettuce and tomato? Not even cheese?"

I give him a smile and take one of the teas.

"No way," she says.

We both look up to see a woman walking toward us from the direction of the courthouse.

Taylor. She is fresh-faced and pretty—and also a bit ruffled. Her wet hair is pulled back into a bun, her large puffer coat falling off her shoulder, a ton of loose papers in her arms despite her leather messenger bag.

Sam breaks into a wide smile, his face lighting up.

"I was just thinking about you, Samuel," she says.

"What were you thinking?"

"Not that I'd find you sitting on the steps."

She takes him in and I see her start to process. Sam sitting there in front of her, what that means. But it's hard to focus in on her reaction when all I feel is what's happening to Sam, to my brother. We haven't spent much time apart for the last seventy-two hours, and yet this is the first time I've seen him with anything approaching the kind of smile plastered to his face. With that kind of joy.

He stands up to properly greet her, his face flushed, his eyes bright. His shoulders pulled back. Like he wants, above all, to do one thing: impress her.

"We just came from The Acres . . ." he says.

"So not so far?" she says.

"No, not so far."

"Not that close, either, though," she says.

She puts her papers in her bag, reaching out, touching the side of his face.

"Is everything okay?"

Then she looks down, they both do, as if noticing for the first time that someone else is sitting there.

I wave up at her. "Hi. Sorry to eavesdrop. I'm the sister."

"Ah. The normal one." She smiles at me, warm and genuine. "Well, this is long overdue . . ."

Sam opens the bag of warm doughnuts, holds it out for her. "I thought that I'd deliver a little sustenance."

"Oh man, thank you," she says. "It's like you knew how much I needed this today."

She pulls a doughnut out of the bag, drops it straight in the tea, and swirls it around, taking a large bite.

"My case is going south," she says. "Opposing counsel is on the way over to pillage. City people, you know."

"Aren't you one of them now?" Sam asks.

That stops her midbite. "Yeah, I guess I am."

She looks at Sam with—for some reason—an apologetic shrug. Then she moves closer to him.

"I'm so sorry about your father, Samuel. I wanted to reach out as soon as I heard that you lost him, but I also . . . didn't want to reach out."

He looks at her, and for a moment it seems like he is going to tell her the thing that he hasn't wanted me to tell anyone. That he suspects he didn't just lose him, but rather that he was taken.

Except Sam bites that back, forces a smile.

"Thank you for wanting to," he says. "And for not."

She nods. And they share a look, a long look, that I need to turn away from. Because my brother is wearing it all on his face. Call it vulnerability, call it longing. He is wearing what she means to him everywhere. Maybe it's too much for Taylor too, because she clears her throat, breaks the moment.

"I really do need to get inside," she says.

"Okay—"

I stand up, trying to make this exit easier. An exit Sam clearly isn't ready for. And which Taylor seems to need.

"It was nice meeting you," I say.

She leans over, puts her hand on my shoulder. "You too," she says, her voice suddenly low and entirely between us.

"Careful with him," she says.

She says it so softly and so quickly that for a minute I think I've misheard her. But I know I haven't. I want to ask what she means by that—does she mean that she thinks Sam is fragile and so I should be careful with him? Or does she mean that Sam is tricky and I should be careful dealing with him? Or, perhaps, she means both.

Before I can ask, she has turned away from me. She is looking at Sam again.

"I'll miss you," she says.

Then she kisses him on the cheek.

And, like that, she is gone.

# One More Thing We Need to Do

Instead of getting back in the car, Sam walks.

I try to keep up as he turns onto Green Street, then onto Crown. He seems to know where he wants to go and keeps walking at double-time until he gets there—walking straight into Rough Draft Bar & Books, which is apparently partially a bookstore and partially a bar, because he walks past the shelves of books and up to the counter where he orders two IPAs.

"I don't want one," I say.

"That's good. Since they're both for me."

He puts a twenty on the counter and takes both glasses from the bartender, moves them over to a two-top.

"I guess I'm driving home."

He ignores this. "What did you think of her?"

"What does that matter?"

"I'm curious," he says.

Except that he is not actually curious. He is crazy about her in that way that nothing anyone else says matters.

So I try to think of what he's really asking. I try to think of what Taylor was trying to ask of me. *Careful with him.*

"I think that if you don't want it to be over with her, it felt like maybe it's not too late," I say.

"No. It's too late."

He says it with a finality that surprises me.

"How do you know?"

"She got married two weeks ago, for starters."

"What?"

He nods. "The guy is a friend of her older brother's. She says they didn't get involved until after we broke up, but I don't know. I don't know how she defines involved," he says. "He's an orthodontist named Sherman. He runs triathlons and plays the drums in a local band. And he's fucking old. He's older than you."

"Thanks for that."

"You want to meet him? His office is around the corner."

"No, I do not."

"He's got teenagers. She loves them. She loves him. She moved into his house after telling me she would never leave the farm." He pauses. "I thought I was the problem, you know? That our family was too messed up for her, or she didn't want to deal with living in a city, or I waited too long to ask her to marry me . . . but I just thought wrong."

"What do you mean?"

"It was all of those things and none of them," he says. "She just wanted him."

I feel that in my own chest, in my own heart—what is breaking open in him. What he has lost. What, apparently, he is wondering if he ever had.

Two weeks ago. Sam had to come to grips with this heartbreak two weeks ago—two and a half weeks after losing our father. Too soon after deciding that losing our father wasn't what it appeared to be.

I ask the question, gently.

"So . . . why did you want to stop here?"

"Can't help it. She's always where I want to stop."

~

Sam stares out the window.

He is lost in thought. And clearly not interested in talking.

I focus on driving, the snow coming down harder now, blanketing the farmland, fogging up the windshield. We are moving slowly, but I don't want to run out of time. I don't want to drop my brother off without being there for him. And sometimes being there for someone means staying quiet. But sometimes it means telling him the one thing no one else has managed to say.

"Have people been telling you that Dad is still with you?"

He keeps his eyes fixed on the window, not answering.

"Because they keep saying that to me. That he is with me. It sometimes helps to hear that and it sometimes just reminds me how alone I feel since losing him, like I had this invisible safety net underneath me my entire life and now it's just gone . . ."

"I think we hang out with different people."

"What I'm trying to say is that we don't always make the best decisions when we're grieving," I say.

"Meaning what exactly? I shouldn't have shown up to see my married ex-girlfriend today?"

"That. And also you may want to hold off on sending out any wedding invitations until you're sure that's what you actually want."

He turns and looks at me. "I thought we established that you're not the best person to be giving me advice."

"It's not exactly advice," I say. "More like an observation."

As if on cue, my phone starts buzzing. A calendar reminder comes up on the screen: ELLIOT/AUSTIN. It's a reminder for Austin's piano recital. Village Auditorium. 11:30 a.m. tomorrow. I flip the phone over, but not before Sam spots the name Elliot.

"What's that about an observation?"

"I have to get my life in order too. Believe me I know that. But that doesn't mean I'm wrong about this."

"Fine. So your observation is that I shouldn't move on with my life because we lost Dad?"

"No," I say. "My observation is that I think you are settling for a life you don't actually want."

I try to think of how to say it so that he hears me, what I see when I watch him. What became apparent to me when I saw Tommy watching him too.

"I think you don't really want to work at the company. You certainly don't want to devote your life to it."

"I'm good at my job."

"I'm sure you are. That's different from doing it for the right reasons."

"What are you talking about?"

"What if I could promise you that Dad never cared about you staying on at the company? Would you still want to be there now? Because I'm telling you, it was never about you working there. Or working with him. He just cared about having you close."

"You don't know that . . ." he says.

"Except that I do. I also know that there are only so many big hands you can lose before you stop wanting to place a big bet. Your injury, the breakup with Taylor. Now Dad. When do you decide you've lost enough?"

"Is this your version of a pep talk?"

"I'm just saying, extremely gently, that I think Morgan is a part of that same desire. To feel like you are on solid ground. But I'm not sure the ground gets to feel so solid for us anymore."

He looks torn about this, like it's opening something up in him, something he really doesn't want to touch. Which I get. I'm there with him. In this way, at least, I'm right there with him. When you lose too much in quick succession, it feels unmanageable to risk losing anything else.

"I believe, in my gut, that we make bad decisions when we are operating from fear," I say. "Take it for what it's worth. But, it seems to me, that your less-fearful self is still hoping for something else."

"And what's that exactly?"

"A different life."

I expect him to keep arguing. I expect him to say I'm wrong and I'm missing the thread again. But he gets quiet. He opens the window, keeps his gaze on the highway lights.

"You know, not too long after we got involved, Taylor asked me what playing baseball felt like," he says. "I went into this long explanation about how Dad coached my Little League ball team when I was five, the travel teams I played on my whole childhood, how I knew by twelve years old that playing ball was the only thing I wanted to do with my life."

He turns and looks at me.

"But I didn't understand that she wasn't asking for the biography. The history. She was asking what playing ball felt like. No one had ever asked me that before, so I didn't get it." He shakes his head. "And every time I see her, I want to tell her I have an answer now, as if that will change anything."

"Well. Tell me."

"It always felt like a kind of proof." He shrugs. "I know that sounds corny, but it did. Not proof of something so large as God or death, but not so removed from those things, either. Like proof that a given moment was happening. These are my arms and this is my breath and what am I going to do about it? How am I going to work it out to get from here to there? I always had an answer. Without even trying, I had that answer. And after I got injured, I went looking for that type of certainty everywhere. I don't know. Being with Taylor felt like the closest I'd come to finding it . . ."

I take that in as I steer down the Henry Hudson Parkway, New Jersey showing up across the river, Upper Manhattan in view.

"Except maybe now it's the opposite," I say.

"What do you mean?"

"Maybe when she walked away, it left you with the job of trying to prove it to yourself," I say. "That the two of you mattered."

He sighs. "This car ride sucks."

I let out a laugh as he looks back toward the window, signs for Harlem starting to appear, the sparkly lights of New York City coming through the windshield in the distance. I see something come over his face, a sadness he can't quite push away.

"I don't know about how it was with you, but Dad was never big on offering me romantic advice, which made sense, three divorces in. But when Taylor and I broke up, he took me out for dinner and we both drank a little too much and he made this big point of saying that you only get so many chances."

"Chances to do what?"

"To fix what you get wrong."

That hits hard. The truth of it.

"Dad said that?"

He nods. And I try to picture our father offering that up. Our father avoided weighing in on our personal lives. Which made me wonder if he was talking about Sam's personal life, or if a little too much alcohol had him talking out loud to himself. And if that was the case, what in his own life did he think he'd gotten wrong? That he still hadn't been able to fix?

I shake my head, not sure how to figure that out. "That doesn't sound like Dad," I said.

"Why do you think I remember it?"

## *Thirty-Four Years Ago*

"You like him. I can tell."

Cory had a new boyfriend. Liam and Rachel had run into them in front of Liam's office building, of all places. Cory and the boyfriend were coming from a matinee of *Lost in Yonkers,* Neil Simon's new play. The fact that Cory had taken him meant something. Did it mean something that he was waxing eloquent on all the reasons he hadn't loved it? Liam had trouble focusing on what his reasons were. He had trouble focusing on anything except the boyfriend's hand, holding Cory on her waist, holding her at the bone there.

Now, two days later, they met for lunch in Central Park. She wouldn't tell him much.

"And he wants to get married?" Liam asked.

"No one is talking about that yet but you."

"I thought you didn't believe in marriage."

"That's not what I said. I never said that."

"Except that you did."

"What I said was that marriage isn't what was going to save you and me. A legal document or what have you. The only thing that saves two people is what always saves two people."

"Which is?"

"Showing up."

"I show up," he said.

"Exactly," she said. "So what are you worried about?"

She laid back on the grass, the sun hitting her face, shining on her bare shoulders, her hair. He stared down at her.

"How can you be with someone who doesn't like Neil Simon?"

She covered her eyes with her arm. "I could be wrong, but I think people have survived worse together."

"Cory . . ." he said.

"I don't go by Cory anymore. That's an old nickname."

"Okay, fine . . . whatever your name is," he said.

She laughed.

"As much as I hate to admit it, he seems like a good man," he said.

"He does not think the same about you."

She shrugged, like it was beside the point. Because really it was. Then she took her arm off her eyes, sat up onto her elbows. She met his eyes.

"The thing is . . . I've never lied to him. Not about you and me, not about any of it. I just think . . ." she said. "It's only fair to him, and to me, for us to find a new shape to things between us."

"So we will."

He didn't hesitate. He would never hesitate. This was what they did for each other, after all. Figured out whatever workaround they needed to fit into the other's life. Even if he knew—didn't she know too?—it should really be the other way around. You could argue, in the ways that mattered most, it was.

And, anyway, it was beside the point. Everything but them was beside the point as far as Liam was concerned. Whatever Cory wanted—however she wanted to make room for him in her life—he would meet her there. Forever.

"I just want you to be happy," he said.

She leaned in, touched his face. First with the front of her hand, then with the back.

"Come on," she said. "Don't start lying now."

# Who I Used to Be

It's 11:00 p.m. when I get back home, and the light is on in our bedroom.

I open the front door and put down my bag, get a glass of water from the kitchen, sit down at my drafting table. I start going through the emails from the day, replying to any that seem urgent. I reset a few meetings, calming a few clients, as much as a late-night message can.

I am careful to move quickly. But as I head up the stairs, the light in our bedroom goes off. And by the time I walk in, Jack is lying on his side, facing away from me.

I tiptoe into the bathroom and wash up. I take off my clothes. I slip into our bed, beside him. I'm relieved to be in from the cold. I'm relieved to be beside him.

I know he's still awake. I can feel it, in the space of his breaths. I can feel it on his body. Maybe he is trying to give me a break from a conversation neither of us feels good enough to have. But it feels more like a check-in—a final check-in—to see if I'll be the one to do it. For the first time in a long time. If I'll cross the divide.

Even in the beginning, I crossed the divide without equivocation. Like an instinct. I just wanted to be closer to him. I still want that, except not enough to overcome it. The part of me that insists on keeping still.

I don't like that I'm thinking about the beginning. In my experience that usually happens when you are approaching an end you don't want. Why are beginnings and endings so intricately linked in that way? Maybe because they aren't the opposite of each other. Their DNA is actually the same. They are the two things we all try to fix.

Either way, I don't move toward him.

Either way, this is how you begin to fail.

~

I dream of my father.

If I believed differently—if I would allow myself to believe differently—I would say that it was less a dream and more him visiting.

I can smell him. The blend of him. Peppermint and fresh coffee and forest, courtesy of the soap he always used. In the dream, he is wearing jeans (which he rarely wore), and he has grown a beard.

I reach out and touch it. It's scraggly and soft and very long. It doesn't feel at all like it belongs on him. But he gives me a kiss on the forehead. And it's *him*.

*Hello, my love*, he says.

I think we are on dry land, but then the water comes in fast, covering our ankles, moving toward our knees. We are on the cliff together. Windbreak's cliff. And my father takes my hand and starts walking toward the edge.

*Dad?* I say. I'm pulling him back toward me. *Dad, don't.*

*Too close,* he says. *That was too close.*

I say, *I'm so happy that I didn't miss you.*

He says, *Almost, Nora-nu. You almost missed me.*

He says, *Don't miss this too.*

# A Hundred Roads Lead to Goodbye

In the morning, I find Jack in the kitchen.

He's waiting for me in jeans, no shirt on, his hair still wet from the shower. I feel a surge of love, just looking at him, and the desire to move toward him, run my fingers through his hair, hold close to his skin. But I also feel the weight of last night's quiet, of his unanswered request that we talk, of the fact that, at this moment, he isn't moving toward me, either.

I take a seat at the counter and he puts a hot mug of coffee in front of me, a plate of cinnamon toast for us to share.

"I'm glad you slept in," he says. "You needed it."

He stays on the other side of the island. But he leans forward as I wrap my hands around my coffee mug, take a sip. He leans toward me.

"Are you still heading into the city today?" he asks.

"The city?"

"Don't you have Austin's recital this morning?"

"How do you know that?"

It's coming out more defensive than it should, probably because I'm feeling defensive.

"Our calendar."

I shake my head. "Sorry. Yeah, I promised him so—"

"You promised Austin?"

It's a question and it's not. "Yes, Jack. I promised Austin."

He nods and starts to say something, but he stops himself. Which is when I feel like I should do it for him.

"The recital's about supporting Austin," I say. "Not about Elliot."

"Is it?"

He says it less with judgment or antagonism and more with curiosity.

"Yes."

"So what's the part about Elliot?"

He is waiting for me to answer. An actual answer. But I'm guessing he also knows the answer isn't going to get us anywhere better. Not now. Which may be why he clears his throat, keeps talking.

"Look, I just needed you to know that I made a decision," he says. "I'm going to help Becker out."

It takes me a second to process what he's saying. Becker is his friend from culinary school, the owner of the two-star Michelin restaurant in northern California, the friend who asked Jack to take over her restaurant while she's on maternity leave.

Jack has decided to take this on. Three thousand miles away.

"I've been trying to find a good time to tell you this, but maybe there isn't one," he says.

"How long are you going for?" I ask.

"I don't know. A while."

"What's a while?"

He shakes his head. "She needs to walk me through and properly transition the team, and she's at thirty-three weeks, so this all needs to happen pretty quickly . . ."

My heart is racing so fast that I'm having trouble taking in what he is saying. I'm finding it hard to even believe that we are here. But of course we are here. I've driven us here, haven't I? Into a corner we both want to get out of.

"Jack, come on," I say. "Nothing has happened with Elliot. I'd never do that to you. To us."

"This isn't about Elliot. I mean, it's certainly not helping anything, but I'm not threatened by him," he says. "And I get it. All the loss. Your mom blew a hole through you. Fuck, it blew a hole through me. And now your father too. It's too close together. It's all too close together for anyone to know how to process it."

"So your answer is to leave?"

"My answer is to give you some space," he says. "Because it's not working for you with me here."

"That's not true."

"Maybe it will make it easier for you to be on your own . . . or pivot. Or to start fresh."

"So this is about Elliot?"

He doesn't answer. But I feel him pushing up against it—what he won't allow me to deny that I'm doing, what he won't watch me give away.

I fight the tears that are filling my eyes. He walks around the counter, sits down beside me. And when he starts talking again, his voice is low, even lower and gentler than usual, as if it's taking all his energy to say it. For both of us.

"What do you want, Nora?" he says. "Because I want you to have it. Honestly. Whatever it is."

Time. That's my honest answer. I want time. Except I don't just mean I want time to feel better, to feel like the world isn't slippery and lonely. I also want the time he can't give me, that no one can give me, the time I'll never have again. With my parents, here again. With Jack, when loving him, when loving anyone, felt lighter. When I didn't simultaneously feel it in my bones, the fear of it primal and real now. The moment I'll lose him too.

"I want to believe that we're just stuck," Jack says. "At least that's what I've been telling myself. But I've been telling myself the wrong thing. Because it doesn't matter, either way, if I can't get to you anymore."

"Jack, I'll work on it," I say.

"I don't want you to have to work on it. I want you to want it. I can't do it another way."

It isn't a threat. It's the opposite of a threat. There's no guilt, no shame. It's just a promise.

He reaches out and takes my hand, his fingers crawling their way through mine.

I look down, my eyes too fogged with tears to know which fingers are his and which are mine.

"I really don't want you to go," I say.

"That's not the same thing as wanting me to stay."

# Falling Fatalities

Jack leaves for the restaurant, and the house goes silent.

I sit on the bed and stare straight ahead at the photographs lining the fireplace mantel. Framed candid shots and Polaroids and photo-booth strips, glimpses into our last couple of years together: photographs of the two of us in our backyard and at friends' weddings, on a bike-riding trip upstate with my mother. I even have a framed photograph of us at thirteen years old. I found a copy of our eighth grade yearbook and there it was, a class picture in woodshop. We were on opposite ends of the first row. Jack was smiling at the camera, but I was looking down the bench toward him. Jack likes to joke that I was definitely looking past him at Hudson Ricci, the kid to his left, who everyone had a crush on. But I know it was Jack. Even then, I knew.

I can go to see him, I think. I can fix this. I just need to stand up. My phone buzzes, stopping me, an unknown number on the caller ID. For a brief moment, I get to tell myself it's Jack calling from the restaurant's landline. Jack saying he's not going. Jack saying we can figure this out. Stay there. Stay where you are. I'm on my way.

But it's a woman on the other end of the line. Her voice terse and serious.

"This is Dr. Susan Clifton. I received your email. I work with Lanie Robertson."

Dr. Susan Clifton. The second of the two forensic pathologists.

I sit up taller, focus in. "Dr. Clifton," I say. "Thank you for the call. I really appreciate you getting in touch."

"Of course," she says. "Though I'm not sure how much help I'm able to be. I took a look at the files you sent. And, to be perfectly frank with you, most aspects of your father's fall lend themselves to multiple interpretations."

"Okay . . ."

"I think the investigators were correct to rule out self-harm," she says. "The fall pattern is consistent with someone caught off guard, as was the angle of contact. Forgive the bluntness. But, I do have to say, their other conclusions feel premature to me. With falling fatalities, it's quite difficult to ascertain with any degree of certainty whether a fall from a great height is due to an accident or foul play because the fall pattern is similar."

"So why did they conclude there was no foul play?"

"That would be my question as well. Unless they were privy to information I was not. There don't seem to be toxicology reports here or proper blood splatter analysis. Your father was cremated, correct?"

"Correct."

"Unfortunately, that really limits what we are able to determine now. There is usually a story that emerges. But without his body, I can't be of much help."

*A story emerges.* That language stops me. And something else does.

"Dr. Clifton," I say. "What do you mean by 'most aspects'?"

"Excuse me?"

"You said most aspects lend themselves to multiple interpretations." I say. "Some aspects are more definite?"

"Certainly there are a few things I would characterize as—"

"Suspicious?"

"Requiring further investigation."

"Like what?"

"There was a large contusion on his left cheek, which he could have sustained in an altercation before the fall. If we had access to the body, I'd be better equipped to study that and to see if they missed any foreign DNA under his fingernails . . . I also think the velocity with which he seems to have fallen suggests it was the result of a push. On an accidental fall, I would expect him to land closer to the cliff's edge . . ." She pauses. "But, to be honest with you, the most compelling pattern piece to me, at the moment, is the fact that everyone is pretending they know anything with certainty in a very uncertain situation."

"So without a body, is there anything left for me to do?"

She pauses, the air between us thick. "As a clinician, I don't know. But as a daughter? You may want to go back to the scene of the fall again. Sometimes things emerge that you can't see on the first or even the second visit."

"And you think that's worth doing?"

"I can't promise you it will be fruitful, but yes."

I take a moment to steady myself. "And if it were your father, and if you were making an educated guess, you think he was pushed?"

"I'll say this. I can't tell you he wasn't."

~

I call Sam's cell, but it's Morgan who picks up. She starts talking over me.

"Thank goodness it's you," she says. "I need you."

"Okay, but I have to speak to Sam first. It's a bit of an emergency."

"You have an emergency? I have an emergency! We need to meet you at the brownstone ASAP. Sam wants to move up the wedding."

I think I heard her wrong. I'm still focused on Dr. Clifton. On the scope of my father's fall. The angling.

"So you and me just need to triage," Morgan says. "Focus on the roof deck and how to get that ready. I need a detailed lighting plan, obviously. Also, maybe we like . . . erect a cool outdoor staircase or ladder that people have to climb up to the top?"

I try to process what she's saying. "What are you talking about?"

"You know, a way to avoid guests walking through the unfinished house. I don't need the judgment."

"Is Sam there, Morgan? Can you get him, please?"

She calls out to Sam. "Nora's on for you!"

I hear his response coming at me from another room in their apartment, from an echoing distance. "Not a good time," he says.

"Not a good time?" I ask, as though he can hear me. "Tell him to pick up the phone."

"He's walking out the door already," she says. "Let me send you some inspo pics. Ten a.m. tomorrow at the brownstone, okay?"

Then she hangs up.

~

I sit at my drafting table, turning over everything Dr. Clifton said to me. Her suspicions, her uncertainty.

Her words to me: *a story emerges*. I learned the same early on in my training on how to think about building out a space. A column isn't just a column. A pillar isn't just a pillar. It doesn't just have to interact with the rest of the building but also with the story of what the building needs to do. Who, at the end of the day, am I hoping the building will save? Who do I need it to hold?

I study my father's will again, going back over the deed and property notes for Windbreak. What am I missing? Who was my father trying to save? Who was he trying to hold?

I zero in on Jonathan's name on the bottom of several of the documents. Jonathan Reed, Noone's general counsel, who clearly has access to everything. Jonathan, who is the only person with a legal obligation to keep that information privileged and private.

I shoot him an email anyway. I ask him to give me a call when he gets to the office, that I have some questions about Windbreak, about next steps for me to take possession. These aren't the questions I have, but they are questions that he won't try to avoid answering. Questions that, it seems, are in his fiduciary responsibility to try and answer.

Then I get on the subway and head to Austin's recital.

When I get off at Bleeker Street, my phone buzzes. It's Jonathan.

I walk toward Austin's school as I listen to him say hello, listen to the false lilt in his voice.

"It's quite straightforward," he says. "You're free to take possession of Windbreak when you are ready. Or if you'd prefer to explore selling, I can help you with a local real estate agent and prepare the sale from here."

I have no intention of selling, but I also don't want to get into that discussion. Because he'll want to know what I'm going to do with a cottage across the country and I don't have a good answer yet. I just know that I'm not ready to give up the piece of my father I seem to have held on to.

"Jonathan, was there ever anyone else?" I ask.

"How do you mean?"

I mean, who else did Windbreak matter to the way it mattered to my father? Who may have been there that night with him? Who may have been there because my father mattered to them in a way that was so deep and painful that it ended on the edge of that clifftop?

"I'm asking if it was always my father's intention for me to get Windbreak or did that plan change too?"

He is quiet, his silence steely. And I wonder if I'm imagining it in the silence or if it's actually there. The anxiety.

"Nora, I'm not really at liberty to go over the whole history."

"Should I take that as a yes, then?"

I've arrived at Austin's school. The auditorium doors are open, family and friends heading inside. I see Elliot racing toward the entrance from the other direction, still in his hospital scrubs, holding a present for Austin

"If it's helpful to know," he says, "your father always wanted to take care of you."

"That's not answering my question, is it?"

"It's the best answer I have," he says. "Your father wanted to do the right thing, for you, for your brothers. For everyone he loved. He was nothing if not loyal."

A teacher comes out and starts to swing the auditorium doors shut. I click off the call and race inside.

It isn't until the curtain goes up, Jonathan outside my grasp, that I find the question I want to ask. The question he didn't answer. The question no one will answer.

Loyal to whom?

## *Thirty-Two Years Ago*

"Think of it as starting over again," Liam said.

"Starting what over again?" she asked.

They were out at Windbreak. He had purchased the house over a year ago, but this was Cory's first time seeing it. The two of them standing in his empty living room, taking it in together. Liam getting to see it through Cory's eyes.

"This is the way for you to get it back," he said. "California. Everything that was taken from you."

"Nothing was taken from me."

"We'll grow old here."

She laughed. She couldn't help it. "You're deranged."

"I'm not saying we will be here every day . . ."

"Oh, you're not?"

He ignored her tone. "I'm just saying, in our way, we will."

She gave him a look, not insulting either of them by saying it. All of it. She had been married for a little over a year. And Liam had a little girl whom he loved. He didn't want to do anything, to risk anything, that meant he'd be apart from Nora.

In so many concrete ways, he and Cory had never been further from living in this house together. And still, being there with her, it was the first time Windbreak felt real.

She walked into the center of the room, pointed to the bay window that looked out over the yard and the ocean and the rest of everything.

"If this were my house? That's where the bookshelves would go," she said. "I'd build in large, white bookshelves, wrap them right around that window, sit there all day."

He leaned against the wall, crossed his arms over his chest. He'd been waiting for this moment. He tried not to smile.

"They're already on their way," he said.

She turned back and looked at him. "You're lying."

He shrugged, like it was no big deal. "Custom-made white bookshelves, like you showed me in the photograph."

"The photograph?"

"Of your graduate school apartment. The bookshelves you had at the firehouse. The ones you said you loved."

She didn't say anything, but he could see the tears forming in her eyes.

"These are a bit nicer than those, but same idea."

She walked toward him, quickly, deliberately. She moved straight into his arms.

"Well, before you get too excited, I did blow the whole furniture budget on the bookshelves," he said. "So hope you don't mind sleeping on the floor tonight."

She started laughing. He could feel her smile against his shoulder, mixing in with her tears. Happy tears, but tears all the same.

"You're infuriating when you're proud of yourself."

"I know," he said.

She was still in his arms, her cheek against his neck. He rubbed her back and tried not to cry himself. Was it seeing her this happy?

How he loved to make her happy. But there was also the other piece—the sadness that lived between them now, that he couldn't control, not anymore. The not knowing exactly when they'd be alone like this next.

He paused, breathing her in. "They do say that sleeping on the floor is good for your back, at least."

"Who are they?"

"The guys who sold me the bookshelves."

# A Musical Interlude

After the recital, Austin is surrounded.

He has a mess of people all there to support him. His mother is there and her fiancé, a mix of cousins and friends. I give him a hug, and I feel him instinctively look behind me for my father. My father who normally would be there with me.

"Are you alone?" he asks.

Before I answer, Austin blushes, embarrassed that he has forgotten my father has died. Or, maybe, just confused by it. I bend down and meet his eyes, kiss him on the forehead. *Don't feel badly,* I silently say. I forget too. All of us grown-ups still forget all the things that we wish we didn't have to remember.

"What do you say?" I ask. "Hot chocolate next Thursday?"

He nods, his smile growing big again. "Deal."

I start to slip out the back exit when I feel a hand on my back. Elliot. He is handsome in a way that is startling, even in his hospital scrubs, even with his two-day shadow, his eyes tired from last night's late hospital shift.

We walk out to the street together. "Do you have time for a quick cup of coffee?" he asks.

I think of his hand on my back, my desire to burrow into the comfort he is bringing me. Then I think what it's already cost me to even consider that.

"I can't," I say.

I shake my head no. And maybe it's the way I look at him, the finality, that stops him. Because he tilts his head, and it seems like he registers that I'm not just talking about coffee. I'm talking about the rest of it. This dance we've been doing since we've reconnected, what it has set the stage for us potentially to do.

I need to stop it now, if for no other reason than this. Even if I don't know how to reach toward Jack, again, even if it may be too late, the least I can do is stop reaching away from him.

Elliot sits down on the ledge. He is almost awkward sitting there, as much as someone that tall and handsome can ever be awkward, his legs taking up half the sidewalk, his arms clasped in front of him.

"This is causing problems?"

"That's not on you," I say.

"I think at least some of it is," he says.

He shrugs, and I know he is trying to take the blame for reaching out to me again after my father died. But it doesn't matter. The fault here is mine to hold alone.

I take a seat beside him and try to think about how to say it. There is the part that he knows too. How comforting it is to see what I see in his eyes. Our shared sadness. The shared knowledge of what has been lost. My father, Elliot's friend. This is why talking to Elliot has felt simpler, more manageable, than leaning into Jack. This is why I've been connected to him again. Elliot knew the best of my father. I wanted to be around that a little longer.

Then there's the other part of it, the part I'm just starting to understand myself: sometimes a goodbye can feel interrupted. My goodbyes to both of my parents were. The two of them were there one day, gone the next. No warning. And, in a way, the first time Elliot and I said goodbye was incomplete. Even if I was starting to figure out then that we were meant to be friends, our relationship ended because we were trying to do the right thing for his family. To honor his wife's request to try again. Maybe that's also what we are doing here. We are rectifying the incomplete endings that we can.

But it doesn't mean the goodbye was wrong—not the first time, and not this one. One way or another, we needed to find our way to this moment. We were supposed to find our way to this moment. Where we say goodbye again to the idea of us, in a way that sticks.

"Can I ask you something?" I say.

He looks up at me.

"You know when I called you the other day and asked you about the last time you saw my father? I feel like you didn't want to get into what really happened. What you guys really talked about. Am I wrong?"

He pauses, his eyes getting serious, his jaw clenching in spite of himself. "Nora, it's not what you think . . ."

"Okay, so tell me what I'm missing."

"Well. We talked about you a little bit," he says. "He knew that you needed some space from him. He was a bit heartbroken too."

"Because of my mother?" I say, confused.

"No, other things. But he got it. He really did. I'm saying it badly because I can't get into it all. For ethical reasons . . ."

"Ethical reasons? Was he sick? What was going on with him?"

He is quiet, and I know he is holding back from saying what he thinks he can't share.

"He wasn't sick. I just . . . I'm just trying to say that he knew how much you loved your mother," he says. "He knew how loyal you were to her. And he valued that."

Jonathan's words come into my head: *Your father was nothing if not loyal.*

"I think the important thing is that he loved you so much, Nora," he says. "He didn't blame you for pulling back from him. He didn't blame you for anything."

"Who did he blame?"

"At the end of the day? Just himself."

## *Thirty Years Ago*

"You're losing the thread," Cory said. "She's awful."

"Why don't you tell me how you really feel?"

They were sitting at a small restaurant near Rockefeller Center, the ice-skating rink busy outside the windows, the Christmas tree lit up and bright. Cory had just met Sylvia for the first time. Sylvia, who had interviewed Liam for a luxury travel segment she was doing for her morning show and with whom he was subsequently spending too much time. It wasn't a planned meeting, between Cory and Sylvia, of course. Not that it would have gone better if it had been.

"Not to point out the obvious, but you're the one who decided we shouldn't be together," Liam said. "Get married, the traditional way."

"Spare me. I didn't want to marry you the way that you're capable of being married. And apparently, I was correct about that. Sylvia doesn't hold a candle to Rachel. Wow, what a cliché you are."

"Never been like that with you."

"Only because I refuse to allow it to be."

She pushed her plate out of the way. They were sharing a bowl of seafood pasta, a bottle of house wine. She wasn't touching any of it. Her hair was piled into a bun on top of her head, her eyes tired and puffy. And, now, they were narrowed in anger. But she looked beautiful. She looked impossibly beautiful every time he was lucky enough to be sitting across from her. If anything made him a cliché, it was that he felt that way.

She leaned toward him. "You don't see the way Sylvia is coming for you, but she is," she said. "And you are going to move to the dark side before you even know you are there."

"We should be together. Really together."

"You've got to be joking."

"I'm serious."

"You're serious? Okay, I'm married, and you're married, and all you're focused on is your new friend who is not going to stand for you being married for much longer. Mark my words on that. And just to be clear, I don't blame Sylvia for that. You're the one letting it happen. Correction, you're the one making it happen, Liam. Because it's easier than admitting it."

"Admitting what?"

"I'm not doing this," she said.

"Admitting what, Cory?"

"The reason this works, that we still work, is that you don't owe me anything. That we don't owe each other anything."

"That's where you're wrong. Maybe for the first time, you're actually wrong. We owe each other everything."

She motioned to the waitress for their bill. And then she stood up. She was done sitting there with him. She was done with this part.

"Where are you going?"

"To the Carlyle," she said. "To get a proper drink."

"I think it's you," he said. "I think it's you who likes to keep us here. Because it's safer. Because you've decided it's safer. It's easy to sit across from me and judge my choices when the only choice I really want isn't available."

"How convenient for you."

"Please sit down."

She was already putting on her coat. She was already moving away from him. "No. Fighting with you is boring," she said. "I love you too much to sit here and fight."

"Then listen to me."

He tried to think of how to say it so she would hear him. She didn't want to hear it, not anymore. She didn't want to hear that it was time they do this another way.

"What if I'm ready?"

"To stop fighting?" she said.

"Cory . . ."

"Then you can come for a drink."

# Where It Started, Where You're Going

I don't go home.

I try to reach Sam again. When he doesn't pick up, I pass by my stop. I take the subway to Avenue H. My father's old neighborhood.

My father made no apologies about how eager he was to leave Midwood behind. He found it funny that his only daughter chose to live so nearby a world he couldn't wait to leave. And that I loved it.

But, no matter how fast he fled from here, my father seemed to love a piece of Flatbush too. I could see it in how he would light up when he talked about Midwood. And he liked showing me around his old stomping grounds, taking me to the places he and Uncle Joe used to frequent, to their old neighborhood hangs.

Now I walk down Bedford Avenue, on my own, and work to remember. I pass his high school, which is letting out for the day, Brooklyn College standing pretty and tree-lined right across the street. Uncle Joe had gone to school there. They were the first two kids in their family to go to college—my father to Yale, Joe a couple of years behind him to Brooklyn College.

The two of them reunited after graduation to live together in Manhattan. The two of them always found their way to each other and spent their lives, one way or another, by each other's side. *Your father was nothing if not loyal.*

If he had been loyal to anyone, wasn't it Joe?

I turn on Twenty-Eighth Street and head to my father's childhood house. This small yellow house with green shutters, plants lining the outside porch.

I have never been inside. I walk up to the front door and ring the bell. A young mother answers the door in a tank top, a rose tattoo sleeve covering her left arm, her baby son on her other hip. She looks me up and down, an unexpected visitor, the last thing she needs today.

She keeps the screen door closed. "If you're selling something, you've come to the wrong place," she says.

"No, nothing like that," I say. "And I'm so sorry to bother you. But my father used to live here."

"Oh. Are you Mr. O'Malley's daughter?"

"No, Liam Noone. His family sold to the O'Malleys."

"Like thirty years ago?"

I nod. It was closer to twenty years ago, but I don't correct her. One of the first things my father did as soon as he could afford to was to pay off his parents' mortgage. Then, when his father's knee got bad enough, he convinced him to retire and moved them (and Joe's mom) into a waterfront condominium in Naples, Florida. Midwood, finally, and for good, behind him.

"Would it be weird if I came inside for a bit?" I ask. "See his old bedroom."

"Very," she says.

I turn and start to go. I hear the screen door squeak open.

"But come on in anyway."

~

There are only two bedrooms upstairs.

I peek into the smaller room, which is now home to the baby and his older sibling. I try to imagine what it might have been like when my father was here—a bunk bed where the crib is, a small wooden desk instead of a blowup truck bed. The window doesn't let in a lot of light. But it looks out on the alley, and there's a rusting basketball hoop and two kids playing an intense game of one-on-one, running fiercely, no room for any cars trying to get by.

The closet door is open, the smell of baby detergent and fresh diapers hitting hard. I flick on the light. And I notice there are etchings on the wall. The marking of someone's height. It could be my father's. It could be the kids who lived here after him. There are no initials to indicate whose height is being measured, no names beside the lines. But I run my fingers along all the markings anyway, reaching up to the top height line.

And then I see it, just above the top height line. A small stenciling in the wood. Two little hearts sandwiching the bubbled-out names:

Cory & Liam

I run my fingers along the ridges, run my finger through his name.

This is when I hear the young mother clearing her throat. She is standing in the doorway.

"I just looked up your father. He did live here."

"You thought I was lying?"

"I thought you were taking a long time."

I point to the markings in the wood. "I love that you kept this. This plank with all the markings on it."

She shrugs. "Closets are pricey."

I want to ask her if I can make her a trade. I will design her a new closet, build it out, if I can come back and take this wood plank. The height etchings that may or may not be my father. The little love note that is. But it's not just the plank I want. It's the feel of this place, of this room. It's what lives beneath the surface, lives in the history—despite how far he ran from it, from here. Him.

"He looks familiar to me, your father," she says. "I think he came by too. Not that long ago, actually."

I turn and look at her. "When?"

"Six months ago, maybe? Maybe longer. I don't really remember exactly. And I can't be sure it was him, but I think so."

"He came to see the house?"

"I guess. He didn't introduce himself, though. He stood outside on the sidewalk for a bit. He was with a woman."

"A woman?"

She nods. "I went to the door, but they'd already left."

I turn back toward the closet, take in the Cory & Liam again. I try to figure out what my father was doing here. Who he was doing it with.

She clears her throat. "So my other son is on his way home from soccer practice and I'm going to need the nursery back," she says. "Unless you're willing to offer up one of your father's hotel rooms for bedtime."

# Not All Houses Are Homes

I plan to walk home.

I head down Ocean Avenue, circling onto the side streets. But as soon as my house is in view, I see all the lights off, Jack not waiting for me inside. And I keep going.

Maybe it's knowing that Jack is still at the restaurant. Maybe it's not knowing if he is coming home at all tonight. That is like him, after all. After he did the hard part of letting me know the plan, he may decide not to come back when I'm there too. He's not going to do anything to make it harder on both of us.

So I head over to Tilden and hail a cab. We take the tunnel and head up to Perry Street. And I hop out at my father's apartment.

The doorman has me on a list of approved visitors and takes me upstairs, unlocks the door.

The apartment is all windows and water with expansive views of the Hudson River. But the apartment itself feels empty. There are no mementos lining the countertops, no family photographs. The art on the wall is neutral, the furniture untouched. Had it felt like this when he lived here?

The front door clicks open, and I turn to see my father's third wife, Inez, walking in with a roller bag. She always looks beautiful, but especially tonight, dressed in a pantsuit, her makeup done, her long dark hair pulled into a low ponytail.

"Nora!" she says. "They didn't tell me you were up here."

She puts her bag against the wall and starts walking toward me, her arms outstretched for a hug. Inez hasn't lived here since she and my father separated. So I'm somewhat surprised to see her here now. And yet I'm not entirely surprised. Inez and my father were still the closest of friends. Why wouldn't he want her here whenever she wanted to be?

She gives me a hug, then pulls back, takes me in. I wasn't particularly close to Inez when she and my father were together. Part of it was the aftershock of Sylvia. But something shifted when she and my father decided to separate—and then when I got to know her now wife, Elizabeth. I've spent more time with them as a couple than I ever did with Inez and my father.

"I had a dinner uptown," she says. "I'm just staying for the night."

"Of course, I can get out of your way."

She waves me off. "There's no rush. I'll make us a drink."

She heads over to the bar cart and starts to pour two small whiskeys.

"Luna has a stomach bug, so Elizabeth stayed home with her," she says. "But I don't love being here on my own, to be honest."

She hands me one of the tumblers, and I take a long sip.

"I was feeling the same before you walked in," I say. "It looks different in here than I remember."

"Different how?"

"Did someone move my father's things out of the apartment? It just feels so . . ."

"Depressing?"

I laugh. "I was going to say bare."

"Well, I know he wasn't spending a lot of time here recently."

"Mostly Windbreak?"

She nods. "Mostly Windbreak. At least as far as I know."

"Inez, may I ask you something?" I say. "Did my father ever discuss Cece Salinger with you?"

"Only a bit. She was quite interested in the company a while back if I'm remembering correctly."

"But he wasn't interested in her romantically?"

"Cece? I don't know. I don't think so. From what your father told me, that was all ancient history. Like when they were twenty years old. Unless there is something we don't know. Which, I suppose, with your father is always possible." She takes a sip of her drink. "Why are you asking?"

"I'm just trying to figure out why he was spending so much time at Windbreak. She lives out there. It feels like maybe that had something to do with it . . ."

"Well, I seriously doubt that had anything to do with Cece," she says. "As far as I know, he just preferred being there. I mean, didn't he always prefer being there? That was his home."

*His home with whom?* I want to ask. *And what am I supposed to learn from the fact that it's now mine?*

She takes me in, her eyes filling with concern. "You okay?"

"Sure."

"'Cause you don't seem it."

"Was he seeing someone toward the end? Someone that I didn't know about?"

"Your father?"

I nod. If he were involved with someone new, Inez and Elizabeth would certainly know before my father would have shared it with me. But, as she starts to answer me, she shakes her head instead, stopping herself.

"What?" I say. "Please say it."

She puts her drink down and walks over to me, gently squeezes my hand. "I'm going to tell you what your father would say if he were here. Your father loved you. He loved all of us, the best he could. I think it's better to leave it at that."

"Better for who?"

She shrugs. "That's always the question."

# Aspect Ratio

"I thought we were meeting at the brownstone tomorrow," Morgan says.

I'm standing in the doorway of her and Sam's loft. She is photo shoot ready in a sheer minidress, full makeup, clad once again in her blue boots.

"I'm just looking for Sam," I say. "Is he here?"

"We're actually on our way out the door."

This is when Sam walks up behind her, puts an arm around her waist. He is also dressed to the nines in a dark blue suit, a vest beneath it. Everything about him looks rested and put together. It makes me even angrier that he didn't return my calls. All five of them.

"Why are you so sweaty?" he says.

"I ran here," I say.

"From Flatbush?"

I cross my arms over my chest and glare at him, Morgan looking back and forth between us.

"Morgan, would you mind giving us a minute alone, please?" I say.

He kisses her on the cheek, softly. Kindly. "I'll be ready in five, babe," he says.

Morgan heads inside, and Sam turns back toward me.

"What's going on with you?" I say.

"What's going on with you?"

"Why didn't you call me back all day?"

He points in Morgan's direction. "I've been busy," he says. "And we are about to head out for a fundraiser—"

I ignore this. I ignore him.

"We need to go back to Windbreak," I say.

"What are you talking about?"

"There's nothing at Dad's apartment. There are a few family photographs, sure, but there's really nothing personal. The scrapbooks, the photographs, all the things that made him *him,* separate from us, separate from the families, that was at Windbreak. He kept everything that mattered to him at Windbreak."

"We were there."

"Then we missed it."

"You're worse than me."

"We need to go back."

"Not happening."

"I also went out to Midwood," I say. "And you know what's crazy?"

"That you went out to Midwood?"

"There were more things that felt like our father there, in the house he hasn't lived in since he was a teenager, than an apartment he lived in until a month ago. How does that make any sense?"

"It doesn't," Sam says. "He didn't even like growing up in Midwood."

"There's one way it adds up."

"What's that?"

"We are missing the thread. The thread that starts all the way back there and ends on the cliff that night."

"You sound crazy," he says. "And that's not enough of a reason—"

"How is this for a reason? The forensic pathologist got in touch with me. She thinks you could be right. She is suspicious too. More than just suspicious."

"Nora."

"Sam, whatever it was, whatever part of his history he couldn't seem to leave behind, that holds the key to the rest of this. I'm sure of it. It's what's behind whatever happened to him that night."

He starts fidgeting, sliding from foot to foot, looking into his apartment in the direction of where Morgan went.

"Look, I'll call you tomorrow, okay?"

"Not okay. Do you hear what I'm telling you?"

He shakes his head. "You don't get it. I was wrong. You were right. I've been trying to figure out who Dad was. Or maybe I just haven't been able to accept that I didn't get to know him the way I wanted to when he was still alive. But nothing happened on the cliff that night."

"You believe that?"

"I believe I got carried away."

"Carried away with what?" I ask.

"All of it . . ."

He pauses, like it hurts him, like I'm hurting him, to make him say this part. To make him look at this thing he suddenly wants to pretend doesn't exist.

"I couldn't sleep last night," he says. "Yesterday got me all messed up. All that shit you were saying to me in the car. I'm on a path, you know? This is pulling my life apart."

"Oh, now it's my fault?"

"No, it's mine. But I need this to stop."

"Why? So you can marry someone you barely know? Work a job that doesn't inspire you the way playing ball did? Get drunk at some fancy party tonight that you'll pretend you don't hate?"

"Who are you to say what I'll hate?"

"Someone who's been listening to you."

This is when he starts to close the door.

I catch it with my hand, hold it open. "No. No way. You're the one who dragged me into this and now you're just going to bail?"

"You're surprised by that? Isn't this the part where you tell me you're not surprised?"

I look at him and I can see it—what's going on with him, what he is desperate to shut down. He doesn't want to know what he is starting to know about himself. Because he doesn't want to do the uncomfortable work that comes when you accept something needs to change. The uncomfortable work that comes with knowing that change means showing up for yourself in a new way.

But I refuse to simply judge him for that. Because I look at him and I see something else too. I see that he expects my judgment. Why wouldn't he? All these years that we've been kept at a distance from each other and I've done nothing to reach out to him—to reach out for him—he's been playing the role too. He's been playing the role that's more comfortable to him. The role of someone who doesn't care. So, I try something else.

"Look, let's do this differently, okay? Let's just decide that starting now we are going to do this differently. For each other. And for Dad."

He looks at me, and his eyes soften. And I think I've reached him. I think I've reached my brother. But he shakes his head, turning away.

"This is all I can do," he says.

Then he shuts the door, leaving me in the hallway, all by myself.

## *Twenty-Four Years Ago*

"This is not going well," Liam said.

"Well, who on earth asked you?"

Liam laughed, Cory flicking a paintbrush in his direction. They were at Windbreak, at the end of a rainstorm. They had both been in Los Angeles for work and they found an excuse to meet here for a couple of days. (Didn't it always end with them finding an excuse to meet here for a couple of days?) Cory was hanging wallpaper in Windbreak's living room. Bird-patterned wallpaper.

She didn't want his help, so Liam was standing beneath the ladder, watching her work, watching that wallpaper go up. He didn't particularly like it. The birds seemed wild, dangerous. And hadn't his mother always said that birds inside a house were bad luck? Nevertheless. Cory loved it, so up it was going.

Cory stepped up higher on the ladder, readjusted the level. "I think that looks pretty good."

"That makes one of us."

She smiled at him, reached for her razor knife.

"You know," he said, "the books, the views, the ugly birds . . . This seems like a perfect room for you to write in."

He felt her body tense. "It would be, I imagine. But it's not my room."

"The wallpaper says otherwise."

She let out a laugh.

"Do you ever think about writing?"

"Liam—"

"What?"

"Don't think that I don't see where this is going," she said. "Just because Sylvia is spending a suspicious amount of time with her personal trainer . . ."

"He's not her personal trainer. He's her friend's personal trainer."

"Forgive me. Just because Sylvia is being Sylvia, that still doesn't mean you get to question my life choices."

"I love your life choices. I love every choice that has brought you to still be standing here in this room, on this ladder, in those very adorable overalls and old lady glasses . . . somehow and miraculously not done with me quite yet."

"Oh, believe me, I'm getting closer."

He smiled at her. He knew he needed to tread carefully. Her work was a source of contention for them. He wanted to remind her that when she interviewed with Sally, it was supposed to be temporary. The corporate world, the long hours, the stress her job put on her—that was never supposed to be the long-term plan. She'd made plenty of money now to do what she wanted to do. Why wasn't she doing what she wanted to do?

"I think someone might say that I'm hitting a nerve," he said.

"Don't give yourself so much credit," she said. "Besides, who says I'm not still writing anyway?"

That stopped him. "Really?"

"Yes. Really."

"How did I not know that?" he asked.

"There are a lot of things you don't know about me."

He put his hands on the ladder. She stepped down several rungs and turned toward him, so that his hands were right over her head, encircling her. His face inches from her face. Just the two of them breathing in that air, like a halo, like a safety valve.

"I pray every day that's not true," he said, sincerely.

"Okay. Well." She met his eyes. "Do you remember Mrs. Dixon?"

"Mrs. Dixon?"

"Sophomore English. Had lots of turtle paraphernalia in the classroom."

He never had her as a teacher, but he searched his memory to properly place her. Fidelity is who you tell your stories to. He could feel how important it was that he really showed up for this one.

"With the red hair, yeah?" he said. "She made Joe join the literary review or she was going to fail him?"

"Exactly. She had a *New Yorker* writer come into the class to speak to us, a short story writer, and he sat on the floor in front of the class, and he told us that when he's writing his stories, they're each a love letter to one person. A love letter that other people are just peeking in on." She shrugged. "I still think about it when I write and it takes it away."

"Takes what away?"

"Any idea that I should be writing for anyone but me."

"And the person."

"Yes. And the person."

"Who's the person?"

She smiled, not answering. "Don't miss the point."

"Fair enough. Tell me the point."

"I know that it's your favorite pastime, to focus on what should have been, but I don't like to focus on it. It's a waste. And to be honest, it feels like just another thing that gets in the way of you finding it. Holding on to it."

"What's that?"

"Happiness."

"How did this become a referendum on me?"

"You interrupted my wallpaper install."

"So you don't ever think about the alternative life?" He shrugged. "The one where I get to be with you every day and all the babies we've had running around, we are raising them together. And you write in this room all day and at night, I bring us some tea, and sit in that chair there. And watch you work."

"I like my life," she said. "Plus, you're watching me now. And I'm finding it quite annoying."

"That's not an answer," he said.

He pushed the hair out of her face, her thick curls. His fingers running the length of her cheek.

She leaned into him, into his fingers. "The sunset's going to be beautiful when the rain clears. Why don't you go save a spot on the cliff, and when you're annoying me less, maybe I'll come meet you out there."

"You're exiling me? Into the rain?"

"You have boots."

She kissed his wrist, the edge of his palm. Then she turned away from him, headed back up the ladder.

He looked up at her. "For what it's worth, I am happy," he said. "I'm happy whenever I'm with you."

"Good to hear, out you go."

"I'm serious, Cory. How long has it been? Almost thirty years now and there's still nothing that makes me happier than you."

"Oh please. You always get like this when we're here together."

"Well, that's because it's our place."

"It's not."

He started to walk to the porch and the sunset, to give her what she wanted. "If that's true, then I'm taking the wallpaper down as soon as you leave."

# Frequent Flier Miles Don't Get You What You Think They Will

I'm in the last row of the plane.

To get a ticket on the first flight out, there were no other options. I'm sitting between a mom in the window seat cradling her crying baby and a man in the aisle seat drinking straight vodka (at 8:00 a.m.) and shooting daggers at the baby, as though that will help make anyone feel better.

"It might help if I could grab her spare pacifier," the mother says. "Or I should say the spare of her spare. The others are on the ground."

"I'm happy to hold her while you grab it," I say. "Is that weird to offer . . ."

Before I finish speaking, she drops the baby into my arms. I hold her against my chest, cradle her sweet head as her mother leaps out of the seat, climbing over me and past the guy in the aisle, who of course doesn't sit up a modicum, or move his legs out of her way.

The mother reaches for her diaper bag in the overhead bin, searching for the pacifier. Then she crawls back into her seat. But, like a miracle, her baby is quiet and sleeping in my arms.

"Wow," she says. "Impressive."

"Beginner's luck."

She reaches her arms out to take her daughter back, but I see it in her face, the fear that any movement will wake her.

"You know, I don't mind holding her while she's sleeping. If you're comfortable with that—"

"Are you sure?"

I smile and start to say I am when our surly seatmate chimes in. "Yes please! For crying out loud. Hold her!"

I shoot him a look. "We've got this. But thank you."

He shakes his head and looks away. Then I turn back toward the mother.

"I'm good, honestly."

The mother nods, gently touching her baby on the arm. "Thank you," she says, letting out a breath. An exhale. The first of this plane ride.

She gives me a grateful smile. "You must have kids?"

"Not yet."

"But you'd like one?"

I nod. "I would."

"Hmm. You got the person?"

"May have just lost him."

"This is turning into a depressing conversation."

She lets out a small laugh. And maybe it's a bit too loud—the promising sound of her mother—because the baby starts to gurgle in my arms. The mother puts her hand on the baby's back, and she starts to settle again.

"This little one's daddy is having a bit of a hard time adjusting to parenthood, so I'm going to stay with my sister for a bit. Give him a little room."

"That sounds like a needed trip."

"Let's hope. My sister is pretty much the smartest person I know, and she told me to get on the plane. She said if you are looking for answers you can't find, you need to change the question."

That hits me, how true that is. "Sounds like she is operating on a different level."

"Well, she's living with five roommates and they're all unemployed, so . . ." she says. "Bit of a mixed bag."

I smile, adjusting the baby, trying to keep her comfortable. "So, what's your new question?"

"Will my being gone knock it out of him?" She shrugs. "The parts I don't recognize."

I nod. That's what we are often fighting against, isn't it? The parts in someone we don't recognize. The parts we are trying to reconcile. Aren't my current questions, as large and impossible as they are, circling around that exact thing? What happened to my father that I wasn't there to see? What did I miss about who he was? Where do those things intersect?

Also this. What should I be asking instead that will get me to a clearer picture of what happened on the cliff that night? That will get me somewhere better. Meredith Cooper comes into my head: *There are no wrong questions when you're grieving*. Jonathan: *He was nothing if not loyal*. Inez: *He loved all of us, the best he could*.

My mother: *Oh, for Pete's sake . . . It's like you don't know your father at all*.

Maybe. Maybe not. Maybe the question is not only who my father was. Maybe it has more to do with this—for all of us, doesn't it have more to do with this? Who, at the end of the day, did my father wish he could have been?

"So," she says. "Now that I overshared, you go. What's so urgent that you're heading across the country last-minute?"

"How did you know this is last-minute?"

"Middle seat. Last row. What's going on?"

But, just then, the baby's gurgles get louder, and suddenly she is awake, taking me in, a woman she doesn't belong to, and starts clawing to get back to her mother, her cries turning into loud shrieks.

"Cancel that," she says. "You're on your own."

# A Wintery Beach Tells a Story

At Windbreak, I walk the beach.

I start at Loon Point, and I walk east first, as though I'm the jogger. Then I walk down to the Velasquez property and turn back in the direction of Windbreak, as the Coopers did, envisioning the night from that vantage point. I study the exact area where my father was discovered, on the high sand, fifteen feet from the entrance to the rickety stairs, leading up to his property. I look up at the bluffs, take in those stairs from below, take in the next-door neighbor's high wall, my father's gentle palisades.

I try to re-create it. The pattern of it. The order.

What exactly happened that night? If someone pushed him, then where did they go, if not down those stairs, landing on this beach too? Did they jump the fence separating Windbreak from the neighbors? That would have been captured. If they went out Windbreak's front gate, that would have been captured too. Unless someone knew how to erase what was seen.

"Nora?"

I turn around and see an older man in a Yale baseball cap, a white mustache matching the hair peeking out from beneath the cap. Two large dogs are running in wide circles around him.

He looks vaguely familiar to me, but I'm having trouble placing him until he puts his hand to his chest by way of introduction.

“I thought that was you,” he says. “Ben King.”

I smile at him as I remember. This is Ben, my father’s friend from college. The reason my father found himself on Padaro Lane three decades ago. The reason he saw Windbreak in the first place.

“Ben, of course,” I say. “I’m sorry I didn’t recognize you.”

“That’s okay,” he says. “It’s been a few years. I think you were finishing college.”

“Then it was many more years ago than that.”

“They all start to bleed.” He smiles, offers a gentle shrug. “I was really sorry to hear about your father. I hope you’re hanging in okay.”

He blushes in the way that has become familiar to me. In that way I’ve noticed so many of us do when we try to offer sympathies, as if naming the grief will conjure it up, will be the thing responsible for adding to the pain that otherwise could be forgotten. It makes it feel all the kinder to me when someone takes the risk and does it anyway.

“Thank you,” I say. “I appreciate it.”

“Are you staying here for a bit?”

“Just the night, I think.”

“Famous last words,” he says. “This place grabs you fast.”

I give him a smile. And he waves goodbye. Then he starts heading down the beach, picking up a beach stick, throwing it to his dogs. They race out ahead of him, working to catch it.

I watch him for a moment, this man who is so relaxed and happy. Isn’t this who my father wanted to be? A man not unlike this one, not worrying where his next meal was coming from. In a cliffside house with his old life (the old versions of himself) shed, far behind him. But that couldn’t be my father’s story of who he wanted to be, could it? Not when he loved as intensely as he did. Not when he brought

Joe along with him. When he kept all his families close. Not when he was nothing if not loyal.

No. The story was closer to something else. Something about a man holding on with as much force as he also tried to flee. But to what? Which is when it hits me.

Cece. Cece ended up in this storied corner of the coast, hadn't she said her husband was still here, not too far from Uncle Joe? Not too far from my father?

I pull out my phone and do a search for her ex-husband. Davidson Salinger. A sales record listing his address as Sand Point Road. A five-minute drive. Davidson Salinger, a Los Angeles native who graduated from Yale University, where he met his first wife, Cece Kayne.

Yale. This shouldn't be a surprise. Cece had said that she and my father went to school together, but I assumed she'd meant Midwood High. Why did I assume that? Because she had said they grew up near each other. Hadn't she also said that?

I walk back up to the house, taking the steps two at a time, closing and locking the gate behind myself, and running the length of the property to the house. Until I'm inside the house, closing the door behind myself.

The house is freezing, and there are no lights on yet. I've called Clark to come by and turn everything on. He has to do it from a locked power breaker. I have to learn how to do it myself.

But suddenly I don't feel like waiting. I head to the living room, head straight to the bookshelves, pulling several things down from the personal shelf: some of the playbills, the yearbooks, several of the photo albums. I move it all by the window, and into the light and the heat from the late afternoon sun.

He has one yearbook from his senior year at Midwood, one marked the *Yale Banner*, from his senior year there. I check the index in the *Banner* first, searching for any photographs of my father. There are none except for his senior portrait. I start going through the photo albums instead. Some of them are dated in the front, and I look for any that take me back to the late 1970s, when he was finishing college.

The second album I go through has a large group photograph in it. Several of his male friends are in it, but not Ben King. Not anyone else I recognize on first blush, except for my father, looking strong and young, his arms crossed over his chest, his smile large and wide. And looking so much like Sam that it startles me.

I turn the page and see another group photograph. My father is in the center, several friends circled around him. In this photograph, I recognize two people. On the far left is my uncle Joe. And, on the right, the only woman in the photo. A young and very beautiful Cece Kayne. She is standing near my father, but someone else has an arm around her. Maybe this is Davidson Salinger. Maybe it is someone else entirely.

Either way, Cece is leaning toward my father, even though this man is leaning toward her.

I pull the photograph out of the album, staring at all of their faces, holding them in my hand.

I hold it closer, hold him closer, wondering what it is that I can almost see.

# *Eighteen Years Ago*

"I don't want to talk about it anymore . . ."

Cory and Liam were standing in front of track twenty-eight at Grand Central Station. Cory was waiting on the 5:55 train to Dobbs Ferry, where she and her husband had been living for the last few months. He was a visiting lecturer at Sarah Lawrence, and they'd rented an old Victorian house for the semester. It was a house that Cory loved, on a street Cory thought maybe they should move to permanently. She was working less. She was auditing a nighttime poetry class. She was getting on that train to get back to a place that made her happier than Liam did at the moment. He had thirteen minutes to change her mind.

"Nothing is going on with Cece," he said.

"Oh, please! You think that's what I care about here?"

She was angry enough that he knew that was at least partially what she cared about, even if she wasn't going to admit it. Not to him, not to herself. Cece had been a bone of contention between them since the first time she and Cory had met during Liam's senior year of college. Cece and Liam had been in the same residential college since freshman year and had dated briefly before Cory and Liam had reconnected. They had stayed close. Friends, but close.

Cory wasn't a jealous person, but Liam could see that she had a reaction to Cece. It wasn't just that Cece was (quite possibly) the most beautiful woman Cory had ever seen in person. Or that Cece wasn't trying to hide that she still had feelings for Liam, even though she had started seeing someone new. It was that Cece had been dismissive of Cory. Dismissive or threatened or both.

The bottom line was that she hadn't been nice. Not then, and not in their subsequent meetings since.

And now, of all days, Cory had arrived early to her train and saw Liam and Cece having a drink at the Oyster Bar. They were sitting a little too close, drinking their martinis, Cece leaning into him.

"Cory. She made an offer for the company. I had to hear her out."

"And?"

"And I declined."

"You think you deserve praise for that?" she asked.

"Of course not."

Cory shook her head. "You're wasting time."

"Hers?"

"*Mine.*" She met his eyes. "My time. I thought you weren't getting back from San Francisco until next week."

That was the plan. He was opening a property not too far from Pfeiffer Beach, a stunning private retreat with twenty treehouses high up over the ocean, offering unparalleled views of the rock and the water and that rugged coastline. And, of equal importance, offering him a place to hide. And he was—in too many ways—hiding at the moment. Most obviously, from Sylvia, his soon-to-be ex-wife, and from the second family he'd failed. He was even hiding from Cory. Which was to say he was hiding from himself.

"I tried to reach you as soon as I landed," he said. "Check your phone."

"I'm not checking my phone. If you say you called, you called."

"I flew in for Sam's game tomorrow. They made States. I couldn't miss it."

She paused, studied him, as if figuring out whether she believed him. This was the worst part.

"We don't keep things from each other. That was always the deal."

"It's still the deal," he said. "The only reason I didn't mention Cece is because it's a nonissue."

"Because, to be clear, I don't care if you sell to Cece," she said. "What I care about is that you've told me that you never want to sell to anyone. Especially to a place as corporate as the Salinger Group, which will take everything you built and turn it into something you don't recognize."

"I know."

"You shouldn't need me to remind you of that. You shouldn't need anyone to."

This was going the wrong way. But Liam didn't know how to stop it. Because this was about Cece and it was about more than Cece. It was about all the choices Liam was making these days, enduring (as he was) the final gasps of his second marriage.

The conductor called out that the train was boarding, and Cory turned to go. He reached for her arm, tried to stop her. She wasn't having it.

"Would you take the later train? Can we go sit somewhere and talk this through?"

"Are you going to tell me why you were really having a drink with her?"

"What?"

"People say no over the phone, Liam. That's what the phone is for."

He didn't say anything. What was he going to say? She was right. And now he had to acknowledge it to himself. A part of him, a tiny part of him, had wanted to know what Cece had to say.

Cory hoisted her handbag higher on her shoulder and turned to walk down the track. He reached for her arm. He reached quickly to stop her. His skin against her skin. His mouth by her ear.

"Please don't go."

He knew she'd say no. He knew it before the words even came out of her mouth. "I'm not missing my class," she said. "Besides, we aren't getting anywhere good . . ."

"I'm trying to fix that," he said.

She started walking away from him. "Perfect," she said. "Maybe one of these days you'll stop trying to fix the wrong things."

# Too Early and Too Late

I'm watching the sunset on the back porch when Cece calls.

I'm listening to the waves, a cup of tea in my hands. I have no reason to feel peaceful, and yet I'm so peaceful that I don't hear the phone buzz at first. I'm taking in the soft light and the sound of those waves and thinking of Jack. And I'm wishing he was here with me, knowing how peaceful he'd find it too. I consider picking up the phone and calling him, but I feel like I don't get to do that anymore. Not just because I miss him. Not until I also have something different to say.

When the phone buzzes a second time, though, I think for a moment that it is Jack. But it's an 805 number that comes up on my phone, a number I don't recognize, Cece's voice coming at me, her tone clipped and anxious.

"I hope it's alright that I'm calling," she says. "Your uncle Joe told me that you were at Windbreak."

"And how did my uncle Joe know that?"

She gets quiet, not answering. "I thought maybe we could have dinner tomorrow. Talk some things through."

"Is he joining us as well?" I ask.

"I didn't share with him that I was reaching out to you, actually," Cece says. "I was hoping that just the two of us could talk . . ."

I hear a knock on the screen door. And look up to see Clark standing there.

"I'm going to head out," he says.

"Hey, Cece, I'm going to call you right back, okay?" Then I click off and turn to Clark. "Thank you for coming out."

"Of course. It's nice to have someone staying here again."

I give him a smile and stand up, walk over to where he is standing in the doorway. And I reach into my back pocket, Cece's voice still in my head. "Before you go, can I show you something?"

"Sure."

I hold out the group photograph with my father and with Uncle Joe in it. With Cece in it.

"I guess, and I understand if you want to remain discreet even now, but . . . did my father and this woman spend any time together here?"

He reaches for the photograph, reluctantly at first, clearing his throat. But then he looks down at it, scanning the group, landing first on my father.

"Wow, Liam looks so young here," he says.

"I know."

"And a lot like your brother."

"I think so too."

He holds the photograph closer to his face, takes it in. Then he shakes his head.

"But the woman . . . I can't say I recognize her."

"I can pull up a more recent photograph online."

"No. There's no need." He hands me back the photograph. "I never really saw him here with anyone. You kids occasionally, but, more often than not, your father was alone here."

I nod. "Yeah. That's what I thought."

Clark touches the doorframe, running his fingers alongside it. Then he turns to leave, his back turned to me, his voice almost too low to hear.

"He talked about you," he says. "He'd like that you were here."

"I appreciate you sharing that."

I look down, grateful, too grateful really. It means too much to me to hear that my father wanted me here. To hear that this part matters.

"There was one woman who came here with him."

I look back up at him, wondering if I heard him correctly. "Sorry?"

He looks at me over his shoulder, shrugs. "Or at least there was only one woman that I met. That was it."

I hold his gaze, my heart starting to race. He isn't saying the rest because he doesn't have to. He means one woman besides my father's wives, one woman besides his families, one woman who he is guessing shouldn't have been here.

I can see it in his eyes. He isn't sure if it's a betrayal that he's told me or the right thing to do—or, somehow, both at the same time.

"I only met her a few times, and I wasn't sure if she was a friend."

"Did she seem like a friend?"

"Yes. And no."

"Do you happen to know her name?"

He doesn't hesitate. Now that he's gotten this far, he doesn't hesitate when he says it. "Cory," he says. "He introduced her to me as Cory."

Cory. Why does that sound familiar? That was the name etched into the closet. Cory & Liam. I'm sure of it. Could it possibly be the same Cory?

Clark knocks on the doorframe, as if he is steadying himself against what he revealed. And I reach out and touch his arm. "Thank you," I say.

Then I am moving away from him—to the living room, to the bay window and that bird wallpaper, to all the photo albums and playbills and yearbooks that I spilled onto the floor already, that I have yet to put back.

Cory & Liam.

I call Cece back, but she doesn't pick up. I leave a message.

Then I reach for his oldest photo albums—anything that looks to be from high school, anything that looks to be from before that.

And I start to move through.

## *Eleven Years Ago*

It was ten degrees outside.

Liam was waiting for her on the street corner. The windchill was below zero, the snow flurries relentless, but he would wait until she appeared. He'd just left a drinks meeting at the St. Regis, and he was feverish from his scotch and from the hope he would get to see her soon. He knew which subway she took from Midtown to her apartment. He waited by the stop near her office.

Until there she was: barreling toward him in a long trench coat and a cashmere knit hat, her curls flying out beneath it, her cheeks red from the frost.

"What the hell are you doing?" she asked. "Trying to freeze to death?"

But she broke into a smile. She broke into a smile that seeped straight through his skin, the cold forgotten.

He smiled back at her. "Hello to you too."

"You look giddy."

"I missed you," he said.

"I've seen you."

"Not enough."

She shook her head. "How is that possible?"

That was how it was with them recently. Liam the one reaching for Cory, Cory mostly humoring him. There were reasons for that. Cory was coming up on a big wedding anniversary, and she and her husband were talking about spending a year in Paris. They could both work from there. They could also, more importantly, work on their marriage from there. Cory didn't tell Liam that this was the real purpose. She didn't have to tell him. They were going to stay in a friend's apartment in the 6th arrondissement and spend days at La Grande Épicerie and go to London so she could see shows on the West End. Her husband would go with her. He would do whatever it took to try and keep her.

Liam knew this. Just as he knew that it wouldn't be forever. Of course it wouldn't. But it would mean, for a while, he could no longer stand outside the subway in the freezing cold. Just for a chance to surprise her.

He pulled the playbill out of his jacket, a set of tickets to *The Goodbye Girl*. A new revival. She looked down at the playbill in her hand, Neil Simon in large letters.

"You didn't," she said.

"Front-row seats."

"Is this my consolation prize on the eve of your third wedding?"

He laughed. What else was there to do? He was getting married again. Again, and maybe for the last time. Her name was Inez. She was younger than Liam by eighteen years, as though that was the detail that mattered. Here was a detail that mattered: making things official was important to her. Her mother was unwell. He knew Inez wanted her at their wedding while she could still be there. He also knew Inez really wanted children of her own. He wanted to do what mattered to her. She deserved that. There were many reasons that getting married was the right thing to do. Looking at Cory now, he could hardly remember them.

"I'm sorry I'll miss the wedding," she said.

"Are you?"

"Not really," she said. "Though I do like Inez. She's too good for you, to be honest."

"We're in agreement on that."

She linked her arm through his. And they fell into step, heading in the direction of the theater. Suddenly (and like usual) Cory being the one to lead the way.

"Doesn't change the fact that you should possibly consider stopping with the weddings," she said.

"Not a lot of faith that third time's the charm?" he asked.

"I don't make any judgments."

"Thank goodness that's not true."

"I'm just saying, you decided to do this pretty soon after you found out I was leaving the country with my family," she said. "Not to make this about me."

"Mostly everything is, so . . ."

She smiled at him.

"I've been honest with her about you," he said. "As honest as I can be."

"The *can be* is where my questions come in."

She leaned her head against his shoulder, and he felt her do it, take that small exhale. Something like relief. Something like happiness.

"Thank you for the tickets. I needed this today."

"Then you'll be glad to hear that I also have some contraband Junior Mints in my pocket," he said. "Since I know how you hate cutting it too close to the curtain."

"Twizzlers too?"

"Am I new here?"

He pulled the red candy out of his coat pocket, handed her the packet.

"Well," she said. "Now you're just showing off."

# There Is No Language That's Meaningless

I fall asleep, on the floor.

I'm freezing when I wake up. It must be the middle of the night. My arms and legs are covered in goose bumps. My neck creaking awake.

I've looked through the photo albums. I've scoured his high school yearbook from senior year. There were 630 girls in his graduating class, but there was no Cory. Female or male. I don't have it in me to go through the other 3,000 students at the school, not knowing what I'll figure out, even if I happen upon someone named Cory.

So, I stand up to put the photo albums back on the shelf, back in their place, to put all his belongings that I've gone through next to the framed photographs.

Which is when I see it still on that shelf. A thin book. A thin book on which one of those photographs is perched. A thin book I almost missed.

I pull it down off the shelf and stare at its maroon cover.

*Jabberwocky: The Midwood High School Literary Review.*

I start turning the pages until I land on the table of contents. I'm searching for my father's name—a story he would have written, or an essay—something to explain why he kept this journal.

I don't find my father's name there, but I do see Joseph D. Goddard. My uncle Joe, and a short story that he wrote called "The Shortstop."

It makes me smile, thinking of him writing a story. It feels so off-brand that I almost turn to read it. But then I zero in on another name.

Another name that catches my attention. I see two pieces (a poem and a short story) by someone named Cordelia Ryan.

I hold on the name Cordelia. Cory could be short for Cordelia, couldn't it? This could be Cory. It also, of course, could not be.

It's the closest I've come tonight, so I turn to page eight, to read her story, which she's entitled "The Children Go."

But under the title there is a note I close in on. It's a short note, handwritten, all in lowercase. Except for his initials. Except for my father's initials.

*LSN—*
*in case i don't say it later,*
*they're all for you*

My heart starts racing as I keep flipping through the journal. As I flip until I get to the masthead.

As I flip until I find it. CORDELIA G. RYAN. EDITOR IN CHIEF.

There is a photograph beneath her name. A small black-and-white photograph of a young woman sitting on a bench, smiling at the camera in her wire-rim glasses and wrap dress and this long, unruly hair. Her face may be small in the photograph, the curls covering too much of her eyes. I need to turn on the light to see her more clearly.

But I recognize her face, her pretty and familiar face, even before the light goes on. I recognize her before I'm even sure that I do.

Grace.

# — Part III —

A building has at least two lives—the one imagined
by its maker and the life it lives
afterward—and they are never the same.

—Rem Koolhaas

# Sunrise Looks Different from Different Angles

Like that, they reappear.

Snapshots. Poorly developed film. A narrative swinging through the trees. These things (so many of these things) that you only half-noticed because you weren't looking for them. Why on earth would you be looking for them?

You were young. You were looking at yourself.

Eight years old and she is by his side at your school play; twelve and she is having a picnic with you and your father in Central Park, the two of them lying in the grass and laughing. The two of them laughing in a way you can't remember your father ever laughing with anyone else. Fourteen and eighteen and twenty-two. At your father's office, at *their* office, her voice in his background when you call, her bright blue dress, his eyes watching her.

Twenty-seven or twenty-eight. What does your mother say to you after the two of you run into Grace and her daughter, Jenny, in Brooklyn Heights? What does your mother say to Grace, their cheeks touching tightly: *I love you.* What does your father whisper to her at your uncle Joe's birthday party? After she squeezes your shoulder and heads toward him, heads toward him and Uncle Joe. Your father touching her hand as she arrives by his side: *There you are.*

Just last year. After you lost your mother, the last time you'll see Grace. You're with Jack when you run into her. She is walking with your father in Midtown. Her kind smile. His happiness.

What do you see when you look over your shoulder as they're walking away from you? Their eyes back on each other, your father's hand slipping onto her hip like it belongs there.

Because, apparently, it always did.

~

First, I call Sam.

His phone goes straight to voicemail. The beep hits my ears before I even know what to say.

Sam, call me. Sam, I need you.

Next, I call Elliot. It's almost 9:00 a.m. in New York. He's probably already at the hospital. Maybe he's already with patients. But I don't need him to confirm what I'm putting together on my own anyway. What Elliot must have been trying to tell me without telling me. What he discussed with my father during their last dinner, what Elliot meant by ethics, what he couldn't say because it involved a patient. It involved Grace. That's why my father (my heartbroken father) was so attached to Elliot, at least in part. Elliot was helping Grace. Tangentially, perhaps, in an advisory role, maybe, but still close enough to her medical care that Elliot felt like he couldn't ethically discuss it. He couldn't discuss someone that he'd been advocating for, as though she was a patient. Not with me.

Elliot couldn't discuss what my father was still asking him at that last dinner, what he was still grappling with. How did Grace's heart give out for a second time when they were all watching it so closely, watching her so closely? My father couldn't help but go over it. And then go over it again. As if understanding why she was gone would make it any easier that she was, as if it would change that he'd lost her.

Elliot doesn't pick up, the call clicking over to voicemail. Neither does Uncle Joe. I don't leave a message for either of them. I hang up and call Jonathan.

I'm outside now. I am outside on the edge of the property, the sun sharp against the horizon, a slim golden strip.

"Nora," he says. "What can I do for you?"

"Is it Grace?"

He is silent. To his credit, he doesn't ask me what I'm talking about. Cordelia G. Ryan. Cory, Grace.

Jonathan doesn't try and lie. I look down over the white rock and water. I focus on the shimmery gold starting to light the sky, crystal and wild and ready.

I focus. A timeline concretizing in my mind: the loss of Grace less than a year ago (did Paul say it was eight months ago?), my father's unmitigated sadness in the aftermath, his desire to let it all go (anything that reminded him of her, even the company). So why not give it to Cece? Why not give it away. Until his realization that it wouldn't fix it. What had been lost for him. What was broken.

"It's Grace, isn't it? He was going to leave her the company."

He pauses, the air between us thick. "Let's make a time for you to come into the office, okay? We can discuss this in person."

"I want to discuss it now."

"I'm sorry, but I need to call you later," he says. Then he hangs up.

I don't blame him. But I also won't accept it.

I start to call him back.

Which is why I don't hear the footsteps coming up behind me.

Which is why I don't hear that there is someone else, someone walking quickly toward me.

Not until he is right behind me, until he could just lean over and push.

His hand touches my shoulder, jolting me. My breath catching in my throat, a scream caught in my throat. And I turn around.

I turn around, and I see my brother.

"You scared me half to death."

"Sorry about that."

Sam is in a hoodie and old jeans, untied Converse sneakers, everything on him wrinkled and messy.

"I took the early flight," he says. "No one should have to be here alone."

I am already hugging him to me. I am already hugging him tightly, like this is something we do.

"It's Grace," I say.

"What's Grace?"

"All of it."

# San Ysidro Road Leads You Home

Noone Properties' West Coast satellite office is in the Upper Village of Montecito—a quiet enclave in Santa Barbara, not too far from Windbreak, not too far from The Ranch. The office is in a wooded area, on the second floor of a small brick building. Ivy covers the front door. Flowerpots line the small waiting area. Mountain views and treetops sneak in from every window.

We walk past the receptionist and into Joe's office.

He is sitting at his desk, on a phone call. He covers the receiver with his hand.

"Would it kill you two to send a text first?" he asks.

"He was going to leave it to Grace?" Sam says.

But Sam isn't really asking. We know the answer. I put the copy of *Jabberwocky* on the desk in front of Joe.

"What the hell is this?" he asks.

"We know, Joe," I say. "We know they were involved."

Into the phone he says, "I've got to call you back."

He hangs up and starts paging through the journal. He shakes his head, as if in disbelief. Maybe he can't believe that my father kept it. Maybe he can't believe that it's sitting in front of him now.

He looks up at us. Then he motions toward the chairs on the other side of his desk. "Have a seat, then."

"We're good to stand," I say.

"Then you're going to be standing for a while. If you want to know the whole story . . ."

"We wanted to know the whole story last week," I say. "We wanted to hear the whole story before we knew there was a whole story to tell."

"Come on, guys, you know it wasn't my story to tell."

"No, we totally hear you on that," Sam says. "It was a lot better for us to try and figure this out for ourselves."

He crosses his arms over his chest, angry. Hurt.

Joe meets Sam's eyes and sighs. Then he moves to the front of the desk, the side that we are on, and sits down on the edge of it.

"Okay," he says. "What do you want to know?"

All of it, I want to say. Where it all started, what happened next, and how it all ended here.

"They were together in high school?" I ask. "Grace and Dad?"

"Define together."

"You define it."

"Okay, well, first we dated, Grace and I," he says. "Very briefly."

"And then they did?"

He nods. "A lot less briefly."

"But you knew about it?" Sam says.

"About them? Sure. Give or take fifty years."

"So they were in a relationship?" I ask. "That whole time."

He shakes his head, like he doesn't want to answer that. Like he doesn't want to give anything approaching an answer that might hurt me. Because, what does that mean then? In terms of how my father felt about my mother? By, extension, how he felt about me?

But, somehow, it feels unrelated, like this is about something else. Something sad and raw and definite.

Sam rubs his eyes, overwhelmed. "So it was always going to be Grace who Dad left the company to?" he asks. "The whole time?"

"Yes."

Joe says it unapologetically, letting Sam take that in. I turn to Sam and I expect to see pain there. But what I see instead is something like processing. And something like relief.

"You have to understand, your father and Grace . . . it goes way back."

"We got that part," Sam says.

"He brought her into Hayes shortly after he took over, not too long after I joined the company," he says. "She had just moved back from California, and it was supposed to be temporary. But when she came in, it was obvious from the beginning that it wouldn't be."

"Why not?" I ask.

"Your father knew exactly what he wanted these hotels to be. It was a niche that hadn't been executed well until then, and he had the vision. But when it comes to scaling that, in a way that each property is successful on its own, it's all about the messaging. And Grace . . . she was a storyteller, you know. And she understood how to generate that message. She probably understood it better than your father. Certainly, he thought so."

He pauses. And I think of what Sam said to me in the car—how alive my father seemed at work. And I start to recalibrate why that was. It wasn't just what he got to do there; it was who he got to do it with.

"All of which is to say that she was really great at her job. Not just the marketing. But the branding. Communications. All of it. And she made him better at his."

"So when did you find out?" Sam says.

"About what?"

"When did you find out he was going to leave the company to her?"

"Officially? Probably five or six years ago. Somewhere around then, but I always assumed."

"You assumed?" Sam says.

"I did, Sam. I assumed. Like I said, he needed her. Though that sounds binary, like it worked one way. And it wasn't. It worked both ways. They were . . . in it together. So I always knew that was going to be what your father wanted to do."

"You sure about that, Joe?"

"What are you getting at, kid?"

"Dad didn't just fall that night," he says. "The night that he died."

"What are you talking about?" He looks back and forth between us, taking that in. "You think someone hurt him? That's what you're saying?"

Then his eyes narrow, hearing what Sam didn't exactly say.

"And you think I had something to do with that?"

"I don't know, Joe," Sam says. "You gave your life to this company, and it was never going to be yours and maybe you got mad about that. That it wasn't going to you. That he was giving it to a woman you were with first—"

"Oh you've got to be kidding me. I knew that was his plan. And I knew about them for fifty years. The whole time. Do you know how many girlfriends I had in high school?"

"So then it's just a coincidence that you tried to convince him to sell the company to your current girlfriend?"

"That had nothing to do with me. That was all your father. He didn't want to do it without Grace. He didn't want to do much of anything without her. I didn't discourage it, but he needed something easy after Grace died. He needed to be done with it. And Cece was eager to do it. She'd always wanted the company. Did I broker that? Absolutely. At your father's request."

"And you weren't mad when he reneged on selling to her at the last minute?" Sam asks. "At losing your last chance to be in charge?"

Joe stands up and moves right in front of Sam, inches from his face. Sam moving in the rest of the way, their noses practically touching, Sam clinching his knuckles, Uncle Joe clinching his wrist.

"Fuck you, kid."

I step between them, putting a hand on each of their chests, pulling them back apart.

"Guys, take it down," I say. "Just, slow down."

Sam looks at me and pulls back. Uncle Joe is still shaking his head, but he calms himself too.

He sits back on the edge of the desk, leans in toward Sam.

"Look," Joe says. "I know it's hard to hear, but it wasn't about you and Tommy or your abilities or any of that. He just . . . couldn't. Everything he did was for her. This was the one thing he got to do with her every day. And he couldn't keep doing it himself, not in her absence. The one thing your father couldn't figure out how to do in his entire life was to be without her."

He pauses, looks back and forth between both of us. And I feel the pain that must have existed for my father—for him and for Grace—that they were together and they weren't together. Why would anyone make that choice? But I start to hear the answer without Joe needing to say it, as if anyone needs to say it: the reasons that you move away from the people you love are sometimes the very reasons you wish you could move toward them.

"The point is, ultimately, he decided it wasn't fair. He decided you and your brother deserved your shot to do with it what you would."

"Or maybe not. Maybe he just ran out of time," Sam says. "Why else would he have called Cece the night he died?"

"Guess that was possible. But he seemed pretty settled in his decision. Besides, there was a much simpler explanation."

"And what's that?" Sam asks.

Before Uncle Joe can answer, I do it for him.

"He was trying to reach you," I say.

He nods. "He was trying to reach me. I have bad coverage at Cece's. He must have been trying to get to me for something."

He motions to me.

"I probably should have told you all of this," he says. "Cece certainly thought I should have. But I was reluctant to do that, to be honest. I just didn't know how we could tell you any of this while also protecting the things, I think, he didn't want shared . . ."

I see it in his eyes, the sorrow there. And I understand, suddenly, what our uncle Joe was trying to do until the end—he was trying to protect our father. It's what he's still trying to do now, the only way he knows how.

"You have it," I say.

"Have what?" Joe says.

"His cell phone."

He holds my gaze, for a minute, not replying. But then he walks around his desk and opens the bottom drawer, pulls a cell phone out.

"When I went to Windbreak, that next morning, I found it in the bedroom," he says. "Your father and Grace had gone to such lengths to keep their relationship private, to hold it just for themselves. I didn't want . . . It felt like the least I could do to help them keep it quiet now."

He turns the phone over so we can see the home screen. A picture of Windbreak stares back at me—a picture of the view from Windbreak's porch. The sun setting over the ocean, the edge of his favorite chair. It's my father's phone. Our father's phone.

"Take it. Clearly you think I'm hiding something, so take it. Look through the whole thing. See for yourself."

He starts to hand me the phone, but I wave him off. I have no intention of opening it now. I don't want to see what my father was trying to hold on to for just him. And for her.

But Sam, apparently, feels differently. He drills me with a look and takes our father's phone out of Joe's hand.

"I'll take that, thank you."

I look down at the phone in Sam's hands, at that screensaver, that photo of Windbreak staring back at me.

"I'm going to try and put aside how insulting it is that you think I could ever hurt your father," Joe says. "I know better than anyone how easy it is to confuse grief for guilt."

I look back up at Joe, those words penetrating. Confusing grief for guilt. He isn't wrong. It was easy to think that Uncle Joe was guilty of something, to misread his behavior as suspicious—to misread his sadness as remorse.

And when you are grieving, guilt lives inside your sadness, doesn't it? The guilt lives there like an unfortunate side effect of what you haven't done. You haven't saved who matters most.

"But you believe this too?" Joe says. "That something happened that night?"

I meet his eyes, a new clarity coming to me.

"I do," I say.

And it's true. The whole pattern is gnawing at me, moving closer to me. My father's own words coming back to me. Our first night at Windbreak together, on that cliff together. *Windbreak doesn't just belong to me*. Which is when I get there.

"Joe, how about Windbreak?" I say. "Was he going to leave that to her too originally? To Grace?"

He nods. "A long time ago. But, for as far back as I remember, it was always going to you."

"Why?"

"Grace didn't like to be there without him any more than he liked being there without her." He shrugs. "And your father knew anyone else would sell it. Figured you wouldn't. Figured that maybe you would know what to do with it. How to build something as beautiful as that land is."

"He told you that?"

"He did. He told me that."

I nod, a memory floating back in. That conversation with my father, one of our last, when he wanted me to come with him to Windbreak, when he'd asked for my opinion on renovating the property. *I'm looking to make some changes*. Now I knew why he suddenly wanted my opinion—he wanted me to be invested in Windbreak, to start thinking of it as mine. Because that had been his place with Grace. And now that Grace wasn't there, Windbreak mattered less too.

It catches me all at once, the breadth of it, what I've needed to know. And everything clicks into place. The clues now connected, weaving together in their intricate layers, circling their unifying force. Grace.

Grace, Cory. My father's before, and his after. The person he most wanted with him at Windbreak. The only person he ever wanted to be with. How reductive and yet how true. As if he is the only one to get to claim that.

That's when I realize there is someone else, someone who also wanted to claim that. To claim that what they built was the love that counted more. Because just as you can confuse someone's grief for guilt, you can do the opposite.

You can think their guilt is grief.

That's what I saw on someone else's face, isn't it? It was guilt. He felt guilty for what he'd wanted.

He felt guilty for where it led him.

To the last place he should have been.

The edge of a cliff.

A cliff and a love and a final goodbye, which, despite the ring still on his finger, still didn't get to be his.

I turn to my brother. "I know who was there that night."

## *Five Years Ago*

"You should probably know, I'm leaving it to you."

They were at the office, late at night, sharing Chinese takeout and a bottle of Sam Adams Utopias that someone had sent Liam as a gift. Everyone else was long gone for the day. Jonathan, Tommy, the assistants.

Joe hadn't even come in today. He was still celebrating his birthday. It was the third night celebrating his birthday: night one with his daughter, Diana, night two the Perry St party that Liam had thrown for him, and now (night three) he was spending alone with the woman he'd started seeing. Though Joe was reluctant to discuss it, she was the first woman he had felt this way about in decades. She was only recently separated from her husband. This woman who Joe was worried might not be ready to be separated from her husband for good. Liam knew it was Cece, even if Joe didn't want to mention it yet. He'd mention it when it felt more solid and sturdy, perhaps. When it felt right.

"What did you just say?"

"I said, I'm leaving it to you. Of course."

Cory put her chopsticks down, looked at him. "I didn't ask for that."

"Why on earth would you need to ask?" he said. "I built it with you. And it's only because of you that it became what it has. It belongs to you as much as it belongs to me."

"Oh my lord, if you do this . . . "

"It's already done. You will be the majority owner, named as CEO and chair of the board. I'm just letting you know."

"Your boys are going to lose it."

"They'll be fine. They'll be minority owners and have a seat at the table. And obviously, when you retire, I hope you will consider letting them take over. But that will be up to you."

She held his eyes, so he would hear her. So he would hear this part. "If you do this, Liam, it will out us, one way or another," she said. "You know that. Everyone will wonder."

He took her in. "So let them."

"Easy for you to say."

He wasn't sure he would say that it was easy, but he understood her point. He and Inez were already separated. And it was, despite how trite it sounded, the best for both of them. They were closer now than when they were pretending to be something that never quite worked. He was grateful that their time together at least cemented for Inez what she wanted, and it cemented for him that there was only one room he belonged in (as though he needed that cemented)—this one, with Cory.

"How about you?" he asked. "Will it cause problems for you?"

He held her eyes, waited. She started to say something, but then stopped herself. Paul was spending more and more time out in California, Southern California, which he knew she preferred. Paris hadn't fixed it, whatever they hoped something outside of them would fix. They were still friends. Good friends. But that's who he was to her now. She wasn't open to discussing this with Liam, though, not in any detail. Liam knew she wouldn't be open to that until Paul came to terms with it too.

"No. I'm not worried about that," she said. "Not exactly."

"Then it's settled."

She tilted her head, considered. "Maybe I should be insulted that no one suspected all this time," she said. "Probably helped that you've kept yourself fairly busy marrying other women."

"Who knows who suspected what? Joe certainly has an idea."

"Well, I would say so."

She smiled at him. How he lived for it, that smile. What it did to her eyes, her skin.

"Why are you telling me now?" she asked.

He wasn't sure. There were many things he could point to. The end of marriage number three. Joe's big birthday. The fact that he drank too much of that expensive beer on an empty stomach. All of it, none of it.

"I kept it to myself for more than thirty years. That seems long enough." He shrugged. "Plus, I'm not getting any younger."

"Easy there. You're only two years older than me . . ."

"Two and a half years," he said.

"My point is, I'm not sure how much security putting me in charge will get you."

He shook his head. "That doesn't matter."

"What doesn't?"

"Anything happens to you, that's it for me," he said. "I fold up the tent."

She smiled. "Is that so?"

"It is."

He nodded, serious suddenly. His eyes sharp and hurting. "I have no desire to be without you."

"My darling, this is turning into a pretty morbid conversation for a Tuesday night."

"What would you like to talk about?"

"I don't want to talk about anything," she said. "I'm hungry, and I would like to eat in peace before we have to get on the phone with Hawaii. I think we can't avoid flying out there next week, but Sam's doing some good work."

He sighs. "Sure. I'm still not convinced it's work he should be doing. Not that he's open to that conversation."

"Maybe time will tell that, one way or another . . ."

"Maybe."

He reached for the beer and started to pour them each a little bit more. But she took ahold of his arm, looked into his eyes.

"I have no desire to be without you, either, for the record," she said.

"Where's this record?" he said.

"Pour me the rest of that beer, and maybe I'll tell you."

# New York City Misses You

When we land in New York, we go straight to his apartment.

The ornate art greets us, the steely lobby, the familiar doorman. He is helping a resident with her dinner order. He waves us up as we walk by.

"Are you sure about doing it like this?" Sam asks.

"No," I say.

But we are already getting on the elevator. We are already heading up.

Paul opens the door. He is in a sweatshirt and cargo pants. Bare feet. The day is behind him, he thinks. He is home, where he feels safe, a bourbon already in his hand.

"We know it was you, Paul."

This is what I say before he says hello.

"You know that what was me?"

"We know it was you on the cliff that night," I say.

Paul looks at me, and then back and forth between us. He looks genuinely surprised. Genuinely confused. And for a moment, for a grateful last moment, I get to think I'm wrong that it was him. That when I texted Meredith Cooper a photograph of Paul, she was also wrong that he was the jogger on the beach. That Uncle Joe was wrong that Paul owns a house in Malibu, up in Point Dume, where he spends at least half his time.

I get to believe, for that final moment, that all the signs pointing me here were signs that should have been pointed somewhere else. That I'm about to owe Paul a big apology. That I'm about to go home.

But then I notice it. His hand is shaking. The hand holding the bourbon. The hand with his wedding ring still on it.

"It's up to you what you want to do here. We can go straight to the police and let them figure out the rest," I say. "Or, I suggest, you let us in."

He gets quiet. His eyes dropping.

Then, slowly, and all at once, he steps out of the way.

~

"You've got to understand," Paul says. "None of this started with me."

This is how he begins. We are sitting on leather couches across from each other. Sam is standing by the windows, the large windows, Manhattan visible in the distance. Sam hasn't said a word since we've walked in, since he's come face-to-face with Paul. I know he is using every drop of his energy to try and stay calm. I can feel his energy from across the room. I try to settle him from where I am. I meet his eyes and silently ask him to trust me. I see him inhale, and I turn back to Paul.

"I met Grace back when we were in graduate school. She was studying creative writing and I was getting my master's in photography. But she was living with a couple of friends in my program, and so I'd see her around that first year. I actually met her a bunch of times and she never remembered me, which probably got my attention . . ."

He doesn't say the rest. That when he walked into a room, most people remembered him. And here was someone who couldn't have cared less.

"Anyway, one night, my friend and I were drinking in the living room, it wasn't even late, like eight thirty or something, and Grace came out of her bedroom and told us to take our party somewhere else. She was really calm about it, but she meant business. And I was done. I mean totally smitten. Weird reason to be smitten, maybe. But it didn't matter. She wasn't interested and she made it clear she wasn't interested, and so we became friends. Until she moved back to New York to take care of her folks, and we lost touch . . ."

He clears his throat.

"But then when I ended up in New York, we reconnected. She was different. Like a grown-up. Or maybe that's not a good categorization. She was always pretty grown up. But she was more settled in her skin. She was working with your father by then, and she was happy. She loved her job or working with him, or both. And we started spending time together. And I knew, she never lied, she told me that her relationship with your father was . . . complicated. I don't know if I took that as a challenge? I hope not. But I don't know." He pauses. "I just loved her. And I guess I believed that I was better for her than he was. How could I not be better? I was offering her all of me. But the audacity of me, to think that you can apply that kind of logic to love. That logic has anything to do with it."

I watch him.

"I guess what I'm saying is that I don't blame Grace. It's unfair to blame her. I walked into it with open eyes. I knew. I just thought that eventually it would add up to more. My loyalty to her. And at times it felt like it did. Once we were committed to each other, she changed the parameters of their relationship. At least for a time, I believe she did. But that didn't change how they were together. The way she looked at him. So I don't know . . . what does it mean to be faithful if you love someone else anyway? Loyalty doesn't trump love, not in the end."

I feel that in my gut. In my soul. The pain he had to work through that he ended up on the wrong side of that equation. On the wrong side of someone else's love story.

"What happened that night, Paul?" Sam asks.

"In her will, Grace had asked . . . She had asked that her ashes be scattered at Windbreak. I had been putting it off." He takes a deep breath. "We were separated at the end. When she had the heart attack, that complicated it for a little while. But it's fair to say that we'd been separated for the better part of the last few years. We were still friends. Good friends. In the end, we ended up back at the beginning . . ." He considers. "But it made grieving, and how to even think about grieving, even more complicated. All of which is to say it took me a long time to finally get out to Windbreak. To finally honor that wish."

He looks up at me.

"Grief does crazy things," he says. "That's not by any means an excuse."

"It's just a fact," I say.

He nods. "It's just a fact."

"How did you get in?" Sam asks.

We both turn to him, standing by the window ledge, as if remembering he is there. His eyes flush, wet.

"The stairs from the beach. Grace had taken me in that way once, a long time ago. She also had the code written down. It was with her instructions in the will . . . " He pauses. "Your father wasn't supposed to be there. That's why I picked then to go. He was supposed to be at an event for Inez. I knew that because I received an invitation from her as well. I confirmed your father would be attending. If you check with his office, you will see that I made that call."

I nod, knowing that is true. Inez had said as much. Our father had made a last-minute decision to bow out. He decided to get on a flight to be at his favorite place instead.

"I had just finished scattering her ashes when he must have seen me. When he came up behind me. He startled me. And we got into it. Not because I was there, exactly. He wasn't surprised that I was there, not when I explained why. But he seemed . . . so broken. It made me mad. I was just so mad. When we were younger, I was mad at him for not choosing her. I never understood why he didn't give everything up to be with her. Maybe she didn't see it that way, but it felt to me, it always felt to me, like he never chose her. Just her. No one else. And fuck him for that . . . except standing there with him, I realized I'd been wrong."

"About which part?" I say.

He shrugs. "He was loyal to her," he says. "He belonged to her as much as she belonged to him."

He looks away. And I start to picture the scene. A rainy night. A man taking those steps two at a time up to the last place he wanted to be. Still, there he was. Because he wanted to honor his wife's last wish. He wanted to scatter her ashes where he knew she wanted them to be. Despite himself. Because he knew what he never wanted to let himself know. What he always knew. He knew where she belonged.

"We argued a bit," Paul says. "I don't even remember what was said exactly. He was angry to just see me there like that. I was mad because he wasn't supposed to be there. That I couldn't even have this without him, in the background. My whole life, this guy in the background . . . But I turned away and started to leave. I just wanted to get out of there. And then your father . . . he called out after me. I think he was trying to apologize or make it peaceful. He said how much Grace cared about me. Like I needed him to say it. Except, apparently, I did. Because it leveled me. It absolutely leveled me. So I walked back toward him."

He shakes his head, lets out a disbelieving laugh. Sam moving away from the window. Sam moving closer to us, to me. As if he knows we need to be together. We need to be together to take in this part.

"I keep going over it, what I heard him say then. He was talking real softly because he wasn't exactly talking to me. But he needed someone to know. And she wasn't there to hear it anymore. He said, *I can't figure out how to be without her.* And it was worse than anything else. The pain. The pointlessness of it all . . . And I just . . . it tipped me over, you know? In my mind, this whole time, he was to blame. And it was somehow worse that I couldn't blame him anymore, either. And I pushed him. Yeah, I did push him. But I didn't mean to push him over the edge. I didn't mean to kill him. I didn't mean . . ."

Paul wipes at his face, tears sliding down his cheeks. He tries to stop them, the tears he doesn't feel he deserves to shed. But he can't. He is crying so hard that he can't even talk anymore.

Sam moves away from him, from both of us, holding his knuckles so tight that they're turning white. His eyes fill with tears too, as much as I see him trying to fight it, angry tears that are starting to spill down his face.

I turn back to Paul. And I can start to see the rest of it without anyone saying it—without Paul saying it. The shock of it. My father there one minute, gone the next. Paul's heart racing. No one there to hear it.

The aftermath. My father disappearing in the night sky. What just happened? How did that happen? What had he just done?

The world moving into a weird slow-motion, and also going faster than it ever had before: Paul taking the steps down to the beach, two at a time, calling 911. Getting to my father, to *the body*, just as the couple did. The couple and their loud barking dog. They're also on the phone with 911. The EMT holding her hand over my father's pulse, shaking her head. She is shaking her head at her husband.

Paul is running before he even knows he's running. Before he can think about the rest of it. Get out of there. He has a pregnant daughter, Grace's pregnant daughter. He's about to have his first grandbaby. There's nothing he can do now even if he stays. The EMT is holding her hand on his chest still, her husband is talking to 911. We have no pulse. We have a broken skull, a broken brain. There's nothing left to do for him. There's nothing, at all, to do. But, for his daughter, his granddaughter—for *Grace's* daughter and granddaughter—he can get away from there.

He looks up at me, needing me to hear this part. "I'll do whatever you want now. We can go to the police together. Not that you should have to bear that burden. But just tell me and I'll do it . . ."

What can I tell him? Probably not what he wants to hear: that I can feel how heavy the word *burden* sounds coming from his mouth, the weight of it surrounding him, visible in his skin and on his hair and in his smell. What he has lost, what he never quite had.

That I understand, looking at him, the grief we carry, that small hollow circle. We can love someone and they love someone else. We can spend a lifetime trying to understand them, without accepting they weren't really ours to understand. We can look someone straight in the eye and never bear witness to the most private part of them—the part they saved just for themselves.

But, oh to know it now, to know the part that my father saved for himself. To know what made him move and turn and breathe.

She loved you, Dad. Didn't she? That was her life. And, despite all the noise, all the beautiful and necessary noise, loving her was yours.

So I do what you would do if you were here. What you would do for her.

I reach out slowly. I take his hand.

# The East River Shows You Everything

We walk for a long time.

We are too stunned to do much else. So we walk the tree-lined streets of Brooklyn Heights, moving slowly but deliberately away from what we just went through. Neither of us speaks for a while, like it will break something to say it out loud, like it will make it real.

Then, Sam turns to me. "Do you believe him?" he asks.

We have just circled around to the promenade. The Brooklyn Bridge is not too far in front of us, the East River and Pier 6, downtown Manhattan lit up with its night-lights.

I think about what I saw in Paul's eyes, the sorrow there and the regret. That was the last thing he wanted. All of this is the last thing he wanted.

"I do believe him," I say. "If that makes it any better."

"Which way is better?" he asks.

But then he lets out a breath. Because it does make it a little better. It makes it better to let our father be in peace now. It makes it a little better to put the bigger pieces together.

Pieces help. They help to make you whole. They strip away the shock. They strip it away until, slowly but surely, the shock isn't your entire story. Even when the thing you truly want—the thing my brother and I both still want—is the thing we can't have anymore. Our father standing here with his mysteries intact. Closer, and farther, at the same time.

"I just miss him," Sam says.

I turn and meet his eyes.

"It catches me off guard. How much I miss him."

I nod. "Me too."

"Will it get easier?"

I think of my mother, who has been gone longer. I think about how being without her feels like being without my skin. You might only notice it when you touch something. But you're always touching something.

"Kind of," I say.

"You're such a liar. But I appreciate it."

I laugh, and he leans against the railing.

"Paul knew, didn't he?" Sam asks. "I mean, he told us himself that he walked into it with open eyes. But I guess he just . . . needed to see it for himself."

"To see what?"

"Where he stood."

That hits me. Because I think Sam is correct. I also don't think he is just talking about Paul anymore.

"Maybe he just loved her," I say. "So he really didn't want to think about it . . . what he was up against."

"Can't really blame him for that," he says. "Who wants to think about what they're up against?"

No one, I want to say. No one wants to think about what we're up against. And with love, with standing up and trying to love anyone, we are up against ourselves too. We are up against our heartbreak and our pasts and our ideas about how things should be. We are up against our most primal pain, like a living-breathing barricade, blocking the space between where we've gotten stuck and where we most want to go.

Sam gets quiet again, looks out at the river. I know him well enough now to know what's living for him somewhere in the silence—that beneath our shared grief, he knows what he is up against—how brave he is going to need to be before he gets to where he wants to go. As if what's next is going to be one thing and not a multitude—a multitude that will only reveal itself on the other side of what he's about to give up. His position at the company, his engagement, the dream of steady ground. It's all unsteady, from here on out. Accepting that, just maybe, can bring on its own blessing. For him. And for me.

Loyalty doesn't trump love. That's how Paul said it, isn't it? But what a thing, what a rare and precious thing if you have both. Loyalty and love, swirling together. What have I been doing? Except trying to escape what you can't escape. Because when you do have both, you have everything to lose. And, eventually you will lose it. You will be separated. That is the cost of loving anyone. It doesn't mean you don't do it. You do it anyway. And you pray.

"I'm not moving to Brooklyn, am I?" Sam asks.

I shake my head. "No. Never."

"*Never* seems a little dramatic, but I take the point."

I smile at him. His face is too much like my father's to be easy for me, at least yet. But I take him in anyway because I can already feel the ways I can help him to get there—to a place that's better.

It's selfish, really. Because in this moment, in this newfound hope, my own grief starts to lift.

Sam keeps his eyes on Manhattan while it's still in front of him. I move closer to him.

"We did the right thing tonight?" he asks.

It's a question and it's not. But I put my head on my brother's shoulder, like that's something we do. Which is when it occurs to me that maybe it is now.

"We did the only thing," I say.

This is how we agree that it's time to go home.

## *One Year Ago*

"Let's get out of here," he said.

Cory looked over at him. They were standing on the curb in front of his childhood home, near the mailbox. They were supposed to be on their way to their high school for Liam's fiftieth reunion. Liam had wanted to stop here on the way. He had wanted to ask the new family to let them in for a beat, so he could take Cory inside and check out his childhood bedroom. The closet. Cory & Liam. He wanted to see if it was still there. The doorway where he first met her. He wanted to stand beneath it. He wanted to hold her hand.

"Wait, what are you talking about?" Cory said. "Do you want to ditch the house visit? Or the reunion?"

Liam was looking through the small living room windows at the family inside. A family with young children, watching cartoons. He didn't know them at all. This wasn't even the family who had bought the house from Liam's parents. This was the family after that family. He hadn't been inside since this home had become theirs.

"Both. Neither. Yes."

Cory bit back a smile. "You do know you're the one who suggested this misbegotten adventure?"

"I do know that, yes."

"And what did I tell you when you suggested it."

"That I'd want to call it off."

She started to laugh. "Look at who is becoming predictable in his old age."

He turned to her and smiled. "Well, you look pretty tired tonight anyway."

"A woman loves hearing that."

"That's not how I meant it," he said. Then he leaned over and took her hand, kissed her on the palm.

"Forgive me," he whispered.

And, like that, he wasn't just talking about tonight. He reached into his coat pocket. And he pulled out a ring. It was the same ring he wanted to propose with on the night before she left for graduate school in California. It was a ring he had almost pulled out a dozen times since.

"What are you doing?"

"Asking you to be my wife."

"Oh, for crying out loud. You've got to stop this. I'm *fine*."

He was quiet. She didn't want to hear him. She did look tired, though. He would fight that battle later. He would call her doctor. He'd check in with Elliot too. He would insist she take more time off.

He gave her a smile. "It's not too late."

"I won't have it. This kind of regret. Let's just say we did the best we could and leave it at that."

"Don't you want to just do it already?"

"Do what?"

"I want to wake up with you every day," he said. "As many days as we have."

She drilled him with a look. "Must we do this, what, every six months? Every year?"

"I wish you wouldn't minimize this . . ."

"You're the one minimizing it by suggesting we should be a different way."

He met her eyes, trying to figure out how to best make his case. How could he explain it? It wasn't that he needed it to be another way between them. It was that he needed her. Always had.

"Ask me when I bought this."

"No."

"Please ask me."

She tilted her head, took him in. "No. Because you're just going to give me an answer that makes me want to not be mad at you anymore, and quite frankly, I'm in the mood to be mad at you. It's cold out here and these shoes were an error. And the family is watching us through the window. The mom looks suspicious. And look at the little boy. He wants to know why two old weirdos are standing outside his house. We're going to make him cry."

She stepped off the curb.

"Let's go."

"I bought it the day after we met," he said. "You walked out of my bedroom wearing that green dress and I bought it the next day from Mr. Parker on Avenue A for eighty-five dollars and fifteen cents."

She turned back to him.

"That's why I wanted to come back here tonight, to ask you what I should have asked you then."

"The day after we met? That would have gone well."

Cory stepped back onto the curb. Then she reached out, ran her finger around the ring. The band. There wasn't a diamond there. There wasn't even anything to look at. It was just a band. A gold-plated band. It wasn't even real gold all the way through. Mr. Parker took pity on him by discounting it.

"It's perfect," she said.

Then she took her hand away.

He held out the ring, closer toward her. "For God's sake, Grace, it's been half a century, take the damn thing."

She smiled. He never called her Grace, not when they were alone, except when he was starting to get mad.

"As tempting as it is to be wife number four, I have no desire to marry you, my darling."

"Well, thank you for that."

"You're welcome."

He closed his fingers over the ring, not saying anything. His childhood street was lantern-lit behind her. His past, his present. How easy to say she was wrapped up in all of it. How inadequate. She *was* all of it.

"I hated the idea of the reunion anyway," she said. "So that's not a loss. But you got me all dressed up, so let's do something. Should we stop by Sheet Music? Get some dinner? I'd like to meet Jack."

"You haven't yet?"

"Just that time on the street . . ."

"You're going to like him. He's a good guy. He really is."

She put her arm through his as they started walking back toward his car. "That's some faint praise."

"No, it's not that. He's the person for her, I don't doubt that." He shrugged. "I still just like Elliot a lot."

"Hmm," she said. "For Nora or for you?"

He laughed. "Touché."

He opened the car door and Cory started to step inside. "Also, I need to try this strawberry pizza I keep hearing about."

"So let's go and get it for you."

Liam went to put the ring back in his coat pocket. This was when she put out her hand. This was when she stopped him.

"I'll take that, thank you."

She took the ring from him, cupping it in her palm. She didn't put it on, not in that moment, but she did take it. Then she smiled up at him. That smile.

"No wedding, that's a nonstarter," she said. "But, together, in the same house? We could do that."

He nodded. "I think we have the house."

Grace sat down in the passenger seat, pulling her dress in tightly around herself. "Okay, then."

She said it so casually, he could have missed it. *Okay, then.* After all this time, like it was that simple.

Perhaps it was that simple. Wasn't that what love could be, after all? Whether it takes you a minute to get there or a lifetime to make it so. At the end of the day, it's still better when I'm with you.

He leaned down, held his nose against hers, breathing her in.

"Nice to know you're not sick of me just yet . . ." she said.

"No. Not just yet," he said. "Not ever."

# The Spring Menu

It's a beautiful restaurant.

It's in a small, shingled house on the side of a dirt road, surrounded by vegetable gardens and beehives and an outdoor firepit—an outdoor firepit where those lucky enough to procure a reservation sit and drink predinner cocktails.

The only way you would know it's a two-star Michelin restaurant, and not someone's home, is the small wooden sign on the edge of the front walkway. EST. 2012

I sit at the bar and order dinner. Four courses are sent out. They're perfect. My favorite dish is apparently new to the menu. It's a twice-cooked flatbread with fried tomatoes and crisped anchovies and spicy greens. Which, in a way, is the fanciest lettuce and tomato sandwich I've ever been lucky enough to have. In another way, it's something else completely.

The point is this: my favorite dish, as always, is his.

After dessert, I ask if I can speak to the chef. I say I'd like to pay my compliments in person.

"He doesn't really like to do that," the waiter says.

"Would you tell him that I know him?" I say. "I'm a regular at Sheet Music. Tell him if he wants me to leave I will."

The kitchen is stunning. It's Nordic in design with Dekton countertops on the workstations, a pitched low-slung roof.

Jack is standing by the far windows, rinsing his hands in an enormous farm sink. He is in his chef's whites and a baseball cap. He's grown a beard. I hate it. I almost can't breathe seeing him in person.

The waiter calls out to him.

He looks up. And when he sees that I'm the person standing there, he takes a step forward. Then, rethinking it, a step back.

"It's you," he says.

"It's me."

He nods a thank-you to the waiter, who walks away and leaves us alone by the sink, by those large windows. There is a foot of space between us. It may as well be a mile. It may as well not exist.

"Dinner was excellent," I say.

"Long way to come for a meal," he says.

"I've actually been spending some time at Windbreak, which made it a little easier."

"Windbreak?"

I nod. "I'm working on a couple of projects in Santa Barbara and in Ventura . . . And I'm fixing up a house nearby. For my brother actually."

"How's that been going?" he asks.

It's been going well, I can honestly say. Sam is doing well. He's interviewing for a scouting job with the San Francisco Giants. He's planning on flying back to New York to see Tommy's babies, who are due any day now. We both are planning on it.

"Good," I say. "And you know . . . better than being home without you."

He offers a small smile. It's small, but it's there. Then he bites his lip, the smile disappearing.

He looks at me, waiting to hear what I've come here to say. I had an eight-hour drive to decide where I want to start.

Eight hours, four courses, Jack in front of me again.

*I'm just wondering,* I want to say. I'm wondering if you'll forgive me. I'm wondering if you even think there is anything to be forgiven. I wonder if you want to come to Windbreak and see if you want to live there with me for a while. We could open Sheet Music West down by the beach. Stay for as long as you like. Or, you know, stay for as long as we both shall live.

Before I say any of that, he must know I want to say all of it. Because he looks at me with those eyes, open again, willing to listen. It's who he is. It's who we are to each other. And I know if this doesn't work, if he doesn't want to try again—if it's his turn to not know exactly how to bridge the distance—it will still be like that between us. Ten years from now or twenty. He'll still be the person I get to be certain of before I remember why. He'll still be the person I recognize before I even know who I see.

So I keep it simple.

"I was just wondering if, after work tonight, you'd like to go and get some ice cream."

He lets out a small laugh. Then he wipes his hands on the towel at his waist. And he moves toward me.

His voice is low and thick and gentle. "We might have to drive for a while," he says. "To find anything open . . ."

"I don't mind a drive."

He puts his hand on my cheek, his face against my face. "No?" he says.

I shake my head no. His skin against my skin, his forehead against my forehead. I'll hold us there for as long as I can. For as long as the earth and the sun and the sky conspire to let me, longer than that, if I ever figure out how.

"Then that sounds nice," he says. "That sounds perfect."

# Acknowledgments

I started writing this book in 2021. But I'd been thinking about Liam and Cory's story for many years before that. I am so grateful to Suzanne Gluck and Marysue Rucci for your excitement as I found my way to the story I wanted to tell here. Thank you for your insight, guidance, and astute feedback; for our Wednesday phone calls; and for all the countless ways you make every page bolder and better.

I couldn't be more grateful to Simon & Schuster and Marysue Rucci Books for giving my work such an amazing home. Thank you, especially, to Jonathan Karp, Libby McGuire, Richard Rhorer, Elizabeth Breeden, Jackie Seow, Jessica Preeg, Clare Maurer, and Emma Taussig; to Selina Walker and my incredible publishing team at Century in the UK; to Laura Bonner, Matilda Forbes Watson, Lane Kizziah, Paige Smucker, and Ari Greenburg at WME; to Jamie Feldman; and to Liz Biber and Meredith O'Sullivan at Lede.

Sylvie Rabineau, twenty years in and I still hope to be like you when I grow up. Thank you for making so many dreams come true.

This book owes an enormous debt of gratitude to Scott Dunlap of NBBJ for sharing his expertise on neuroarchitecture; to Brandon Sampson and Liz Leber; to Katherine Eskovitz for the legal expertise; and to Kate Capshaw, who shared the documentary *My Architect: A Son's Journey* at an integral moment.

I'd also like to credit the teams at Wildflower Farms, San Ysidro Ranch, Ventana Big Sur, Hotel Jerome, and Las Ventanas for providing research assistance and inspiration. And Noah Kahan, whose gorgeous songs kept me company during the writing this time around.

For reading drafts and providing thoughtful insight, thank you: Emily Usher, Allison Winn Scotch, Lawrence O'Donnell Jr., Wendy Merry, Stephanie Abram, Liz Squadron, Jonathan Tropper, Shauna Seliy, Jennifer Garner, Dana Forman, Allegra Caldera, Sasha Forman, Emma Destrubé, Lexi Eskovitz, and Brenda Serpas. And a special thank you to Kira Goldberg for her early belief in this novel.

Thank you to the Dave and Singer families and my wonderful friends for reading random paragraphs and forgiving me for carrying loose manuscript pages wherever I go and for offering so much love and support; and to the readers, booksellers, bloggers, reviewers, and librarians who continue to lift up my novels. Thank you for reaching out, thank you for wanting to talk about books and plays and poetry together, thank you for making bookstores my favorite place to be. My heartfelt gratitude to you for all of it.

Lastly, my loves.

Jacob, my favorite boy, favorite research cohort, favorite everything. Nothing in this world makes me happier than watching you play baseball. Except for watching you be you. I absolutely love being your safeness, kid. And I love every single thing about you.

Josh, I get to do the work that I love because you're the kind of husband and father that you are. Thank you for that. Thank you for your belief in me. Thank you, more than anything, for telling me all of your stories. I will take care of them, and you, with everything I have. Forever.

# About the Author

Laura Dave is the #1 *New York Times* bestselling author of several novels, including *The Last Thing He Told Me* and *Eight Hundred Grapes*. Her novels have been translated into thirty-eight languages, and six of them, including *The Night We Lost Him*, have been optioned for film and television. She resides in Santa Monica, California.